With awe *described the wild beauty that surrounded them.*

By the time they'd reached his ranch, Carly was forced to look at him in a different light. He wasn't a simple small-town sheriff. Devlin McAllister was a complicated man.

It didn't make any difference, she told herself. She wasn't here to pass judgment on him. She was here to get to the truth of her brother's death, twenty years ago. And no matter how interesting Devlin McAllister was, no matter how much she was attracted to him, it didn't change a thing.

The McAllisters had never paid for killing her brother. And she was here to make sure they were finally brought to justice.

Dear Reader,

Happy New Year! And welcome to another month of great reading from Silhouette Intimate Moments, just perfect for sitting back after the hectic holidays. You'll love Marilyn Pappano's *Murphy's Law,* a MEN IN BLUE title set in New Orleans, with all that city's trademark steam. You'll remember Jack Murphy and Evie DesJardiens long after you put down this book, I promise you.

We've got some great miniseries titles this month, too. Welcome back to Carla Cassidy's Western town of MUSTANG, MONTANA in *Code Name: Cowboy.* Then pay a visit to Margaret Watson's CAMERON, UTAH in *Cowboy with a Badge.* And of course, don't forget our other titles this month. Look for *Dangerous To Love,* by Sally Tyler Hayes, a book whose title I personally find irresistible. And we've got books from a couple of our newest stars, too. Jill Shalvis checks in with *Long-Lost Mom,* and Virginia Kantra pens our FAMILIES ARE FOREVER title, *The Passion of Patrick MacNeill.*

Enjoy them all—and be sure to come back next month for more of the most exciting romantic reading around, right here in Silhouette Intimate Moments.

Yours,

Leslie Wainger

Leslie J. Wainger
Executive Senior Editor

Please address questions and book requests to:
Silhouette Reader Service
U.S.: 3010 Walden Ave., P.O. Box 1325, Buffalo, NY 14269
Canadian: P.O. Box 609, Fort Erie, Ont. L2A 5X3

COWBOY WITH A BADGE

MARGARET WATSON

Published by Silhouette Books

America's Publisher of Contemporary Romance

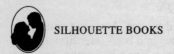 SILHOUETTE BOOKS

ISBN 0-373-07904-4

COWBOY WITH A BADGE

Printed in U.S.A.

Books by Margaret Watson

Silhouette Intimate Moments

An Innocent Man #636
An Honorable Man #708
To Save His Child #750
The Dark Side of the Moon #779
†*Rodeo Man* #873
†*For the Children* #886
†*Cowboy with a Badge* #904

† Cameron, Utah

MARGARET WATSON

From the time she learned to read, Margaret could usually be found with her nose in a book. Her lifelong passion for reading led to her interest in writing, and now she's happily writing exactly the kind of stories she likes to read. Margaret is a veterinarian who lives in the Chicago suburbs with her husband and their three daughters. In her spare time she enjoys in-line skating, birdwatching and spending time with her family. Readers can write to Margaret at P.O. Box 2333, Naperville, IL 60567-2333.

For Jimmie. Thanks for your generosity, your support and lunches at Maggiano's. But most of all, thanks for your friendship.

Thanks to my brothers-in-law, Robert Schafer and John Schafer, for the information about the shotgun, and to Rique Campa for the lessons in shooting. I think my ears have finally stopped ringing!

Chapter 1

The red Jeep Cherokee took the last turn into Cameron, Utah, going much too fast. A plume of dark red dust trailed behind it and the roar of its powerful engine echoed off the buildings. Devlin McAllister narrowed his eyes as he watched the car from the window of his office. When the car slowed abruptly and pulled into a parking space across the street from the office, Dev pushed away from the paperwork he'd been trying to finish and jammed his hat onto his head. The driver of the Jeep obviously needed a reminder about the speed limit in Cameron.

Before he reached the car, the driver's door opened and a woman slid out. Slamming the door, she leaned against the car and stared at the buildings on the other side of the street. Tension seemed to ripple down her slender back, and she put up a hand to absently brush at her dark red hair, ruffled by the wind.

Devlin stopped a few feet away, waiting for her to turn around. But she didn't seem to realize that he was there. As he watched her, he wondered what she found so fascinating about the storefronts of his town.

He waited to get her attention, irritation expanding in his chest.

But before he could say anything she turned and saw him, and the words caught in his throat.

Her dark red hair had been pulled back into some kind of braid, but the wind had teased loose several wisps that now curled wildly around her face. Her vivid green eyes watched him with a guarded expression, lingering on his khaki shirt and badge. "Can I help you?" she finally said. Her voice, low and husky, was a perfect match for her sleek, elegant frame and the sophisticated clothes she wore. It was a voice made for satin sheets and long, hot nights.

Devlin grabbed for his composure. "Can I see your registration and driver's license?"

"Is there a problem, Officer?" Her voice surrounded him with the taste of sin.

It had to be the heat of the late summer sun that had his blood stirring in his veins. Unable to look away from her, telling himself to back off, he finally said, "That car of yours has a powerful engine, Ms..."

"Fitzpatrick. Carly Fitzpatrick." She held out her hand and Devlin hesitated before he reached for it. He knew instinctively that touching her would be a mistake.

"Devlin McAllister. I'm the sheriff of Cameron."

As his fingers wrapped around hers, he felt her tense. Her hand was small and vulnerable, cradled in his palm. It was as delicate as a baby bird, all soft skin and fragile bones. It didn't feel like it belonged to the self-assured woman standing in front of him. Wanting to hold on, he let her hand go and rocked back on his heels.

"You were going too fast when you rounded that last turn into town."

Sliding her hand behind her back, she slowly smiled at him. The curve of her lips held a dare, but in her eyes he saw relief. "It's a failing of mine."

A response flickered deep inside him, unbidden and unwelcome.

Deliberately squashing it, he glanced down the street. "Be more careful. We watch out for our kids here in Cameron."

The smile faded from her face as she let her gaze wander over the buildings around them. Devlin saw her hand tighten around the strap of her purse, then she lifted her chin. "That's very commendable, Sheriff." Her voice was expressionless and her face a careful blank.

His first impulse was to move closer, to protect her from the pain that filled her eyes. He wanted to see her smile again.

He took a step backward instead. "Pay attention to the speed limit on your way out of town. I'd hate to have to give you a ticket."

Carly seemed to shake off whatever ghosts had surrounded her as she straightened her shoulders. "I'm not going anywhere."

"I beg your pardon?"

"I'm not passing through. I'm staying here in Cameron." Her mouth curved slightly. "Maybe I was going too fast because I was happy I'd reached my destination."

"So you've come to see the attractions of southern Utah?" He found himself too anxious for her answer, waiting to hear her say she would take in the sights and be gone in a few days.

She shook her head, the smile fading. "I'm a journalist. I'm here on business."

Damn. The last thing he wanted to see was another reporter in Cameron. But she had been staring at the office of the *Cameron Weekly Sentinel.* "Are you here to buy the newspaper?"

She twisted to look over her shoulder, but before she turned away he saw a look of profound sadness on her face. "Your town newspaper is for sale?"

"It has been for a couple of years."

She stared at if for a few moments, then turned back to him. "No, I'm not here to buy your paper. I'm from *Focus.*" She reached into the Jeep ATV and handed him a business card embossed with the logo of the national news magazine. "I'm here to do a story on Cameron."

Slowly he looked up to stare into her eyes. Behind the quiet confidence that surrounded her he sensed an uneasiness, a wariness being held tautly in check. "Why would you want to do that,

Ms. Fitzpatrick?'' He heard the soft menace in his voice, but he didn't allow his eyes to move from her face.

She swallowed once but didn't flinch or look away. ''Cameron has been in the news lately, and it looked like an interesting town. The kind of place people might want to visit. And *Focus* was looking for a small western town to feature as a tourist destination.''

Anger blossomed in his chest and he crumpled her card in his hand. He'd had his bellyful of reporters in the last couple of months. ''Cameron isn't interested in being a tourist destination.''

Those cool green eyes of hers didn't waver. ''Are you so sure, Sheriff? Are you authorized to speak for the town?''

In spite of his anger he felt a flicker of admiration for the way she stood up to him. He tried to smother it. ''I'm speaking as someone who's lived in this town all my life. We like Cameron just the way it is.''

Her glance touched deliberately on several of the more run-down buildings along Main Street. ''Do you?''

He felt himself flush. ''We don't need tourist money. There are too many strings attached.''

''And what kind of money would come with absolutely no strings attached?'' She quirked an eyebrow at him and rested her hands on her hips. The elegant jacket she wore fell open, revealing a filmy white shirt with a hint of lace underneath it.

Another, stronger emotion replaced the anger, gnawing at him with the sharp teeth of hunger too long ignored. He clamped down on his imagination and looked away. He would not allow himself to want this reporter.

''You're wasting your time here. Once people find out why you're in Cameron, no one will be interested in talking to you.''

''That remains to be seen, doesn't it?''

She stepped sideways and slid back into the Jeep. The white shirt tightened against her for an instant, outlining the swell of her breasts, and Devlin felt the heat scorch his body.

''Thanks for your advice,'' she said, giving him a cool smile. She turned the engine on, and the Jeep purred beneath her hands. ''Oh, by the way, maybe you can tell me where this is.''

She reached over to the other seat and straightened, studying a slip of paper. "I'm staying at Melba Corboy's. The address is..."

"I know where Melba lives," he interrupted. Thank God. If anyone could drive a nosy reporter out of Cameron, it was Melba Corboy. "Take the next left then the second right. It's the third house on your right."

She set the paper down and stared over at him. Her eyes were level with his, making it impossible not to read the challenge in their green depths. "I'll see you around town, Sheriff."

"That you will." He stepped back and watched her drive away, keeping carefully under the speed limit. Her car turned the corner and disappeared. After a few moments the sound of her engine died away and the dust settled back onto the street and Cameron looked no different than it had a half-hour earlier.

But it had changed. The air quivered with possibilities and Carly Fitzpatrick's face lingered in his memory. His body throbbed with a need he wanted to dismiss, but couldn't. Yeah, something had changed in Cameron. And he didn't like it one damn bit.

Several hours later, Carly eased the Jeep into a parking space on Main Street and cut the engine. She sat in the silence for a moment, looking at the buildings lining the street. Vague memories stirred, but they brought nothing but remembered pain. Resolutely she pushed them away, focusing instead on the present. She excelled at that. Pulling out the brochures she had collected before she arrived in Cameron, she scanned the list of businesses for a restaurant.

The only one she found was called Heaven on Seventh, which meant it was a couple of blocks from Main Street. She'd done her homework before she arrived in town, and she knew the layout of Cameron. Sliding out of the Jeep, she closed and locked the door and headed in the direction of Seventh Street. She might as well take a look around town while she was looking for dinner.

More than a few of the buildings she passed looked old and faded. In spite of the sheriff's words, this was a town that could use some tourist money. As she thought of Devlin McAllister, she caught herself glancing toward the sheriff's office. She hastily looked away, but not before she'd scanned the windows for a glimpse of the man.

Remembering the tall sheriff with the golden hair and gray eyes, and her unexpected reaction to him, she forced herself to walk faster. She would not be sidetracked from her mission in Cameron by anyone, and especially not by a McAllister. As she rounded the corner onto Seventh Street, she forced herself to slow down and relax. Could there be any greater irony than the fact that the first person she met after arriving in Cameron was a McAllister?

Only the fact that she'd been immediately attracted to him, she told herself grimly. But that was nothing she couldn't handle. She'd stay away from him and do the job she'd come here to do. And who knows? She might actually write an article about the town, too.

Spotting several trucks on the street in the next block, Carly realized she'd almost found the restaurant. When she pushed open the door, though, she stopped in her tracks.

Flower-filled baskets hung from the walls and the windowsills and decorated every table. Their sweet fragrance mingled with the smell of good food, creating a heady perfume she wanted to simply stand and inhale. As she looked around the restaurant, she noticed that the ceiling was painted to look like a blue sky, with wispy clouds she could almost swear were drifting past.

"Pretty amazing, isn't it?"

Jerking her gaze away from the ceiling, she realized that Devlin McAllister was standing in front of her. He was holding his hat and his golden brown hair gleamed in the lights twinkling down from the ceiling.

Carly forced herself to look away and glance around the restaurant again. "It's beautiful. Is the food as good as the decor?"

"It's better. Janie is a wizard when it comes to food."

"Evening, Sheriff." A perky teenaged girl holding a stack of menus smiled up at him, and Carly watched him smile back. Laugh lines crinkled around his eyes and his face was transformed by a dimple in his right cheek. Her finger itched to trace the dimple, to feel the bristly roughness of his five o'clock shadow. Appalled at herself, she curled her fingers into a fist and took a step away from him.

"Table for two?" the waitress asked.

The sheriff shot Carly an amused glance, then shook his head. "Two singles, please, Mandy."

The girl furrowed her forehead. "We've only got one table open. You look like you know one another. Are you sure you don't want to share?"

"Go ahead and give Ms. Fitzpatrick the table. I'll take mine to go," the sheriff replied.

Carly noticed the flash of disappointment, quickly hidden, in his gray eyes, and had a sudden revelation. Of course he wouldn't want to eat dinner in his office. As sheriff, he probably spent too much time there already.

She heard herself say, "I don't mind sharing if the sheriff doesn't."

Mandy gave them a wide smile and said, "Far out. This way, please."

When she turned her back, the sheriff put his hand on Carly's arm. "Are you sure you don't mind?"

She couldn't speak. The heat from his fingers burned into her arm, sending waves of sensation through her. Staring at him, listening to the blood roaring in her ears, she completely forgot what he had asked her. "I beg your pardon?"

"Are you sure you want to share a table with me?" He had dropped his hand and taken a step backward, and she wondered if he'd felt the crackling tension that enveloped them, too.

"I don't mind." She struggled to regain her composure. "I can pump you for information about Cameron."

His face hardened. "It sounds like you never forget you're a reporter."

"I'll never forget why I'm here," she told him, then turned away to follow Mandy before he could read anything in her face. No, she wasn't likely to forget why she was here. And she wasn't likely to forget that it started with the McAllisters.

By the time they'd studied the menu and placed their order

with the grinning Mandy, Carly had managed to slip back into her role as a reporter. But before she could ask Devlin a question about Cameron, he leaned back in the booth and gave her a smile. The reappearance of the dimple made her toes tingle.

"I thought Melba Corboy was supposed to feed you dinner."

The slow tumbling of her stomach had nothing to do with food. "Why didn't you warn me about her cooking?" she asked.

His smile turned into a grin. "You never asked for my opinion. There are probably some people who'd like the food she serves."

"Maybe someone who hadn't eaten in a month." She shuddered. "And even then it would be iffy."

"Melba does like her grease," Devlin said, and this time he laughed. "Wait until you try her breakfasts."

"The experience of a lifetime, I'm sure," she said, and found herself smiling back.

Something flew between them and lingered in the fragrant air of the diner. Carly shifted uneasily on her seat, but couldn't make herself look away from Devlin. His gray eyes held hers, but she couldn't tell what he was thinking.

"There are a few other places you can stay in Cameron," he finally said. "I can give you a list of the boarding houses."

Carly shook her head. "I couldn't do that to Ms. Corboy. I already gave her a deposit for the first two weeks. I'll tell her that my schedule is going to be irregular and not to count on me for meals. Then I'll make it a point not to be around at dinner."

Devlin watched her for a moment. "You don't want to hurt that old bat's feelings, do you?"

She heard the disbelief in his voice. "What's wrong with that?"

He shook his head. "Melba is the meanest, most ornery, most cantankerous person in Cameron. She was a teacher before she retired, and she still scares me. And you're worried about hurting her feelings?"

"I made an arrangement with her, and I'll honor it." She'd seen the list of boarding houses in Cameron, and she had deliberately chosen Melba Corboy's. The reason why was no business of the sheriff's.

The sheriff leaned back against the vinyl cushion of the booth and watched her with unreadable eyes. "What do you know? A reporter with some ethics. I didn't realize such a creature existed."

He stretched his long legs out next to hers and the heat swirled around her, trying to catch her in its grip. She deliberately shifted away from it as she worked to rein in her temper. She wouldn't accomplish what she'd come here to do if she let him provoke her. "I didn't realize that small-town reporters were so ruthless and hard-driving, Sheriff McAllister."

His eyes flickered in acknowledgment, then he gave her a reluctant smile. "Touché, Ms. Fitzpatrick. But since all good reporters do their homework, I'm sure you know we don't have any reporters here. The *Cameron Weekly Sentinel* is on its last legs. We're lucky to get it printed once a month."

She didn't know that, and she struggled to hide her sadness at the news. Had her family's legacy come to such an ignominious end? "Then where did you get your bias? Or is it just more of the popular media bashing?"

He scowled and sat up straight, leaning over toward her. She wanted to lean away from the intensity that poured from him, but she forced herself to face him.

"You came to Cameron because of what happened here a couple of months ago, didn't you?"

No, she didn't, but the incidents had been a convenient cover. "Yes," she lied smoothly.

"Well, so have a herd of other reporters. They've been harassing my citizens, following them all over town to get their so-called stories. They've trespassed on Grady Farrell's ranch and followed Becca Farrell on her veterinary calls. They've snooped around Damien Kane's house. There have been a couple of near accidents because of them, and they act like we should be honored to have them here. I have no respect for reporters because the ones who've been in Cameron don't deserve my respect."

"I was once shaken down for a bribe by a police officer in Los Angeles. Does that mean I should expect the same from you?" she asked, crossing her arms in front of her chest.

He stared at her for a moment. She was amazed when the dimple on his cheek flashed at her again. "Touché again, Ms. Fitzpatrick. You're right—all reporters are not the same. I'll remember not to underestimate you."

She didn't want his admiration, she told herself. And she didn't want the awareness that she saw in his eyes, or the tension that still swirled around them. All she wanted from Devlin McAllister was justice. And she would get it.

"Tell me about Cameron," she said, deliberately leading the conversation onto safer ground.

His eyes darkened and he scowled at her. "We're a small, quiet community and we want to stay that way."

"I'm not planning to change that. Cameron is a town that caught my interest and I thought the readers of *Focus* would be interested in it, too."

He leaned forward again. "You write about Cameron in your magazine and before you know it we'll have a steady stream of damn fools coming to town and the shopping malls and fudge shops will follow them. Or else they'll want to commune with nature, and that's even worse. We don't have the resources to go hunting for them when they get lost in the mountains or fall off the cliffs."

"You make all tourists sound like idiots and incompetents."

He rubbed his hand across his face, and her fingers tingled when she imagined what the stubble of his beard would feel like. Shaking herself, she sat up straighter and tried to concentrate on his words.

"Hell, I know they're not," he said, and his voice was weary. "But we're not equipped to deal with tourists in Cameron. Where would they stay? At Melba Corboy's?"

At that, he grinned at her, a slow, lethal weapon that set her stomach to twirling again. "That's the solution right there. You go ahead and write all you want about Cameron and give everyone Melba's address. It won't take long before the tourists stop coming."

She couldn't stop herself from laughing. "You're wicked, Sheriff."

"No, ma'am, but I sure would like to be."

His eyes gleamed as bright as silver, and a shiver chased itself up her spine. God help her, she wanted to know how he defined wicked.

"What can you tell me about your crime wave here in Cameron last July?" she asked, determined to ignore her body's response to him.

The grin faded and he leaned back in the booth. "I'm sure you've read everything that's been published about our excitement."

"I have," she admitted. "I wouldn't be here if I hadn't. But I'd like to hear your spin on it."

"Hell, there wasn't any spin. Facts are facts. Damien Kane was hiding three people from hired killers here in Cameron. Two of the dirtbags came looking for them, and they ended up in our jail. Then we had the situation with the Farrells at the same time. Sy Ames used to own the Flying W Ranch. He sold it to Grady Farrell, and when Farrell moved to town he met up with Becca Johnson again. They'd known each other years earlier, when they were both kids, and the sparks started to fly again. Sy took exception because he had his eye on Becca, and he tried to kidnap her. He didn't succeed. End of story."

"So why did it become a national news story?" she asked.

Devlin's face darkened again. "Because they both happened at the same time, and someone saw an angle to exploit. 'Even small towns aren't immune from crime wave.' 'Big city woes come to small town.' I think they wanted to make their readers feel better by pointing out that they aren't alone."

"Don't you think that might be a good thing?" she asked gently. "Point out to people that crime can happen anywhere?"

"I suppose it is." His voice was hard. "But I don't want to put the people of Cameron at risk doing it."

Carly swallowed once as she watched Devlin glance around the restaurant with a proprietary eye. Caring about what happened to the people of Cameron was the last thing she expected to hear from a McAllister.

"I can't promise that my story won't step on any toes, but I'll try to do it gently." His gaze snapped back to her and he watched her with narrowed eyes. "I'm not going to back down, Sheriff. I came here to do a job, and I'm going to do it."

Before he could answer, Mandy slid two plates onto the table in front of them. For the next few minutes, neither of them spoke. Finally Carly said, "None of the guide books mention how wonderful the food is. This is fabulous."

"Janie is a genius in the kitchen."

"Who's Janie?"

"She's the owner of Heaven on Seventh." He glanced toward the kitchen. "I'd introduce you, but Janie's kind of leery of strangers. And she doesn't like reporters." His mouth curled up into a grin. "You should have heard what she said to some of that bunch that was here earlier when they tried to take her picture. It curled my hair."

Picturing an older woman wielding a spatula like a weapon, Carly smiled and asked the sheriff an innocuous question about Cameron. After only an infinitesimal pause, he answered her, and they spent the rest of the meal talking about his town. Carly was surprised at the depth of feeling he clearly had for Cameron and the people who lived there.

"You really love this town, don't you, Sheriff?"

He set his fork on his clean plate and leaned forward again. "Of course I do. I've lived here almost my whole life. I know everyone in town and on the surrounding ranches, and this is my home. I don't ever want to live anywhere else. As far as I'm concerned, Cameron is as close as you can get to heaven on earth."

"If you've lived here your whole life, what basis for comparison do you have?"

"I was in the service." The words came out clipped. "I spent some time in California, in big cities. Enough time to know it wasn't for me. I couldn't wait to get back home."

There was a story here. Carly could smell it. Her reporter's nose had never failed her yet. But she forced herself to ignore it. His years in the service had come long after the time she was interested in, and therefore weren't relevant. "Then maybe you could show me around the town sometime, Sheriff. Let me see it from your perspective."

He nodded slowly, and she wasn't sure she trusted the gleam in his eye. "I'd like to do that, Ms. Fitzpatrick. And the name's Devlin. Or Dev. We don't stand on formality here."

"I'm Carly."

She felt as if something intimate had passed between them, something more private and personal than just the exchange of first names. She always told her subjects to call her Carly. It made them feel more comfortable and made it more likely they'd tell her something they'd rather keep hidden.

But she felt, in some subtle way, that the sheriff had turned the tables on her. Like he knew her strategy and was going to use it against her.

Turning her head, she looked for Mandy and her check. Devlin McAllister wasn't going to worm her secrets out of her. They were too important—her purpose here was too important—to let that happen.

"Let me walk you back to Melba's."

Devlin's voice interrupted her thoughts. "Thanks, but I drove. I parked over on Main Street. I thought I'd take a look at the town on the way here."

After paying the check, Devlin held the door for her, and they emerged into the soft light of early evening. "So what did you think of Cameron?" he asked.

"I don't think there is a more beautiful spot in the country. As I drove here, the mountains and the canyons took my breath away. It's hard to believe no one knows about Cameron," she answered. But she had. She'd known all about Cameron. And she hadn't remembered the beauty. Her only memories of Cameron were filled with pain and ugliness.

"That's us. An anonymous small town in a spectacular setting. We want to keep it that way."

As they turned the corner onto Main Street, his elbow brushed her arm. Even through the silk of her jacket she felt his heat, and the current that jolted between them. It tried to hold her captive, to pull her farther into his orbit, but she forced herself to move away. And she wanted to put more than a physical distance between them.

"You're not going to stop me from doing a story about Cameron, Sheriff."

He looked down at her, and even in the fading light she saw the flash in his eyes. "I wouldn't dream of trying. I just have one suggestion for you. You treat the people in Cameron the way you'd want to be treated if this was your home, and you won't have any problems, Ms. Fitzpatrick."

His words were a small dagger in her heart, but she swallowed and plastered a smile on her face. "That's just what I intend to do, Sheriff."

Cameron *had* once been her home, until the McAllisters had killed her brother.

Chapter 2

Devlin walked into Heaven on Seventh the next morning badly in need of coffee. Sleep had eluded him the night before, and the darkness had tormented him with vivid memories of Carly Fitzpatrick. When he managed to doze off, he'd been awakened by hot, needy dreams and snarled sheets.

"Everyone's here already, Sheriff." Phyllis, the morning waitress, greeted him and nodded toward the corner booth where his deputies were seated. Devlin grunted a thank-you and headed toward the table.

Sometime during the past couple of years his morning meeting with his deputies had migrated to the restaurant. The scenery was a definite improvement and the coffee was a hell of a lot better than the sludge they brewed at the office. Devlin slid into the last seat at the booth and reached for the mug Phyllis had already left at his place.

His hand froze halfway to his mouth. Carly was sitting between two of his deputies, smiling and talking, and all six of the deputies were hanging on her every word.

Slowly he lowered the coffee mug to the table. "Good morning, Ms. Fitzpatrick."

She tossed him a casual smile. The jolt it caused in his chest didn't help his temper. "Hi, Sheriff. Your deputies were welcoming me to Cameron."

"I can see that." He worked to gather the threads of his temper. "Did they tell you this is a business meeting? A private business meeting?"

Her mouth curled up in what he already recognized as her challenging smile. "Don't worry, Sheriff. I'm not looking for Cameron police secrets to splash across the cover of *Focus*. I wanted to meet the rest of the sheriff's department because I thought it was the polite thing to do. After all, I'll be working in your town for a while."

"We'll be sure to watch out for you, won't we, officers?" he said to the deputies.

There were eager nods around the table, and Devlin scowled. He suspected that he and the deputies had different ideas about the term "watch out for."

"I'm sure we're all anxious to see what you're going to write about Cameron," he continued, watching her carefully.

"You'll be the first to know, Sheriff."

If he hadn't been watching closely he wouldn't have noticed her knuckles suddenly whiten, or the way her eyes hardened and narrowed.

He was trying to figure out what it meant when she gathered up her purse and a small notebook, then slid out of the booth. When she stood up the smell of oranges and exotic flowers surrounded him, driving all other thoughts out of his head. He gritted his teeth and fought to control his body's reaction. Her scent had played a too-vivid role in his dreams of the night before.

"Have a good day, Sheriff," she said. She walked away without looking back.

None of the deputies would meet his gaze. In spite of Devlin's irritation with Carly, his mouth twitched into an involuntary smile. Clearly they'd all worked for him long enough to recognize the signs of his temper.

"Let's get down to business," he finally said, beginning to eat the food Phyllis had set down in front of him. "What happened last night that we need to know about?"

Ben Jackson, the deputy who'd worked for him the longest, was the first to speak. The rest of the deputies relaxed and began talking, but Devlin couldn't concentrate on what his men were saying.

Carly hadn't left the restaurant. She'd taken another booth and ordered breakfast, and Devlin could see that she consumed as much gossip as food. While his deputies continued to speak, he strained to listen to Carly. He simply wanted to know what she was asking, he told himself. And what people were answering.

"What do you think, Dev?"

The voice of his newest recruit interrupted his thoughts. Devlin had no idea what Matt had asked. As he turned back to his deputies, he could feel his face reddening. "I'm sorry, Matt, I wasn't paying attention."

The deputy repeated his question, and Devlin answered him. Forcing himself to concentrate on the status reports from all the men, he did his best to ignore Carly and her questions. But a part of him stubbornly refused to pay attention to the details of the traffic stops from the night before.

He didn't have to turn around to know that Carly was still in the booth on the other side of the restaurant. He felt her presence so acutely that she might as well have been sitting right next to him, he thought with disgust. He swore he could distinguish her perfume lingering in the air, taunting him with her essence. When he found his mind wandering away from what his deputies were saying once again, he stood up.

"Sorry, fellows, I'm not good for much this morning. If there's anything important, catch me back at the office. If it'll keep, save it 'til tomorrow."

The deputies filed out, one by one. Devlin was surprised that Ben Jackson stayed behind.

"Is something wrong, Ben?" he asked.

Ben's dark eyes watched him. "You tell me. What's going on with the Fitzpatrick woman? Trouble?"

Ben always saw too damn much. Devlin sighed and rubbed his hand across the back of his neck. "No more than the usual reporter, I guess. I'm just damned sick of them."

He watched as Ben focused his gaze on the woman across the room. "She looks determined."

"Yeah, she is. And smart, too. If she wants to make Cameron into a tourist destination, we'll be swarming with minivans and whining kids within a year."

Ben shifted his gaze back to Devlin. "You couldn't keep your eyes off her this morning."

Devlin managed a careless shrug. "She's an attractive woman. And last time I checked, I still had all my working parts. It doesn't mean I'm interested. Hell, she's a reporter from New York, for God's sake."

Ben shook his head. "Sometimes the heart ignores what the head is telling us." He froze for a moment, his eyes following someone behind Devlin, and his face suddenly became expressionless. Then he shifted on the vinyl cushion of the booth and deliberately turned back to his boss.

Dev twisted around in his seat in time to see Janie, the owner of Heaven on Seventh, disappear into the kitchen. He turned back to Ben. "Are you speaking from experience?"

"I'm simply telling you what I saw." He paused, and a twinkle lightened Ben's normally sober expression. "But I'm thinking that the next few weeks might be very interesting."

Devlin scowled as he pushed away from the table, leaving most of his breakfast uneaten. "Go ahead, have your fun. Just remember that what goes around, comes around."

The twinkle disappeared from Ben's face. "Not in this case, Dev."

Devlin threw some money on the table for a tip, paid for his breakfast, then headed outside. As the door to the restaurant shut behind him, he heard the sound of Carly's laugh, low and husky, over the other sounds in the restaurant. Clenching his teeth, he caught himself before he could turn around and look at her.

As he headed back to the office, he drank in the scent of the Utah morning, savoring its crisp, clean taste. Although the sun was still low on the horizon, the bright blue color of the sky and the lack of clouds warned that it was going to be another hot day.

He couldn't stop himself from glancing back at the restaurant. Things were heating up, in more ways than one, he acknowledged grimly.

Out of the corner of her eye, Carly watched Devlin leave Heaven on Seventh. She was talking to an older woman but she caught his hesitation at the door, noticed the way he stopped himself from turning around. Deliberately focusing her full attention on the woman, she waited until she was sure he was gone before glancing back at the door.

She'd talked to several people in the restaurant that morning, but the whole time she'd been aware of the sheriff, sitting at the table in the corner. She'd heard his voice as a background to her own conversations, easily picking it out from the threads of other voices in the room. When a glance at the door assured her that he was gone, she turned back to the older woman with a smile. Now she could concentrate on her own work without distractions.

"What you ought to do is check at the newspaper office," the woman said, and gave her a gentle smile. "You can learn an awful lot about a town from their newspaper."

"Thanks," Carly replied. "I'll do that." She'd intended to head over to the newspaper office today, anyway, but she was pleased by the advice. She wanted the people of Cameron to feel comfortable talking to her. It was the only way she'd get to the bottom of the tragedy that had occurred here twenty years ago.

Pushing away from the table, she smiled at the woman she'd been talking to. "Thanks for your advice, Gladys. I'll see what the paper has to say."

"You tell Ralph Hanson that Gladys Jones sent you over," the woman instructed her. "He'll take care of you."

After paying for her meal, Carly headed back to Main Street and the newspaper office. It was across the street from the sheriff's office, but she wouldn't allow herself to look for Devlin McAllister. She'd already spent far too much of her precious time in Cameron thinking about the sheriff. Unless he was going to help her with her search for the truth, she couldn't afford to think about him. And being a McAllister, the truth about the incident with Edmund was probably the last thing he was interested in.

Carly hesitated before crossing the street, staring once again at the office of the *Cameron Weekly Sentinel.* Just as they had the day before, memories squeezed at her heart. Vague pictures of her father, tall and smiling, swirled in her head, but they were far too blurred and hazy. The memories of her mother in the newspaper office were more distinct, as were those of her brother. She pictured Edmund at a typewriter, looking up to grin and wink at her when she wandered into the office.

Forcing the images out of her mind, she crossed the street and opened the door. She was very good at ignoring everything but the job. It was one of the reasons she was a damn good reporter. Stepping into the dimness of the newspaper office, she smiled at the gray-haired woman sitting at a desk by the door. "Good morning," Carly said.

The woman peered at her with barely concealed suspicion. "You're a stranger. What do you want?"

Carly felt her smile faltering as she said, "I was hoping to look at some back issues of the paper."

The woman scanned her from head to toe, then said, "You're not here about a bill?"

"No, ma'am," Carly replied, but filed the information away. She pulled out one of her business cards and handed it to the woman. "I'm here to do an article about Cameron, and Gladys Jones suggested that I start by looking at some old town newspapers."

The woman examined the card thoroughly, then finally set it down on her desk. "I'm June Hanson. My husband Ralph owns the paper. Did you want to talk to him?"

"I will eventually. Right now, I just want to get a feel for the town and its history."

"I suppose that would be all right." June's tone was grudging. "I'll show you the files."

June Hanson led her down a narrow stairway into the basement, which was filled with file cabinets. "They're all here."

Carly looked around, hoping the files were in some sort of order. If not, she would be spending a lot of time down here. "How far back do the papers go?" She held her breath, waiting for the answer.

June shrugged. "Ralph bought the paper from Joe Whitmore's widow almost twenty years ago. Although he was the editor before he bought the *Sentinel,* I'm not sure he saved the issues from back then. All the issues we put out are here. There might be some from Whitmore's time way in the back, but they're ancient history." June gave her a sharp glance. "You wouldn't want to look at those, would you?"

Carly forced a smile on her face. "I'm interested in Cameron, Mrs. Hanson, and right now I'm not sure what direction my story will take. I may want to look at some of those old issues."

June looked as if she wanted to say something, but she compressed her lips and looked around the room. As her gaze drifted over the file cabinets, she finally said, "Good luck finding what you need."

Luck was what she would need, Carly thought several hours later. She'd managed to find the most recent issues of the *Cameron Weekly Sentinel,* but there was no sign of the copies from twenty years ago. And those were the issues she was interested in. She needed to know what had been happening in Cameron in the weeks before her brother was killed, and what had been written about his death. When the dust made her sneeze once more and she realized she was getting a headache, she reluctantly replaced the papers she'd been looking at and headed up the stairs.

Before she reached the office she heard the low rumble of Devlin's voice drift down to her. Pausing, she listened closely but couldn't make out what he was saying. Was he warning the Hanson's not to talk to her? Adjusting the strap of her shoulder bag, she bounded up the rest of the steps.

"...remember that you have rights, Ralph," Devlin was saying. "I think you need to get yourself a lawyer and find out what those rights are." She heard the rustle of paper as she approached the door. "Give me that phone number and I'll make sure that the phone calls in the middle of the night stop."

All three of them turned to face her as she walked into the room. June Hanson and a heavy-set, gray-haired man she assumed was Ralph flushed with embarrassment, but Devlin's eyes hardened when he saw her.

"Listening at keyholes, Ms. Fitzpatrick?"

She angled her chin and stared him down. "I've been looking at old newspapers in the basement. I had no idea you were here until I was halfway up the stairs."

He must have seen that she was telling the truth, because his eyes softened. "I apologize, then." He turned to Ralph. "I'll talk to you later about this," he said.

Instead of leaving, he lounged back against the door and watched her. She refused to let him see how much his regard flustered her. Deliberately turning her back on him, she held out her hand to Ralph Hanson.

"I'm Carly Fitzpatrick, Mr. Hanson. Thank you for letting me look at your files."

The older man hurried forward to shake her hand. "Welcome to Cameron, Ms. Fitzpatrick. I'm Ralph Hanson." He shot his wife a worried glance, then looked back at Carly. "My wife told me you were here from *Focus* to do a story on our town." He drew himself up straight. "If there's anything you need, anything at all, you let me know. Members of the media have to stick together."

"Thank you, Mr. Hanson." Carly gave him a smile and wondered at his nervousness. It must have something to do with whatever they were discussing with Devlin. "I appreciate your help. I'll want to come back and look at your old issues again, if I may."

His smile faded slightly, but he nodded vigorously. "Whenever you like, Ms. Fitzpatrick."

"Please, call me Carly," she said. "And thank you. I'll see you tomorrow or the next day."

Devlin held the door for her and followed her outside. Once the door was closed behind them, he moved to stand in front of her. "I'm not going to allow you to write about the Hanson's problems, or anyone else's problems, for that matter."

She cocked her head as she watched him. The last thing she'd admit was that she had no interest in exposing the problems of anyone in Cameron, with the exception of her brother's murderer. The only thing she was interested in had happened twenty years ago. But instead of telling him that, she said, "And how are you going to stop me?"

Resting his hand against the building, the sheriff leaned toward her. She'd never felt particularly small before, but Devlin's long, rangy body made her feel tiny.

"If I thought that was what you were going to do, I'd hound you mercilessly. You wouldn't be able to go anywhere in this county without having me as a shadow." His mouth quirked up, but there was no humor in his face. "Surprising as it may seem to you, the people in Cameron trust me. If I told them not to talk to you, they'd listen. Clams would be a lot more talkative than the folks around here."

He meant every word he'd said, Carly realized. He thought she was a threat to the Hanson's. In spite of herself, she softened just a little. How could she not respect a man so fiercely determined to protect the people in his town?

"Believe me, Sheriff, I'm not interested in hurting anyone. I'm not going to detail anybody's problems in *Focus*. That's not why I'm here." The irony tasted bitter in her mouth. The only people who could consider her a threat were the McAllisters.

He didn't move, but she felt him relax a little. "I'm glad we understand each other."

She almost smiled at that. He didn't understand a thing about her, and if she had her way, he never would. Not until she'd accomplished what she came to Cameron to do. And when that happened, Devlin McAllister wouldn't be looking at her with that hunger in his eyes. No, when she'd finished in Cameron, after she'd exposed his father as a murderer, hate was the very best she could expect from Devlin.

But it wasn't hate she was feeling from him right now. The frost that had filled his gray eyes had melted, and now they gleamed with an unmistakable heat. The air hummed with anticipation, and although he hadn't moved any closer to her, Carly's

skin prickled with awareness. When one side of his mouth curled
up in a smile, her heart began a slow, tumbling roll.

"There's something I've been thinking about, Carly," he said.

His low voice rasped against her nerve endings, awakening
them. He said her name like he was savoring the flavor of it,
weighing its taste on his tongue. Her pulse speeded up as she
watched him.

"What's that?" She couldn't believe that the breathless voice
belonged to her.

His smile was slow and sensual, and she had no doubt what
was on his mind. Something tightened inside her, sending a wave
of sensation crashing through her.

She saw the instant that he recognized her response. His pupils
darkened and the flash of heat from his eyes seared her. Then he
straightened and took a step backward. "I promised you a tour
of Cameron," he said as he shuttered his face. "I have some free
time right now. Are you interested?"

She struggled to regain her balance, to steady herself. For one
wild moment she questioned whether she had imagined the message in his eyes. Wondered, humiliated, if her own wishful thinking had put it there. Then she saw that his breathing wasn't quite
steady, that his hands shook slightly as he crossed his arms in
front of his chest.

Shoving her own hands into her pockets to hide their trembling,
she gave him what she hoped was an impersonal smile. She could
be as smooth and unaffected as he was trying to appear. "I'd love
a tour of Cameron," she said, and was proud of the fact that her
voice barely shook. No one who didn't know her well would
notice. "If you're sure it's not taking you away from something
you need to do."

"I'm at your service."

A tiny part of her, a part that appalled her, wished that his
words were true in every sense. *This has to stop,* she told herself
wildly. She refused to be attracted to Devlin McAllister. But that
tiny part of her mocked her, nudging her to move closer to Devlin.

Swallowing, she looked around town to remind herself what

was at stake. When she could answer him coolly, without any of the heat that burned inside her, she turned back to him.

"I'd like nothing better than to get your impressions of Cameron, Sheriff. I'll be greedy and take as much time as you can give me."

He looked down at her, and the heat was gone from his eyes, as well. "Why don't we start here, on Main Street? Later I'll drive you around the county."

An hour later they were back in front of the sheriff's office. They'd walked from one end of Main Street to the other, then toured several of the side streets. Carly knew her hair had long since begun to unravel from its braid and perspiration sheened her skin. The intense sunlight had beaten down on her until she'd felt as if the heat had sunk its fangs into her and shaken her thoroughly. It hadn't seemed to bother Devlin at all.

"Why don't we stop in my office and get something to drink?" he asked.

"That would be wonderful." She sighed in ecstasy as the cool air of the air-conditioned building flowed over her heated skin. "I'm not used to this kind of heat."

"Give yourself a few weeks. You'll hardly notice it." He handed her a cold can of soda.

"I doubt that." She took a long drink, feeling the coldness trickling down her throat, cutting through the dust. "Thank you. I never knew root beer could taste so good."

He grinned at her as he gulped his own drink. "Nothing like the Utah heat to make you appreciate the simple pleasures of life."

Devlin had maintained a careful distance from her as they'd walked through Cameron. He'd been careful not to brush against her or touch her in any way, but that hadn't lessened her awareness of him. Now as he leaned casually against a scarred desk, drinking from a can of soda, she watched in fascination as the muscles in his throat rippled with each swallow.

Get a grip, she told herself firmly as she stood straight in front of him. She couldn't afford to relax her guard. "Thanks for the tour, Sheriff."

He set the can down, pushed himself away from the desk and leaned toward her. "I thought we were on a first name basis," he said.

She took another drink to give herself a moment to settle herself. "Sorry. Devlin," she muttered. Trying to change the subject, she looked around the spartan office. "You don't have a very fancy workplace here, do you?"

"It works for us. There are only two or three of us on duty at any one time, and we're usually not in the building. Why would we need a fancy office?"

She grinned up at him. "To make the criminals more comfortable?"

He relaxed back against the desk and grinned back. "We want the criminals to suffer. That's why we painted the walls that particular shade of green. Believe me, it doesn't sit well on a stomach that's full of liquor."

"How many arrests do you make in Cameron?"

His smile dimmed. "Back to your reporter mode?"

"Actually, no. I was just curious." She was shocked to realize that it was the truth. She hadn't thought about her story at all. She was asking merely to find out more about Devlin.

"Sy Ames, and then the problem with Damien and Abby Kane's nieces were the most serious situations we've had here in a long time. Damien was protecting Abby and her nieces from mob-hired hit men, and that was a first for Cameron. Mostly we get cowboys who get drunk and disorderly down at May's, or kids who get bored and do something stupid. There isn't a real big criminal element in Cameron."

Her mouth curled into a smile. "No desperadoes or bank robbers?"

"No, ma'am. Sorry to disappoint you." His eyes crinkled into an answering grin and his dimple flashed.

Her smile faded as she set her can of soda on the desk next to her. "Cameron is an attractive town," she said.

"Not everyone would think so," he said softly.

"It may not be the most picturesque, but it has heart," she said, remembering Gladys Jones and the other people who had talked to her. It was the last thing she had been prepared to admit. But it was true, she realized.

Devlin's eyes softened. "You're very perceptive to see that. And that's just why I don't want it to change."

Carly slid off the desk she'd been sitting on. "I don't want to change Cameron. I just want to write a story about it."

"Same difference," Devlin said. He set his can down with a snap on the desk behind him. "Come on. I'll show you the rest of the county."

"Are you sure you have time right now?" She hung back, suddenly reluctant to spend any more time in his company. She was far too aware of him as it was.

He'd already started for the door, but he turned to look back at her. "What's the matter, Slick? Are you beginning to realize what you'd be doing to this town if you wrote an article about it?"

Her chin shot up. "Absolutely not. I simply thought you'd have other things to do than chauffeur me around."

"I have my radio. They can get in touch with me if they need to." His eyes narrowed in a challenge. "You've only seen one part of Cameron. In order to appreciate it, you have to see the ranches that make up the rest of our community."

She never refused a challenge. "Let's go, then."

The hot air seared her lungs when she stepped out the door. Devlin gestured to a white Blazer that stood at the curb, and she opened the door and swung herself inside. In a moment they were passing the last houses in Cameron.

"That's the veterinary office," he said, gesturing at a tidy white building that stood on the edge of town. "Becca Farrell is part owner of the practice."

"Do you think she'd talk to me?"

He shrugged. "You can ask."

They drove over the same winding roads she traveled on her way into Cameron, but now Devlin pointed out the individual ranches, told her about the people who lived there. And he knew the name of every mountain, every canyon they passed. He described the wild beauty that surrounded them with awe and wonder.

By the time they'd reached his ranch, the Red Rock Ranch, she was forced to look at him in a different light. He wasn't a simple small-town sheriff. Devlin McAllister was a complex, complicated man.

It didn't make any difference, she told himself. She wasn't here to pass judgment on him. She was here to get to the truth of her brother's death, twenty years earlier. And no matter how interesting Devlin McAllister was, no matter how she was attracted to him, it didn't change a thing.

The McAllisters had never paid for killing her brother. She was here to make sure they were finally brought to justice.

Chapter 3

Devlin shifted behind the wheel of the Blazer as he shot a glance over at Carly. He wished like hell he knew what she was thinking. She'd become more and more quiet as he'd driven her through the valleys and canyons that made up the area surrounding Cameron. At first she'd asked questions about the owners of the ranches, the kind of questions he'd expect a reporter to ask. But since he'd pointed out his family's ranch, and told her that his sister Shea was now in charge, she hadn't had much to say.

Finally she asked, "Do your parents still live on your ranch?"

"My mother does. My father passed away a while ago."

"I'm sorry," she murmured.

"Don't be." He shrugged. "The old man lived his life exactly as he pleased, and he died the way he would have wanted to go. He had a heart attack while he was working. By the time the men found him, he was already dead."

"Did your sister take over because you didn't have time to manage the ranch?"

"Shea?" He grinned at her. "Everybody knew I didn't want any part of the family business. And that was all Shea wanted.

She fought with my father for years about running the place. Managing the Red Rock Ranch is what she's dreamed of all her life.'' He felt his smile dim. ''It was the cause of some bad feelings between my father and me, but we managed to settle our differences. Now Shea and I are both doing what we love.''

There was a humming silence in the car, and Carly didn't look at him. Finally she said, ''I'm glad for both of you that it worked out. You're obviously fond of your sister.''

''I adore her.'' He glanced over at Carly. ''How about you? Does your family live back East?''

''No.'' She turned away to look out the window and he couldn't see her face. ''I don't have any family left. My mother died earlier this year, and my father died when I was a small child.''

''No brothers or sisters?'' he asked.

''No.''

Her voice was clipped, making it clear that the discussion was over. There was more here than she was telling, he realized. He wanted to probe more deeply, to find out her secrets. He wanted to soothe the pain he heard in her voice, pain she tried hard to hide.

Shocked at himself, he tightened his hands on the steering wheel and turned his attention to the road in front of them. There was no way he was getting involved with Carly Fitzpatrick. And he suspected that she wasn't the type of woman who was interested in a brief fling.

''What do you say we head back to Cameron?'' he asked. He knew his voice was tight, but he didn't care. He'd been a fool to bring her out here. He wanted time away from Carly, distance from her. And driving around in the truck, having her sitting only inches away from him, wasn't the way to achieve that distance.

''That sounds good.'' It sounded suspiciously like relief in her voice, and he pressed the accelerator a little harder. It sounded like she wasn't enjoying their enforced intimacy any more than he was.

She hadn't turned to look at him. Still staring out the window, she said, ''Is this part of your ranch, too?''

"No." He glanced at the large herd of cattle huddled close to the tiny stream that ran through the pasture, and his mouth tightened. "That's the Hilbert place."

At that she did turn to look at him. "You don't sound too happy about it."

Staring at the cattle, he shrugged. "I don't approve of his ranching techniques, but he can do what he wants with his cattle. I didn't have much of an opinion about Phil, one way or another, until he tried to buy us out after my father died. When we wouldn't sell, he said some pretty ugly things about the fact that Shea is running the Red Rock. I guess no one gets along with all their neighbors."

"What don't you like about his ranching techniques?"

She sounded genuinely interested, and he looked over at her in surprise. But the interest in her eyes was real. Hell, if it would keep her mind off Cameron as a tourist destination, he'd be happy to give her a ranching lesson.

He turned the steering wheel of the Blazer abruptly and pulled off the road onto the shoulder. Leaning closer to her, he stared out the window at the cattle in front of him. "See how many head of cattle he has on that pasture?"

"There seems to be a lot of them," she said cautiously.

"Too many." He compressed his lips and watched at the cattle milled restlessly around the water. "There isn't enough water running through that pasture for all the cattle he has there. So they stick close to the stream, and that causes problems for the people farther downstream. There's too much waste in the water."

"Why does he do that?" she asked, watching the cattle.

"He needs more water, but he doesn't have a source. So instead of running fewer head, he just crowds more cattle onto the pasture land he does have. He figures he'll make as much money as he can and to hell with his neighbors downstream."

"Can't anyone stop him?" she asked, and he heard outrage in her voice. When he looked at her, indignation sparked in her eyes.

He felt himself soften toward her. "It's his land. There's nothing anyone can do."

"What about the poor cows? Doesn't anyone care they're not getting enough water?"

Smothering a grin, he leaned back and watched her. "They're steers, not cows. And they're getting enough water. It's the herds downstream that are in trouble."

"Those steers don't look healthy," she said, opening her window and leaning out to look at them. A blast of hot air swirled into the car. "They look nervous."

"What does a nervous steer look like?" He had to work to keep from laughing.

She studied the cattle in front of her. "Like these," she said firmly. "Look at how they're all moving around. Someone should do something about it."

"We don't believe in sticking our noses in other people's business," he finally said. "As long as Phil Hilbert isn't doing anything illegal, he can put as many head of cattle on this pasture as he wants to."

Before she could answer, a dusty red truck coming from the opposite direction slowed, then stopped next to the Blazer. Devlin clenched his teeth as Phil Hilbert rolled down his window.

"Admiring my herd, Sheriff?" His voice was mocking.

"We're just looking, Phil." Devlin deliberately kept his voice mild.

"Maybe you're looking for some ideas. I hear your sister needs some help."

Devlin leaned forward, anger flaring. "Shea needs more employees because she's doing so well with the ranch. I doubt she'd want any management tips from you."

The older man's face flushed with rage, but instead of responding he looked over at Carly. "Is this the newest reporter to hit Cameron?"

Devlin knew the grapevine had been at work. "This is Carly Fitzpatrick." He turned to Carly. "Phil Hilbert."

Carly leaned across him. "I'm glad to meet you, Mr. Hilbert. I've been noticing your herd."

Carly's voice was cold, but Phil didn't seem to notice. He gave her an assessing look, then smiled. "I'll be happy to talk to you any time, Ms. Fitzpatrick."

"I'll keep that in mind." Now the frost was unmistakable.

Phil's smile slowly faded, then he slammed his car into gear again. "I'll see you around, McAllister."

Devlin nodded. "Hilbert."

He watched as the other man drove away, going much too fast. Then he put his truck into gear and headed back into town.

"You should have been nicer to Phil. He could give you a lot of information about Cameron." His voice was neutral.

"I doubt I would be interested in the kind of information he could give me."

He slanted a glance at her. "I didn't think you needed to like a person in order to use them."

"Like has nothing to do with it. I can see how he takes care of his animals. I would have a hard time trusting anything he said." She shrugged. "It's not that big a deal."

But it was. Devlin tightened his hands on the steering wheel and pressed the accelerator harder. It was a very big deal. He already knew how important her job was to her. The fact that she was willing to forgo talking to someone who could give her valuable information simply because she didn't like the way he treated his animals said a lot about her. He was forced to reassess his opinion of Carly, and that made her far more dangerous to his self-control. He didn't want to like anything about her. He wanted her to be simply a ruthless, driven reporter who would do anything for a story. He didn't want to see this side of her, the side that jumped to the defense of someone else's animals. The side that would jeopardize her job in Cameron because of those animals.

"It looked like there was a lot more between you and Mr. Hilbert besides your disapproval of his ranching techniques." She watched him carefully.

He shrugged. "It goes back a long way."

She settled back in her seat. "That sounds like a story, Sheriff."

Her interested voice invited confidences, urged him to tell her all about it. He realized it should be a warning signal, and he caught himself before he could tell her the full extent of what was between him and Phil. "You're good," he said with a cool smile.

"What do you mean?"

"You almost had me spilling my guts, and I know what you're up to. God help the unsuspecting citizens of Cameron."

He thought she would take offense, but instead she burst out laughing. "Caught in the act. Sorry, Devlin, I really wasn't trying to pry. And I wasn't looking for fodder for *Focus*. I can only plead guilty to being incurably nosy." She shrugged her shoulders and glanced over at him, her mouth slanting in a grin. "I guess that's why I became a reporter. So I could ask as many questions as I wanted and have an excuse for it."

She lounged against the seat, her hair tousled from the wind and her long, elegant legs covered by brand-new jeans. Her feet, wearing equally new hiking boots, were braced against the console of the car. She looked completely comfortable and relaxed, and a jolt of desire for her struck him with the force of a blow.

He wanted to taste her mouth, to capture the fire he sensed burning inside her. He wanted to slide his hands over the silk of her skin, letting his fingers learn her body. A narrow, black velvet cord circled her neck, disappearing beneath her shirt, and he ached to follow its path. He wanted to lose himself in her, to drown in her scent and her touch.

He was a damn fool. The last thing he wanted was to get involved with a woman who would leave in a few days or weeks. The last thing he needed was to get involved with a woman, period. He'd learned about that trap a long time ago. Deliberately he looked away, pressing on the accelerator that would get him back to Cameron and away from the temptation that was Carly. It would be a cold day in hell before he'd volunteer for anymore sightseeing expeditions.

"I appreciate you taking time out of your day to show me around Cameron." Her low voice echoed in the quiet of the car, scraping over his nerves like coarse sandpaper.

He tightened his hands on the steering wheel, trying to ignore the need that hummed through him. "Don't mention it. I'm never sorry for an excuse to spend time out here."

He wanted to make their trip sound impersonal, like something he would do for anyone. He wasn't sure he succeeded.

Carly turned and looked out the window. "It's so beautiful," she murmured. "I'd forgotten how beautiful it is."

"You've been to Utah before?"

He glanced over at her in surprise. If he hadn't, he would have missed the momentary tensing of her shoulders, the slight stiffening of her spine. "Years ago," she said, and the casual tone in her voice sounded forced. "When I was a kid."

"Is that why you came here to do your story?"

The silence hung between them, stretching out more and more tightly. Finally she said, "It was just coincidence." Her voice sounded stronger. "It was reading the stories about the two little girls and Sy Ames and Becca Farrell that intrigued me. Once I started to research Cameron, I realized it was a place I wanted to write about."

"Where did you visit when you were a child?"

At that she turned to look at him. "The usual tourist places, I suppose. Children's memories are unreliable."

The open, relaxed look had disappeared from her face and she was no longer smiling. Now she looked like the hard, driven reporter he wanted her to be—the kind of woman he wasn't interested in. But deep in her eyes was a disturbing vulnerability, and he had to stop himself from reaching for her.

He recited every curse he knew until the city limits of Cameron came into view. Reminding himself to slow down, he drove carefully toward Melba Corboy's boarding house. But when Carly saw where he was heading, she sat up straight.

"I want to go back to Main Street, if that's all right with you."

"You work late hours," he said, trying to keep his voice neutral.

At that she grinned again. "Working late hours my behind. I'm trying to avoid dinner at Melba's."

He couldn't stop himself from responding to the smile in her voice. Feeling an answering smile creep over his face, he turned the truck around and headed back toward his office. "I didn't realize it was almost time for dinner. That was a close call."

Her rich chuckle filled the car. "Believe me, after last night, I keep track of the time. I'm going to be planted in Heaven on Seventh for a while tonight."

He knew it was insanity, knew it was a mistake, but he couldn't stop himself. "Mind if I join you?"

The air in the car suddenly swirled with tension and unspoken questions. She hesitated for a moment too long, then said easily, "Of course not. I'd enjoy that."

He was a complete and utter fool, he told himself savagely as he parked the car and walked around to open the door for her. His mood didn't improve when she slid out of the car, her snug jeans emphasizing the long, slim length of her legs. He was jumping into a swamp full of alligators with his eyes wide open.

But when she turned to him and smiled, he felt his common sense slipping away. It was only dinner, he told himself. The restaurant would be full of people. What could happen in a crowded restaurant?

Two hours later, Carly brushed past Devlin to step onto the sidewalk in front of Heaven on Seventh. They had been in a crowded restaurant, she told herself. How had it managed to seem so intimate? Why did it feel as though they were the only two people in the room?

Because they'd been so involved in each other it was like no one else in the room even existed, she acknowledged. Neither of them had mentioned Cameron or why she was here. Instead they'd talked about themselves, about their interests and their jobs. And they'd laughed together.

That was dangerous. A shared sense of humor could be deadly. She needed to keep a clear head while she was in Cameron. She couldn't allow anything to distract her, not even the attractive sheriff. Especially not the attractive sheriff.

As they walked down the sidewalk, she tried to stop herself from edging closer to him. Even though there was a foot of space separating them, the heat from his body poured over hers. It wrapped itself around her, shielding her from the cooling air of the nighttime desert and trying to lure her into his orbit.

His scent was sharper here in the clean air, too. Pine and leather blended together until she could smell nothing but him, until the essence of Devlin filled her senses.

She allowed herself to glance over at him, but she couldn't read his expression. His hat shielded his face in shadow. Would his gray eyes be bright silver, as they had in the restaurant, luring her, beckoning her to lose herself in their depths? Or would they be the hard pewter she'd seen earlier in the day, warning her off when she'd asked too many questions about Devlin and Cameron?

She had no idea. But she wanted to find out, and the knowledge disturbed her. She had no time in her life for involvement, and especially not with this particular man. Her body couldn't have picked a worse man to notice.

At the corner she started to turn right and Devlin started to turn left. They bumped into each other, and he reached out to steady her. His fingers curled around her arm, sending tiny shocks sizzling through her skin. His hands were hard and callused, rough against her arm. But she didn't try to pull away.

She stood staring up at him, her heart tripping once then booming in her chest. His hold on her arm shifted, turned into a caress. When he trailed his fingers down her arm and lingered over her wrist, she felt an answering tug deep in her abdomen. And when he smoothed his fingers over her palm lightly before letting his hand drop away, a thrill of desire shivered through her.

"I thought you wanted to go back to Melba's," he said, his voice deep and rough.

She swallowed once, trying to find her voice. "I do."

"Then we have to go this way." He took her arm and steered her to the left. "Melba's place is over a couple of blocks."

Heat poured into her where he held her arm. Her skin tingled from his touch and begged for more contact. She wanted to feel his hands everywhere on her skin and she wanted to touch him. After a moment he dropped her arm, but she was still too aware of him, her body aching, her fingers yearning to explore him.

She wondered if he was aware of the way her heart was pound-

ing. It boomed so loud in her ears she was sure he could hear
every beat. Even the sound of her swallow seemed to echo in the
silence.

She had to regain her bearings, she thought desperately. She
couldn't allow herself to want Devlin like this. "Thank you for
sharing dinner with me."

Her voice didn't sound as firm and detached as she'd hoped.
She sounded more like she'd just tumbled out of bed.

He looked down at her. "It was my pleasure."

His voice was too low, too personal and intimate. It didn't
sound like he was thanking her for dinner, she thought helplessly.
It sounded like a caress.

They were almost at Melba's. As they turned a corner, she
could see the house down the street. Melba had left the porch
light on, and Carly kept her gaze fixed on it. She only had to
make it a few more feet and she could escape into the house and
away from the disturbing sensations Devlin was causing.

When they reached the sidewalk up to Melba's porch, she
turned to Devlin and offered him her hand. "Thank you for walking me home. It wasn't necessary, but I appreciate it."

Instead of taking her offered hand, he rocked back on his heels
and looked over at the porch. "You're not home yet, Carly. I'll
see you to the door."

Without waiting for her to answer, he put his hand in the small
of her back and walked up the porch stairs with her. When she
reached for the door, he slid in front of it, blocking her way.

"Good night, Carly," he whispered.

As he moved toward her she backed up, unable to look away
from his face. When she reached the shadows at the edge of the
porch and her legs bumped against the railing, she put her hands
against his chest. "What do you want, Devlin?"

"One taste," he murmured. "That's all I want." He lifted his
hands and framed her face, and her heart began to pound in her
chest.

He skimmed his fingers gently down her face, their faint roughness searing her skin. His touch was as light as a caress, and

when he lingered next to her mouth, she closed her eyes and shivered.

"Devlin..." she heard herself say. She barely recognized the throaty plea in her voice. It belonged to another woman, one who knew how to seduce a man. A woman who wanted to seduce this man.

Before she could stop herself, before she could think, she slid her hands up his chest and around his shoulders. He felt so solid, so strong. Her hands ached to slip beneath his khaki shirt, to glide over his chest. Her heart raced and desire stirred, deep inside her, as she imagined his skin, hot and slick beneath her fingers.

As he stared down at her, he lifted one hand and swept his hat away. It landed on the floor of the porch with a soft thud. His hair gleamed golden in the faint glow from a distant streetlight, and his eyes were hot and needy.

Slowly he bent toward her, until their lips were barely touching. Even that slight caress made her shiver with need. She wanted to taste him, too. She wanted to feel his hands on her, to know that his urgency matched her own.

Then he groaned and pulled her against him. The hard planes of his body pressed into her, imprinting himself on her. When his mouth came down on hers, his kiss exploded in her mouth. Desire and need, hot and aching, swirled through her. And she felt an equal need in him. His arms trembled as he held her against him. When he moved her backward, pressing her against the wall of the house, the muscles of his leg were rock-hard with tension.

He moved restlessly against her, and she responded instinctively. Her back was against the wall of the house and he stepped between her legs, his body covering hers. He surrounded her. Every inch of her body was touching his, and she still needed to get closer to him. Her lips were fused to his, and as she moaned his name in the back of her throat, she opened her mouth to him.

Need swirled and churned inside her. It was only a kiss, and he'd taken her to heights she hadn't thought possible. Her body ached for him, ached to feel his flesh against her flesh. When he slid his hands down her back and cupped her hips in his palms, pulling her closer against him, she groaned, deep in her throat, and strained against him.

When he moved from her lips and trailed his mouth down her neck, she tightened her hands on his shirt. "Devlin," she gasped.

He lifted his head to stare at her, and in the moonlight she saw the glitter of arousal in his eyes. Slowly he brought his hands up to her face and smoothed his thumbs along her cheeks. Then he bent his head to kiss her again, his mouth consuming hers. She tasted his need and his passion as they melded with hers, all rational thought falling away as she gave herself over to the sensations of his mouth and body on hers.

It could have been minutes or hours when a sound pierced her consciousness. Devlin must have heard it, too, because he tensed and lifted his head. After a long moment he relaxed. "Just a cat," he murmured, but as he looked down at her she watched the heat fade from his eyes, replaced by a careful coolness. "This can't be comfortable for you," he said, his voice a low rumble, and he stepped back until they were no longer touching.

The sudden chill made her shiver. And the coolness in his eyes made her want to run and hide. Instead she straightened her spine and raised her chin. "Thank you again for sharing dinner with me, Sheriff. And thanks for walking me home. I'll see you around."

As she tried to brush past him, he reached out and took her hand. "I'm sorry, Carly," he said, his voice so low it was almost a whisper. "I had no business kissing you like that."

"And I had no business kissing you back. So we're even." She was proud of the fact that her voice didn't quaver. "From now on it's strictly business, right, Sheriff?"

"Right."

For a moment the heat flared in his eyes again, and she couldn't stop the answering surge inside herself. But now that he wasn't touching her, now that the fog of desire was clearing from her brain, she was appalled at what had happened. She had been wrapped around him on the front porch, in plain view of anyone in Cameron. She had been kissing Devlin McAllister, and in a few more minutes it would have gone far beyond kissing.

She mentally thanked whatever cat had made the noise that stopped them. Because she hadn't come here to kiss Devlin McAllister. She'd come to Cameron to make his family pay for what they had done.

Chapter 4

Carly watched as Devlin bent to retrieve his hat, brushed it against his leg then set it on his head. Once again the brim shadowed his eyes, hiding their expression.

She didn't need to see his eyes. The way they'd cooled, the way the silver had turned to stone a few moments earlier, was imprinted on her memory. He wasn't eager to get involved, either. And she was glad, she told herself firmly. It would make everything less complicated. Any involvement between her and Devlin McAllister was doomed to failure anyway, as soon as he found out why she was really in Cameron.

"Good night, Devlin," she said, her voice firm. "Thanks again for the tour."

Beneath the brim of the hat she saw his mouth curl into a mocking smile. "You're welcome, Slick. I was worried there for a moment. I thought the reporter was taking a break and letting the real woman out. I see I was wrong."

"I was afraid the sheriff was taking a break, too. I'm glad that we're both back on track," she answered. She was proud of the coolness in her voice, the lack of emotion.

"Right." He touched his hat and turned away. His broad shoulders blocked out the porch light for a moment, making the night as dark as the emptiness inside her. For a second she yearned to call him back, tell him she hadn't made a mistake. That she'd wanted to kiss him, wanted to do a lot more than that.

Instead she drew herself up straight and watched him disappear into the darkness. When he was out of sight, she sank down onto the porch swing and pushed it into motion. As she swayed back and forth, she thought about Devlin and the McAllisters, about the sister he adored who was now running the ranch, about the father who'd died.

It didn't matter that she wanted Devlin McAllister. She wouldn't allow it to matter. She couldn't turn back now. Even though Devlin's father was dead, she had to know the truth. Her brother's death had cast a shadow over her entire life, and now she needed to be free of that shadow. The only way to do that was to find the truth, to confront it once and for all. She owed it to Edmund, who had died far too young, murdered in cold blood. She owed it to her mother, whose life had changed forever on the night Edmund died and who had died without knowing the truth. And she owed it to herself.

By the time she rose from the swing, the moon had risen and climbed halfway up the sky. Stiff and cold, she walked into the house and up the stairs to her room. When she slipped between the sheets of her bed, she tried to hold onto a faint memory of her brother and nourish it with her plan for justice.

But instead, as she fell asleep, it was Devlin McAllister's face that haunted her dreams.

The next morning Carly slipped into Heaven on Seventh for breakfast and told herself not to look over at the corner booth. She did anyway, and it took only a glance to see that Devlin wasn't there. Six or seven deputies sat around the table, but instead of Devlin, the one she remembered as Ben was in Devlin's seat.

Was Devlin sick? Had he had an accident last night? She didn't realize she was staring at the table of deputies until Phyllis walked over with a pot of coffee and poured her a cup.

"Today is Dev's day off," she said, setting the pot of coffee on the table and whipping out her order pad. "That's why Ben's in charge." She grinned when Carly jerked her head around to stare at the waitress. "I could see the questions on your face. You being a reporter and all, I figured you were wondering."

Carly swallowed once and nodded, embarrassed to be caught staring. "I want to get a feel for how Cameron works," she said lightly. "How many days off a week do the deputies get?"

"They all work five-day weeks. Dev usually does, too, unless one of the boys is out sick. Then he picks up the slack."

"What does the sheriff do with his time off?" She tried to keep her voice casual and light, playing the reporter who's merely curious. But she hungered to know more about the man Devlin was.

Phyllis snorted. "What time off? When Dev's not on duty, he's out at the Red Rock, helping his sister with the ranch chores." She shook her head. "That boy needs to lighten up, if you want my opinion. He's working himself into an early grave."

"I got the impression that he didn't care much for ranch work."

"He doesn't," the waitress said frankly. "Everyone in Cameron knows his heart is in the sheriff's office. But he's not about to let his sister work herself into the ground, either. Shea works more than any ten people I know."

"Couldn't they hire someone to help out?"

Phyllis shook her head. "It's not that easy to find reliable help on a ranch, especially in an out-of-the-way place like Cameron. Plus they can't afford to pay much. They had a young guy there for a while, but I guess he didn't work out. So until someone else shows up who's willing to work cheap, they do it all themselves." From the way Phyllis's face softened, it was obvious she thought highly of Devlin and his sister.

Phyllis took her order and left, and Carly stared down into her coffee cup. So the McAllister's were hard-working people who had endeared themselves to the town of Cameron. It didn't matter, Carly told herself fiercely. Their father had killed her brother. That was the reality. And if the truth changed the way the people of Cameron looked at the McAllisters, there was some justice in that, too. Because her brother Edmund's death had changed Carly's whole life.

After finishing her breakfast, Carly headed back to the newspaper office. She was determined to find the newspapers from twenty years ago and read the stories about what had happened in Cameron in the months before Edmund died. They might give her a place to start, a reason he'd been killed. And the stories about his murder could supply names of people who were witnesses or who knew something about the incident. If it took a week of sifting through papers in the basement of the newspaper office, that's what she would do.

Pushing open the door to the office of the *Cameron Weekly Sentinel,* she saw that Ralph Hanson was at the desk today. She smiled at him and held out her hand.

"Good morning, Mr. Hanson. I'm back to look at your files again."

He smiled back, but she could see that it was an effort. "Good morning, Carly." He hesitated for a moment too long, then waved toward the stairs. "Go ahead and take a look. I'm sorry that the files aren't in better order." His gaze traveled around the office, and Carly glanced around. No wonder the files in the basement were in such a jumble, she thought. Clearly, organization was not the Hansons' strong suit.

"Does it matter how long I stay?" she asked, turning as she started down the stairs.

"What exactly are you looking for?"

Carly shrugged. "I'm just looking. I don't know enough about Cameron to have anything specific in mind. I just want to get a feel for the town."

Ralph studied her, his brown eyes suddenly and surprisingly hard. "Take all the time you want. We want you to say only positive things about Cameron in your article."

She gave him a noncommittal smile and headed down the stairs, wondering at Ralph's reaction. It was almost as if he didn't want her looking at the newspapers, but didn't know how to tell her no.

Then she stepped into the basement room again and looked around ruefully. The answer was probably no more complicated than Ralph's embarrassment about the way he kept his files. Slipping her backpack off her shoulders, she pulled open a file drawer and got to work.

Carly had no idea of how much time had passed when she heard footsteps on the stairs. Jerking her attention away from the file cabinet she was searching, she slammed the door shut and turned to face whoever was coming down the stairs. Had Ralph Hanson changed his mind about letting her look at the files?

But it wasn't Ralph who appeared at the bottom of the stairs. Devlin swung around the corner and stopped, watching her.

For a moment, his eyes softened. Embers of the passion of the night before flared into life, and a shadow of the desire they'd shared quivered in the air between them.

Then she straightened and forced herself to forget about the night before. "Good morning, Devlin. What are you doing here?"

His eyes cooled as he stared at her. "I might ask you the same thing. June Hanson said that yesterday you were looking for papers from twenty years ago. How is that going to help you write an article about Cameron today?"

"Are you asking in an official capacity?" She was trembling inside, but she hoped her voice was cool.

His face darkened. "What the hell is that supposed to mean?"

"Did the Hansons ask you to get rid of me?"

"No, they did not." His eyes flashed at her. "I stopped in because of another matter, and they mentioned you were here. They were concerned about what you were looking for, and I told them I'd ask."

"If the Hansons don't want me here, all they have to do is say so." She gave him a thin smile. "Although I find it interesting that they would object. What are they afraid of?"

He stared at her for a long minute, his jaw tense, his eyes cold steel. Then he sighed. "Hell, Carly, is everyone from New York this prickly? They're older folks with some personal problems. They're afraid you're going to dig out their troubles and splash it across your magazine. Can't you understand that?"

"I already told you I have no intention of publicizing their problems. You can assure them that I'm not snooping into their private lives."

"Then what are you doing?"

"It's called research." She waved a hand at the file cabinets. "This is the history of your town. Where else am I going to get this kind of information?"

He strolled past her and pulled open a file drawer. Pulling out a yellowing copy of the paper, he studied the first page. Then, a smile teasing the corners of his mouth, he handed it to her.

"Is this what you had in mind?"

The tension in the room dissipated as she glanced at the paper, then laughed. "I don't think that's going to make the cut into my story. 'Steer escapes and tramples garden, ruins prize-winning tomatoes and zucchini' isn't exactly cutting edge journalism."

His smile disappeared. "But it's what Cameron is all about. This is the news in our town. Remember that, and you'll be just fine."

He watched her for a moment with unreadable eyes, then said, "I'll reassure the Hansons again. Sorry I disturbed you."

She listened to him walk up the stairs, and heard the low murmur of his voice up in the office. Finally the door opened, and then there was silence again.

Devlin had filled the room with his presence, making it seem more inviting. Now it was a dusty, damp basement again, and she needed to get back to work. Slamming the file drawer shut, she looked around the basement. Clearly the old newspapers weren't neatly filed away.

She finally found them. Hidden in a far corner of the basement, behind the file cabinets and covered by a collection of broken office equipment, she discovered several cardboard boxes, stained and dusty with age. When she dragged the boxes into the center of the room and opened the first one, she was elated to find that the papers dated from the time before her brother's death.

Banishing Devlin from her mind, she sat on the floor for a long time, staring at the issue on top of the box. "Joseph and Marla Whitmore, Publishers," the paper proudly proclaimed. Finally she pulled it out of the box and held it with hands that shook, tracing the names with her finger.

Her parents' names.

Carly checked the date carefully and saw that it was several months before her brother had died. Her father had been dead for a few years by then, but her mother had kept his name on the masthead. She'd always said that it was his paper, anyway. And her mother had never really been interested in publishing a small town newspaper. She'd only done it in order to keep the paper going until her son could take over.

Swallowing the ball of grief that lodged in her throat at the sight of her parents' names, Carly carefully put the paper aside and removed the next issue. It was for the following week, and she felt a tingle of excitement. Were all the papers in order?

They were. Handling the fragile newspapers carefully, she removed them until she found the issue for the week her brother had died. She would go back and study the earlier papers later. Now she wanted to read the stories about her brother's death. She carried several papers over to a work bench and turned on a light.

The story about Edmund's murder was on the front page, but it said nothing about any suspects or motives for the slaying. It just gave the bare facts—that seventeen-year-old Edmund Whitmore had been found shot to death on the McAllister ranch, outside of Cameron. Frowning, she read the story again, certain she had somehow missed the information. But it wasn't there.

She found another story in the next week's issue. This time, the article included the information that Edmund was shot with a slug from a small-gauge shotgun. The authorities were looking for a weapon missing from the McAllister ranch. That was it.

On the last page she found a small obituary. Her mother was listed as a survivor, and her own name was there. Caroline Whitmore, dear sister. The words suddenly blurred as she stared at the yellowed newspaper. At eight years old, she hadn't completely understood what had happened. But she remembered her mother's inconsolable grief and her own confusion. And she remembered the day when she finally realized that she'd never see her loving, happy-go-lucky brother again.

Swallowing her grief and her tears, she set aside the paper containing the obituary and picked up the next week's issue. There was a story on the front page again, but this time it detailed the death of a man described as a drifter. His body had been found at the bottom of a cliff on McAllister land, his neck broken, and it was assumed he'd been the man who killed Edmund Whitmore. The story closed with the information that the gun missing from the McAllister house hadn't been found, and neither had the Whitmore murder weapon. Two weeks later there was a small blurb on an inside page about the case. All it said was the sheriff had decided there wasn't enough evidence to make an arrest in the Whitmore case, but he was looking for more information.

Then, nothing. That was all the information in the *Cameron Weekly Sentinel* about her brother's death. She paged through a number of issues after those, and found a story about her mother selling the *Sentinel* to Ralph Hanson, the editor. Marla Whitmore moving away with her eight-year-old daughter was briefly noted, and after that there was no further mention of the Whitmore family. They might have vanished from the face of the earth, for all the notice they got in Cameron.

Slowly Carly replaced all the old papers in the box, with the exception of the four that mentioned her brother's death. Then she dragged the boxes back to their hiding place. Slinging her backpack over her shoulder, she walked up the stairs, squinting in the bright light.

June Hanson was now at the desk, and when she looked over at Carly her glance sharpened when she saw the newspapers in her hand.

"Find something interesting?"

"Yes, as a matter of fact. Do you have a copy machine I could use?"

June hesitated for a moment, and the expression on her face told Carly she would have refused if she could have thought of a reason. Finally she said, grudgingly, "Over there."

"I'll be happy to pay for copies," Carly said, reaching into her pocket for some coins.

Behind her, June blustered, "That's not necessary," but Carly set the pile of coins on the side of the copier.

It only took a moment to make copies of the four stories. After slipping the still warm sheets of paper into her backpack, Carly cradled the four issues of the *Sentinel* in her arms and headed down the stairs again. "I'm just going to put these back," she called to June.

As she replaced the papers, she heard June's footsteps approach the top of the stairs. "You put everything back where you found it," she called down.

She had every intention of doing just that, Carly thought grimly as she struggled to replace the heavy office equipment that sat on top of the boxes. She planned on studying these papers, and she didn't want them to disappear. And the best way of preventing that was to leave them just as she'd found them. It would take a while for anyone to find the boxes, and that's exactly what she wanted.

When everything was restored to its former disarray, Carly turned off the light and headed back up the stairs. June stood at the top, blocking her way.

"Did you find some interesting story about Cameron?" she asked, her eyes wary.

Carly shrugged, trying to look nonchalant, but she watched June carefully. "I'm not sure. There was a small story about a boy killed on one of the local ranches, and I thought it was something our readers would find interesting. You know, like something from the Old West." Silently she apologized to her brother for trivializing his death.

She expected June to nod and agree, but instead she tightened her lips. "You're trying to make Cameron look bad."

"Not at all, Mrs. Hanson. I know nothing about the story. It just caught my eye." She watched the other woman carefully. "Do you know anything about it?"

"The Whitmore boy had no business out there on the McAllister ranch," she said. "If he wasn't doing something wrong, why was he shot?"

Carly tightened her grip on her backpack and schooled her face to show no expression. "I'm surprised you remembered his name after all these years."

June flushed a dark red. "Things like that don't happen in Cameron. Of course I remembered it."

Carly took a deep breath and moved around the older woman. "Thank you for your help. I'll probably see you again soon."

She hurried to the door before June could stop her. Once out on the street, she took a deep breath of the fresh air. The scent of dust and mold still clung to her, and even in the heat she shivered. The dampness from the basement must have crept into her bones.

Adjusting the backpack on her shoulders, she headed down the street. She needed to sit for a while and think about the newspaper articles she'd found, and what they meant. It was hard to believe that the shooting of a teen-age boy hadn't elicited more of an investigation, especially in a small town like Cameron.

She was so lost in thought that she almost bumped into Gladys Jones as she came out of one of the stores. "I'm sorry, Gladys," Carly said, holding onto the older woman's arm to steady her.

"That's all right, dear." The other woman studied her with shrewd eyes. "It looks as if there's something on your mind."

Carly made a quick decision. The sooner she began asking people about Edmund's death, the sooner she would begin to gather information. And she knew Gladys had lived in Cameron for more than twenty years.

"There is, actually, Gladys. I found a story in one of the old *Weekly Sentinel*s about a young man who was shot out on the McAllister ranch. It struck me as odd, because the young man died, but apparently there wasn't much of an investigation. There was very little information in the paper about it."

Distress filled the older woman's eyes. "I remember when that happened," she said in a soft voice. "His mother was beside herself. She accused the McAllisters of murdering her boy, and the sheriff of covering it up. She was distraught, of course, but several of us wondered. We thought it was odd that everything was hushed up so fast. The sheriff said he was satisfied that the drifter they found dead had killed the boy, and that was the end of it. Marla Whitmore insisted he do something more, but old Bert Pickens just dug in his heels and refused.''

"What happened to the family?" Carly asked, although she knew very well. She simply wanted to keep Gladys talking.

Gladys's eyes clouded. "They sold the newspaper to Ralph Hanson and moved away shortly after it happened. No one in Cameron heard from them again. I've always hoped that Marla and her little girl ended up on their feet somewhere.''

Carly's heart warmed to Gladys. Their move away from Cameron when she was eight hadn't been completely forgotten. "Thanks for telling me about it," she said, trying to keep her voice casual. "If you remember any of the details, let me know.''

"Are you going to write about that incident?" Gladys looked troubled. "That's not the way I'd like to see Cameron represented in the national press.''

Shame swept over Carly for deceiving Gladys. She didn't want to hurt this woman who had been so pleasant and friendly to her. So she forced a smile onto her face. "I'm not sure, Gladys. It sounded like something from the Old West that would appeal to readers. But I think I need more information before I make a decision about whether to use it in my article.''

Gladys studied her for a moment, then nodded. "I trust you'll make the right decision, Carly. I can see that you're an honorable person.''

As Gladys hurried away, Carly stared after her. Was she an honorable person? Did honor include lying to people to get what you needed?

In this case, it did, she told herself firmly. And if it didn't, she was willing to sacrifice some of her honor to get justice for her brother. Apparently no one else in Cameron besides her mother had ever tried to do that.

Carly walked slowly down the sidewalk, trying to decide what to do next. Ahead of her she saw Gladys stop to talk to someone in a dusty blue truck. Gladys smiled and walked away, and a second later the door of the truck opened and Devlin stepped out.

She hadn't been paying attention to his clothing in the Hansons' basement, but here in the sunlight she realized he wasn't wearing his khaki uniform shirt today. Instead he wore a faded blue work shirt with the sleeves rolled to his elbows. His jeans were old and worn colorless at the stress points, and his boots showed the scuff marks and scratches of hard use. And overlaying everything was a coat of fine red dust. When he wiped his face with the sleeve of his shirt, he left a smear of ochre behind.

Carly slowed her steps, but Devlin turned around and looked at her. Almost, she thought uneasily, as if he had some kind of radar that was tuned to her. Just as she had recognized him before he was completely out of the truck.

She was too far away to read his expression, but he waited for her. When she was close enough to see the dust in the creases in his face, he nodded at her. "Hello again, Carly."

"Hello, Devlin. I'm surprised you're still in town. I thought this was your day off."

"It is." His eyes lingered on her for a moment too long, then he nodded toward the store on her left. "This is my last stop. I have to pick something up for Shea."

"You've been busy this morning."

He shrugged. "There's always something to do on a ranch." His eyes hardened as he watched her. "Gladys tells me you've been busy, too. It sounds like you found something more interesting than the story about the steer."

Her chin tilted. "I'm here to do a job, and that's what I was doing."

"Asking questions about something that happened twenty years ago is part of writing an article on Cameron as a tourist destination?"

"I was looking for some history of the town, something that would define Cameron. Do you have a problem with that?"

He rubbed his hand across his face, smearing the dust more. "Yeah, I have a problem with that. One isolated incident from twenty years ago doesn't define any town."

"Could the fact that your father was involved have anything to do with your feelings?" she asked.

A spark of admiration, quickly hidden, flashed in his eyes. "You know how to get to the heart of a situation, don't you?"

"That's what I'm paid to do." She hoped the smile she gave him was cool. "What's your take on the story?"

His eyes hardened, but not before she saw something deep in their gray depths. Something that looked like guilt. It disappeared as he stared at her, replaced by hard resolve. "I was twelve years old when the Whitmore boy was shot. I don't have any take on the story."

"Your father never talked about it?"

"He wasn't a murderer, if that's what you're asking."

"According to the stories in the newspapers, a gun disappeared from your house. And the murder weapon was never found."

This time there was no mistaking the guilt. Or the anger. "The sheriff realized right away that anyone could have taken that gun. There wasn't any other evidence. In this country, a man is innocent until proven guilty."

"You're right." Her voice was cool as she watched Devlin. His face didn't give anything away, but she wouldn't forget the reaction he'd had to her questions. she asked, "Did you know the boy?"

"Only enough to know who he was. Seventeen-year-olds don't usually spend much time with twelve-year-old kids."

Carly gave him a tight smile. "Thanks, Devlin. I appreciate your answers."

"I couldn't tell you much." He studied her, then straightened. "Are you really going to pursue this story? You won't be able to find much out after twenty years."

"That remains to be seen, doesn't it?"

He moved a step closer, close enough that she could reach out and touch him. In spite of the anger that poured out of him, her fingers ached to feel the strength of his muscles again, to bury themselves in the coarse silk of his hair. His eyes flashed at her, but she didn't think it was the same light she'd seen in them the night before.

"Gladys Jones is upset. I don't like to see my citizens upset, Carly. She thinks you're going to write an article slamming Cameron."

She gave him a scornful look. "That should make you happy. Then no one would come here and disturb your peace and quiet."

To her surprise, the anger vanished from his eyes and he grinned at her. "You're a piece of work, Slick. I told Gladys I was sure you wouldn't do any such thing. I was right, wasn't I?"

She wished he'd stayed angry at her. Angry she could deal with. When he gave her that teasing grin, she melted like an ice cream cone on a hot Utah day. Trying to maintain her cool, unaffected facade, she shrugged her shoulders. "I don't know what I'm going to write about yet. I saw the article and it caught my eye. But since you and Gladys have both come after me about it, I may have to look into it more carefully. It looks like someone is trying to hide something."

His grin faded. "Be careful, Carly. You can pick at me about it all you want, but someone else might not take it so well. Other people may not like you writing negative things about Cameron."

"Is that a warning?" she asked, disbelief in her voice.

"Take it any way you want. Just think about what you're doing."

"I've done a lot of that already." He had no idea how much she'd thought about this trip to Cameron.

Before he could answer, a heavy-set man emerged from the store in front of them. "Hey, Dev, Shea called and said you'd be coming."

"Hey yourself, Marv. Do you have that wire she needs?" Dev answered.

"You're all set. Just pull around back and I'll help you get it loaded."

Marv disappeared back into his store, and Devlin turned to Carly. "I have to pick up some barbed wire for Shea. She's waiting for it, or I'd stay and talk to you." He hesitated, then said, "Do you want to have dinner tomorrow? I'll be back at work then."

Her heart began to pound as she remembered how their last dinner together had ended. She knew she should say no, maintain some distance from him, but she smiled and said, "I'd love to."

He nodded. "I'll pick you up at Melba's tomorrow at six."

She watched as he swung up into the truck, his muscles rippling beneath the worn jeans that fit him like a second skin. After he slammed the door, he leaned out the open window to give her another grin. "Give 'em hell, Slick."

The engine gunned once, then he pulled away. She stood staring at the truck until it disappeared around a corner.

She had to accept his dinner invitation, she told herself. After all, it was Devlin's father who had killed her brother. And the guilt in his eyes told her that he knew more than he was telling her. It was her job to find out what it was.

But it didn't feel like she was having dinner with Devlin in order to do her job. The real reason she had agreed to dinner, she knew, was the smile he'd tossed her, the smile that reminded her of how he'd made her feel on Melba's porch the night before.

That was dangerous. That was playing with fire. But she could afford to fly a little close to the flames, she thought as she headed back down to the restaurant. She wouldn't be in town long enough to get singed.

Several hours later, she walked back down the dimly lit streets toward Melba's boarding house. She'd lingered over her dinner at Heaven on Seventh. A number of people had heard she was asking about the Whitmore boy's death, and they all had opinions. Carly had listened to every one of them, taking surreptitious notes.

She had stayed at the restaurant so long that it was completely dark, she realized. She would never have been able to walk alone down a street like this in New York, but here in Cameron, she felt no sense of unease. There were some benefits to small-town life.

Melba had left the porch lights on, as usual. Carly suppressed a grin as she remembered Melba's reaction to her proposal to take her meals elsewhere. She'd seen the older woman's relieved expression, and realized that Melba didn't like to cook. Melba had even grudgingly offered to give back some of her deposit. Carly had declined, knowing that the other woman needed the money, but there had been a marked lessening of the older woman's stiffness. Melba had even smiled at her a time or two.

The front door was unlocked. As she pushed the door shut behind her and locked it instinctively, Carly wondered if anyone in town ever locked their door. She suspected not. Her lips curled up in a smile. Another thing to like about small towns.

The house was quiet and the living room dark. Usually Melba watched television until she went to bed. "Melba?" she called, but there was no answer.

Carly frowned. In the few nights she'd been in Cameron, Melba had never varied from her routine. Standing at the bottom of the stairs, she called up, "Melba? Are you up there?"

The house remained silent. Carly switched on the hall light, then noticed the note propped up on the hall table. Grabbing it, she let out a sigh of relief. Melba had gone to her weekly bingo game.

Smiling softly, Carly climbed the stairs. She didn't realize that there were still people left in the world who were so trusting. It took a lot of faith in the people in your town to leave your house and not bother to lock it. She hoped nothing ever happened to change Melba's trust.

Switching on the light in her room, she slung her backpack onto the floor. That's when she noticed that the rag rug had been kicked to one side. She stared at it, frowning. Melba was too particular a housekeeper to leave the rug like that. And her room had been in order when she'd left that morning.

Out of the corner of her eye she saw something glint off the mirror. She spun around, a gasp caught in her throat.

An ugly red message covered the mirror. The letters looked like they'd been scrawled in blood.

Get out of Cameron.

Chapter 5

Devlin had just finished dinner when the phone next to the dining room table rang. Gulping one more sip of coffee, he reached for the receiver, waving Shea back to her seat.

"McAllister."

"Dev. Thank goodness."

He recognized Ben's voice immediately. And his deputy's tight voice had him taking another gulp of coffee and looking around for the keys to his truck.

"What's up, Ben?"

"I think you might want to come in for this," Ben said. "It's that reporter, Carly Fitzpatrick."

Devlin's hand tightened on the phone as dread snaked into his stomach. "What happened?"

"Someone broke into Melba's place and got into her room."

"Is she all right?" Dev asked sharply.

"She's okay. A little shaken up, I'd guess, although she insists she's fine. She didn't even call me. Melba had to do that. Apparently she got home from her bingo game right after Carly saw the mess."

"Is Carly hurt?"

"No. The intruder was gone by the time she got there."

"What's missing from her room?"

"That's the thing. It doesn't look like anything's gone. Someone just left a message for her, written on the mirror. Get out of Cameron, it said. In red."

Devlin let out a string of curses. "Hang on, Ben. I'll be right there. And don't let anyone else into that room, including Ms. Fitzpatrick."

"I know the drill, Dev. We'll be waiting."

Devlin hung up the phone and headed for the door. His sister had pushed away from the table, and his mother had come in from the kitchen. "What's wrong?" Shea asked.

He ran his fingers through his hair and sighed. "I told you there was another reporter in town. Someone just left her a nasty message on the mirror in her room at Melba Corboy's." He gave his sister a brief hug. "It looks like I won't be able to help you finish stringing that fence tomorrow morning after all. I'll find some time in the next few days, though. Don't you try to do it yourself."

"You've got a job to do." Shea pushed him toward the door. "Don't worry about the fence. It'll get taken care of. Go catch some bad guys."

"I'm serious, Shea. Don't try to handle that fence yourself. I'll have some free time in the next day or two, and we'll do it then."

"Fine." She tossed him his hat, then held the door open for him. "Now get going."

He'd bet a million bucks she'd be out there tomorrow morning stringing that fence. Dev's mouth tightened as he climbed into his truck, then he gave an involuntary smile. Shea had always done just as she pleased. Why did he think she was going to stop now? They needed to hire someone to help out at the Red Rock Ranch, he told himself as he accelerated toward Cameron, and they needed to do it soon.

But he couldn't worry about that now. Tonight he was the sheriff again, not the part owner of the Red Rock Ranch. As he sped through the darkness toward the town, he banished all thoughts of the ranch and allowed himself to think about Carly again.

He hadn't been pleased to run into her in town earlier in the day. The memory of the kiss they'd shared had lingered with him all night, disturbing his sleep and making him restless and distracted the following morning. And he'd been so besotted that he'd actually asked her to have dinner with him.

He was a damn fool, he told himself grimly. And now, if his obsession with her wasn't bad enough, she'd gone and gotten herself into trouble.

He could handle trouble. He could switch off his emotions and solve the problem. After all, he was an expert in switching off his emotions. He did it every time he was tempted to get involved.

He thought about Carly again, coming home to an empty room and a scrawled message on the mirror, and he pressed the accelerator to the floor of the truck.

When he pulled up in front of Melba Corboy's place, Ben's truck was sitting next to the curb. The police vehicle was a grim reminder that a crime had occurred. Dev's truck had barely come to a stop when he jumped out and headed up Melba's walk, practically running.

Melba opened the door immediately. Her face was pinched and tight, and beneath her usual frown he saw real fear.

"Are you all right, Melba?" he asked.

She nodded once, her lips a tight line. "She's in the parlor." She jerked her head toward the left. "She didn't want to call you. Said it wasn't any big deal." Her lips thinned even more. "Someone comes into my house, leaves ugly messages on my boarders' mirrors, it's a big deal."

"Why don't you make yourself and Carly a cup of tea?" he said, steering the older woman toward the parlor. "It sounds like you could both use something hot and sweet."

Melba considered for a moment, then nodded. "I think I will."

Devlin watched her disappear into the kitchen, then he walked into the parlor. Carly sat huddled in a high-backed wing chair, her green eyes huge and dark in her pale face. When she saw him, she sat up straight and tried to smile.

"What are you doing here?" she asked. He heard the false note of brightness in her voice.

"What do you think I'm doing here?" He couldn't keep the roughness out of his voice. "Ben called me and told me about your 'incident.' Why the *hell* didn't you call me yourself?"

Her chin tilted. "I didn't think it was necessary to call anyone. Mrs. Corboy is the one who called Ben. And I think it would have been a bit presumptuous to call you at your home. Isn't Ben capable of handling a bit of graffiti?"

"It's more than a bit of graffiti, and you know it. Someone threatened you."

"There was no threat." A flash of contrariness reappeared in her eyes, and he relaxed just a bit. "Someone merely wanted to tell me what to do."

"I guess they don't know you very well if they thought you would listen," he muttered. He was delighted to see the ghost of a grin flash across her face.

She watched him steadily, and he saw more color come into her face. "This isn't the first time someone has tried to stop me when I've been working on a story, and I'm sure it won't be the last." She looked out the darkened window, and some of the animation disappeared from her face. "It's just the first time it's happened in a small town like this." She looked back at him, and he thought he saw sadness in her eyes.

"When I got here, Mrs. Corboy was gone, but the door was unlocked. Right before I walked into my room and found the message, I'd been thinking about how nice it was that Mrs. Corboy didn't have to worry about leaving her house and not locking the door." She gave a short, humorless laugh. "On the way home from dinner, I was comparing Cameron with New York. I never would have considered walking home alone on a deserted street in New York. I guess I'll have to think twice about it here in Cameron, now, too."

"Cameron is a safe town," he said, crossing his arms over his chest. It was either do that or give into the need to wrap his arms around her, to hold her and comfort her until that lost look disappeared from her eyes. "You *don't* have to worry about walking down the street alone. I'll find out who left this message, believe me.''

"It doesn't matter who left the message." She stood up, and her movements were jerky. "What's significant is that someone thought it needed to be given at all. I've only been here three days, and the only person who's objected to my presence is you. Are you sure someone in the sheriff's department didn't get a little overzealous?''

He was astounded. "You think that me or one of my deputies broke into your room and left you that message?''

"Who else could it be?" She turned to face him, meeting his eyes steadily. "I don't think it was you, personally, but who else has said they wanted me gone? No one. Not one other person has objected to what I'm doing in Cameron.''

"You can't be serious." He wasn't sure whether to laugh or get angry.

She shrugged. "What would you think?''

"I'd think there was someone in town who had a problem with the questions you've been asking.''

This time she moved closer as her eyes flashed green sparks. "The only questions I've been asking in town are about an incident that involved your family.''

A sick feeling began to gather in his stomach. A guilt that he thought he'd dealt with years ago swept over him again. "Carly, that was twenty years ago. I was twelve years old at the time. You can't believe that I had anything to do with the murder of that boy.''

"No, I don't think that." Her voice was suddenly exhausted as she stared out the window again. "But his body was found on your ranch. Your family is involved." She turned to face him again. "And I know how you feel about your family. You were very clear on that yesterday.''

"I'm a law enforcement officer," he said, and his voice was clipped. "I've sworn to uphold the law, and I take my oaths seriously. You're mistaken.''

"I hope so.''

He took off his hat and tossed it onto a chair. "Hell, Carly, can you look me in the eye and say that you think I was responsible for leaving you an anonymous message?"

She didn't want to meet his eyes. It was written in the tense line of her body, in the tilt of her chin that was just a little too defiant. When she did, the green fire of her eyes blazed for a moment, then dimmed. Finally she sighed. "No, Devlin, I don't think it was you. But I don't think it's altogether absurd that one of your deputies thought he was helping you out."

"My men aren't stupid. Why would any of them do such a damn fool thing?"

She actually smiled. "Even a blind person could see how much they think of you. They all worship the ground you walk on. Maybe they thought they were doing you a favor."

"My men know better than that," he said grimly. "But I'll question them. And if one of them is responsible, I'll kick his butt from here to the Arizona border and back. Before I pull his badge and gun."

Her eyes softened as she studied him. "Thank you," she said softly.

"There's nothing to thank me for."

"I think there is. Most people would have defended their employees."

"You notice that I said I would question them, not that I believed you. I have no doubt none of them were involved, but since you asked the question, you deserve an answer."

She nodded once. "That's fair."

He sketched a salute to her. "I try. I know in your mind I'm just a good-old-boy, back-country, hick sheriff. But we manage to do pretty well here in Cameron. For a backward town, anyway."

"I didn't mean to offend you."

He didn't bother to hide his anger. It was one way of getting his mind off how vulnerable she looked, and how much he wanted to protect her. "I'm sure you didn't. Just like I'm sure that a person from New York would never be able to understand our values here, or what's important to us."

Her lips tightened. "I don't think that's fair. People who live in small towns don't have a monopoly on honor."

He smiled thinly. "That's funny. I don't think I ever mentioned honor. Why would you assume that's what I meant?"

She turned away, but not before he'd seen the sudden pain in her eyes. And suddenly all his anger was gone, destroyed by a pair of wounded green eyes. He wanted to snatch back the angry words, but it was too late. He'd allowed Carly to slip past the barriers he maintained around himself, and she'd goaded him into revealing his true feelings. Now, appalled, he could only try to repair the damage. And then reinforce the barriers.

"Maybe you should take a look at the crime scene, Sheriff," she said quietly.

"I'll do that." It was as good a way as any to escape. "I'll be back in a while."

"There's no hurry."

No, he was in no hurry to get back to Carly Fitzpatrick, he told himself grimly as he started up the stairs. She had managed to make him lose control, something that rarely, if ever, happened. And it was all because of the pain he'd seen in her eyes. Pain that he didn't even understand.

Ruthlessly he closed off that part of his mind and walked into Carly's bedroom. "What do you have, Ben?"

The deputy turned and straightened, holding a canister of fingerprint dust. "A lot of fingerprints, but ten to one they'll turn out to belong to Melba or Ms. Fitzpatrick." He nodded at the scrawled message on the mirror. "That was done with one of Ms. Fitzpatrick's tubes of lipstick."

Devlin saw the gold lipstick case, carefully enclosed in a plastic bag. "Any fingerprints on that?"

"I didn't dust it yet, but it's going to be tough to find anything. It's got a textured surface."

Dev swore beneath his breath. "Anything else?"

Ben shook his head. "According to Ms. Fitzpatrick, nothing else seemed to be disturbed. The only thing she noticed out of place was the rug on the floor. It was bunched up, like someone might have slipped on it."

Devlin stood in the middle of the room and let his gaze travel slowly over everything it contained. Carly was apparently a neat person. There were no piles of clothes on the floor, and her toiletries were arranged neatly on one end of the dresser. When he felt his gaze lingering on the feminine bottles with the intriguing shapes, wondering if they would have the same scent that seemed to surround Carly, he jerked his eyes away. There was a pile of books on the table next to the bed, and the bed itself was neatly made.

He stepped out of the room and ran downstairs. "Carly, could you come up to your room, please?"

Carly looked up from the mug of tea she was sipping. "Have you found something?" There was a mixture of hope and fear in her eyes.

"No. I just want you to check once more to make sure nothing is missing."

She set the mug down on a marble-topped table, then walked up the stairs with him. Her subtle scent, the one he'd just been fantasizing about, surrounded him once more, making him remember how she'd tasted the night before. Clenching his jaw, he slowed down so that she moved ahead of him. The scent retreated, but it didn't disappear completely.

Carly paused at the door to her room, and Dev could feel her reluctance to enter it. Finally she stepped over the threshold, but he noticed that she didn't step far into the room.

"You told Ben that nothing's been disturbed besides the message on the mirror?" he asked, watching her closely.

"The rug was bunched up, too. I knew Mrs. Corboy wouldn't have left it like that."

"Did you check through your things?"

"I made sure my computer was all right, and my envelope full of traveler's checks. They were all there."

"So burglary doesn't seem to be the motive."

She turned to him then. "I think the motive is quite clear."

"So do I." His voice was grim. "But in order to be thorough, humor me and check everything else."

It took only a few minutes for Carly to check through the

drawers of the dresser and the small closet. It took a few more for her to check her briefcase and the small bag on the floor of the closet. Finally she stood up. "Everything else is fine. I'm almost positive that nothing else has been touched."

Dev turned to Ben. "Are you finished here?"

The deputy nodded. "I need to label the items I'm taking and make out a receipt for Ms. Fitzpatrick, then I'll be gone." He showed her what he was taking and filled out a piece of paper.

Carly signed the receipt, her glance resting on the lipstick case for a moment. Then she looked away. "You can keep that. There's no way I want it back."

After Ben left, Devlin sat down on the hard-backed chair that stood near the window. "Sit down, Carly. I have a few questions for you."

She sat down on the bed, facing him, and he thought she braced herself for his questions.

"Who did you talk to today about the Whitmore boy?"

"The Hansons, of course, since I looked at their newspapers. Gladys Jones, because I saw her right before I saw you." She looked directly at him, then glanced away. "You, too."

"I thought we'd agreed that I wasn't responsible." His voice was mild. "But if you're still not sure, you can talk to my mother and Shea. They can vouch for the fact that I haven't left the ranch since this afternoon."

A red stain crept up her neck and onto her cheeks. "I didn't mean I thought it was you. I was only trying to organize my thoughts, remember who I talked to after you."

"And who was that?" He strained to keep his voice even, his temper in check.

She shrugged helplessly. "Half the town, I think. I didn't even know the names of most of the people who talked to me."

"Is that what they teach in journalism school? Solicit opinions from every Joe Blow who walks by, but don't bother to get their names or verify what they're saying?" He didn't bother to hide the scorn in his voice. It was easier to be angry, far safer to concentrate on his outrage than to notice the bruised look in her eyes.

"I was only trying to get impressions of what people thought, to find out exactly what happened," she said, and her voice was weary. "I'm not quoting anyone. The articles in your town newspaper weren't exactly brimming over with details."

"Then give me the names you remember." He flipped open his notebook.

Fifteen minutes later he snapped the notebook closed. "I can start with these people. I'll talk to them tomorrow, see if they know anything."

Carly turned around and glanced at the red scrawl on the mirror, then faced him again. "Thank you, Sheriff, but I know the drill, and I'm sure you do, too. No one will know anything. You'll waste a couple of days, and you won't know any more than you do now. Don't bother."

"It's not a bother." His voice was even. "A crime was committed in Cameron, and it's my job to solve it."

A tiny smile flickered on her face, then was gone. "Thank you, Devlin. But don't lose any sleep about it. Believe me, I won't."

She was lying, and he knew it. His anger fell away, replaced by the need to comfort her. "I'll be right back."

In a few moments he walked back into her room, holding rags and window cleaner. After some vigorous scrubbing, the mirror was sparkling clean. Not a trace of the lipstick remained. Only when it was completely gone did he set down the rag and turn to her.

"Melba probably has another room you could take. Can I help you move your things?"

She shook her head. "I'll stay in this room. Melba told me she was going to keep the door locked from now on. I'm sure I'll be fine." She walked over to the window and stared down at the dark street in front of the house. "I hate that this had to happen at Melba's house. I hate that she has to change the way she lives because someone doesn't like what I'm doing."

Her voice was so low he had to strain to hear her. He moved to stand closer. "It's not your fault, Carly."

She glanced over her shoulder at him, then looked back toward the street. He saw the regret in her eyes. "Yes, it is. If I hadn't been asking questions, no one would have felt the need to tell me to leave. And that person wouldn't have violated Melba's house."

"So why don't you stop?"

"Would you stop doing your job if someone told you he didn't like the way you were doing it?"

"Of course not."

The smile she gave him was pointed. "Neither will I."

Carly crossed her arms over her chest and held onto her shoulders. He thought she trembled, although the room still held the warmth of the day. Before he realized what he was doing, he reached out and cupped her shoulders, covering her hands with his. Her fingers were icy, and he felt a shiver ripple through her.

"You're a courageous woman," he murmured, drawing her closer. "I don't like what you're doing, but I have to hand it to you. You don't back down."

"I learned that lesson a long time ago. If you back down, you're going to get knocked down."

He pulled her against his chest, and after a moment the tension seeped out of her rigid shoulders and she allowed herself to relax. Slowly he stroked her arms, and gradually she stopped shivering. Her smooth, soft skin became warm and pliant under his fingers, and suddenly there was a different kind of tension swirling around them.

He slowed his hands, then stopped, but he didn't let her go. His fingers dipped into the bend of her elbow, and he felt her pulse leap under his touch. Her skin heated, and when his hand moved again, he felt her tremble. He didn't think it was from the cold.

"Carly," he whispered, as he bent to kiss the side of her neck. The skin beneath her ear was soft and fragrant, and he lingered there, tasting and caressing. Her breath broke once, then again as he curled his tongue around her earlobe.

He burned for her. Even as he kissed her neck again, every fiber of him throbbed to possess her, to claim her as his own. Need was an aching void at the core of his being, demanding to be filled.

Her scent curled inside of him, wrapping around a place he

guarded fiercely. Closing his eyes, he buried his face in her hair, drinking her in, letting her fill him.

When she turned her head to find his lips with her own, his control broke. Her name a low growl in his throat, he found her mouth and took it. His lips and tongue devoured her, and the essence of Carly filled his head.

She met his desire, kiss for kiss, passion for passion. When his tongue swept into her mouth, she moaned his name and shook in his arms. He wrapped his arms around her to pull her even closer, feeling every bump in her spine burn into his chest, letting his rock-hard erection nestle into the cleft in her buttocks.

Her breasts were inches away from his hands. Slowly he moved his hands upward, until the soft fullness of them filled his palms. Tremors racked through him, but he wasn't sure if it was he or Carly who was trembling more. When he touched her nipples through the rough material of her shirt, they were stiff and swollen. He heard her gasp, swallowed the sound with his mouth.

It could have been hours that they stood there. Every time he brushed his fingers over her nipples, she shook. When he lingered, she moaned into his mouth. His own body was one aching, throbbing mass of need. Every nerve screamed at him to bury himself inside her, to feel the hot, slick center of her welcoming him. She wanted him, he knew, with an intensity to match his own. He felt it in the shaking of her body, in the desperation of her kisses, in the tiny sounds she made in her throat.

Roughly he turned her to face him. Her eyes were closed, her face flushed with pleasure. "Look at me," he whispered.

When she opened her eyes, they were dark, unfocused pools of passion and pleasure. He saw her need in them, the desire that was impossible to hide. He bent to kiss her again, and her mouth met his eagerly.

They twined together, chest to chest, leg to leg. Every inch of him demanded her touch, ached to feel her hands on his skin. He wanted to rip away the barriers of their clothing, to allow hot, needy flesh to join and become one.

But the one part of him capable of rational thought wouldn't allow him to go any further. Cursing his conscience, he forced himself to gentle his hands and his mouth. As much as he wanted her, and as much as she seemed to want him, he couldn't take advantage of her vulnerability.

He was supposed to be helping her. She'd had a shock, and now that the adrenaline was ebbing, she was looking for something to reassure her. Only an unprincipled bastard would make love to a woman under those circumstances.

But he couldn't bring himself to let her go completely, not yet. He had never known such pleasure from merely touching and kissing a woman. And never had a woman in his arms responded the way Carly responded. So he kissed her again, softly this time, and smoothed her hair away from her face.

Her eyes fluttered open, and she struggled to focus on him. "What's wrong?" she asked.

"Nothing's wrong." He bent to kiss her again, and he knew that she could taste his need, his desire in the way his mouth lingered. "I just don't think this is the time or place."

She stared at him for a long moment, bewildered, her eyes still clouded with passion. Then her eyes cleared, and although the passion lingered, he could see the second that she regained control.

She stepped back, touching one hand to her mouth. He wondered if it was still throbbing, if his taste still lingered on her lips. He didn't think he'd ever forget how Carly tasted.

"You're right." She spoke in a low voice, passion making it more husky than ever. "I don't know what I was thinking about."

He watched as she stood taller and tried to hide the desire that still filled her eyes. And suddenly he wondered if she thought he had stopped because he hadn't wanted her enough.

"Don't think that," he said, his voice a low growl in the room.

"Don't think what?"

"That I didn't want you. I've never wanted anything more in my life."

Some of the caution eased in her eyes. "Then why did you stop?"

He couldn't resist touching her. His fingers trailed down her cheek, then slid over her lips, memorizing their shape and texture.

"I have some principles. One of them involves not taking advantage of women. And I would have been taking advantage of you, Carly. You'd just had a shock, and you were looking for comfort. I let it go way beyond the comfort stage."

"Just when I think I have you figured out, you surprise me again," she murmured. She brushed a kiss over his lips, then glanced around the room. Surprisingly, she smiled at him. "At least I won't have nightmares about an intruder in my room. I suspect I'll be having far different dreams tonight."

Her green eyes seemed to glow in the light from the one small lamp, and Devlin had to stop himself from reaching for her again. If he touched her one more time, he wouldn't leave this room tonight.

"I'll see you in the morning, Carly." He paused at the door of her room. "And if anything else happens, call me. I'll be at the office."

He was down the stairs and out the door of Melba's house before he could talk himself into staying. Carly would feel different in the morning, he told himself. She would have had a chance to think about what had happened, and realize it was a reaction to stress, nothing more. He wouldn't allow it to be more.

He drove over to the office, where he found Ben working on the samples he'd collected in Carly's room. His deputy's dark head was bent over his work, and he realized that Ben should have gone off duty a couple of hours ago. But he was still here, working.

It made him remember what Carly had said about his deputies, and how they felt about him. Surely she was wrong. He didn't want to be the kind of man to inspire those kinds of feelings in his employees. He wanted them to do a good job for the town, not for him.

"Tell me something, Ben." Dev tilted back in his chair and crossed his hands behind his head, deliberately trying to lighten his mood. "Do you worship the ground I walk on?"

Ben choked and sputtered on the coffee he was drinking. When he looked at Dev, his dark eyes were wary. "You know I respect the hell out of you," he said cautiously.

"But you don't light candles at my shrine?"

A grin teased the corners of Ben's mouth, and his eyes crinkled. "Hell, no. I'm too busy trying to handle your work and mine to be lighting candles."

"Thank God." Dev tilted his chair upright again. "Carly had me worried there for a while. Let's get busy. It looks like we've got another situation in Cameron."

Chapter 6

The next morning, Carly thought longingly of the pancakes at Heaven on Seventh as she walked into Melba's dining room. But she banished them from her mind as she watched the older woman set a coffeepot down on the sideboard. She needed to make sure Melba had recovered from the night before. "I just want a bowl of cereal and a cup of coffee," she told Melba brightly.

Carly chose a box of cereal from the sideboard and poured herself a cup of coffee, then sat down to eat. Melba joined her a few minutes later.

"Are you all right this morning?" Carly asked.

"I'm fine." Melba compressed her lips together. "Whoever was in my house last night won't get in again. Next time I'll be waiting for him."

"I'm sorry it happened," Carly said softly.

She thought Melba's gaze softened. "It's not your fault, girl."

"They were leaving a message for me. So in a way it is." She set her coffee cup down. She'd get another one, later, at Heaven on Seventh.

"You're just doing your job," Melba said, her voice gruff. "Don't you let one no-account sneak scare you off."

Carly smiled at the woman who'd been her third grade teacher. "Don't worry, I won't."

As she pushed her chair away from the table, she added, "I won't be here for dinner tonight, either." She felt her cheeks warm. "I have a, ah, date."

Surprisingly, Melba nodded at her, a look of satisfaction on her face. "You go and have a good time. I saw the way he was looking at you last night."

Blazing heat scorched her neck and face. "It's not like that, Ms. Corboy."

Melba gave her a look of scorn. "I have eyes, missy. I may be getting on in years, but I can still put two and two together and come up with four. The sheriff is a good man. You could do a lot worse."

Mumbling something incoherent, Carly grabbed her backpack and headed for the front door. When she yanked it open, she nearly barreled into Devlin, who was standing on the other side.

"Morning, Carly." His eyes sharpened as he looked at her and he grabbed her arm. "What's wrong?"

"Nothing's wrong." She swallowed once and tossed him what she hoped was a casual smile. There was no way he could have heard what Melba had said, she told herself. "I was just surprised to see you."

"I thought I'd stop by and see how you and Melba were doing. And ask if there was anything you'd thought of that you hadn't told me."

He was still holding her arm, but his fingers had gentled. Slowly his palm brushed down her arm until he reached her wrist. He circled her wrist with his hand, feathered one finger over her palm, then let her hand drop.

It happened so quickly it could almost be mistaken for a casual touch. Almost, but not quite. She suspected he'd felt her pulse leap in her wrist, was certain he'd noticed her hand trembling.

Just as she'd felt his hand shake before it dropped away from her.

"Melba's in the dining room," she said, her voice huskier than usual. She cleared her throat. "I think she's fine."

He nodded, but didn't take his eyes off her. "Were you headed out?"

"Yes." She gripped the strap of her backpack and stared back at him defiantly, unwilling to tell him where she was going. She didn't want another lecture about the Hansons.

His eyes hardened as he watched her. "Wait a few minutes. I need to talk to you, too."

She sat down on the stairs and listened to the rise and fall of voices from the dining room. From the tone of the higher-pitched voice, Melba was telling Devlin exactly what she was going to do if she caught their intruder. Carly smothered a grin as she heard Devlin's patient, reassuring reply, then her smile faded.

He really did care about the people of Cameron. He didn't have to come back here this morning and see how Melba was doing. But he'd understood that underneath her bluster, the older woman was upset.

It was getting harder and harder to think of Devlin as the enemy. Desire stirred, deep inside, as she remembered their kisses of the night before, but she forced the memory out of her mind. She had to think of him that way. There was no future for Carly Fitzpatrick and Devlin McAllister. There couldn't be. Sooner or later he would find out why she was really in Cameron, and then the passion would disappear from his eyes. All that would be left was scorn and mistrust.

She heard him walking through the parlor and stood up. She wanted every advantage she could get when she faced him.

"Can I take another look at your room?" he said, stopping in front of her.

"Of course." She turned and led the way upstairs.

He hesitated before he walked into her room, and she wondered if his memories of the night before made him stop. She didn't look at his face. Instead, she stepped into the room and stared out the window. After a moment, he followed her.

"Have you found anything missing since last night?" His low voice rippled over her, making her shiver.

Only her tunnel-visioned sense of purpose. The thought shocked her, and she shook her head numbly. "Everything seems to be here."

"Have you looked through all your things?"

"Yes. It didn't take long. I didn't bring a lot with me."

"You believe in traveling light?"

His words were casual, but she heard the intensity beneath them. She turned around to face him. "I always travel light. I never stay in one place for very long."

Their eyes met and held, and finally he nodded. "That's what I figured."

"I'd pegged you for the same type, Sheriff," she said, her voice soft.

Their eyes locked. His mouth flattened, and finally he said, "You're right. I don't travel much, but when I do, I never stay very long."

"Then we have something in common, it seems." Clearly, neither of them had any interest in getting involved. Her heart pounded at the suddenly fierce expression in his eyes.

"I'm afraid that's true." He watched her for another moment, his eyes suddenly hungry, then he turned away. "It would be best if we both remembered that."

"I intend to, Sheriff."

"Good. So do I."

He stood with his back toward her, and she watched as his gaze traveled around the room. The tension in his muscles slowly eased, and finally he turned to face her. There was no hint of personal involvement in his face. Once again he was the sheriff, in complete control.

"Ben didn't find any fingerprints on the lipstick case. We don't have the fancy equipment we'd need to get them, so we're sending the case to the state lab. He lifted a bunch of prints from other things in the room, but they'll probably turn out to be yours or Melba's. I'd appreciate it if you'd come to the office later today and give us a set of your prints."

"Was there something else you needed from my room this morning?" she asked.

His jaw tightened as he looked around the room one more time. "No. I just wanted to get another look at it in daylight. See if anything else struck me."

"I don't expect you to find the person who did this," she said. "In New York, it would hardly be worth calling the police about it. After all, the person who broke in didn't take anything."

At her words his face hardened again. "This isn't New York," he snapped. "This is Cameron, Utah, and we get upset when someone breaks into an old woman's house and leaves threatening messages on the mirrors. You can be sure I'll do my damnedest to find out who did this."

"I'm sorry," she said. "I didn't mean to imply that you wouldn't do your job. I just meant that it's not a big deal. It wouldn't be the first time I've been threatened because of my job."

"It is a big deal, Carly. It's a very big deal." His voice was soft, and he stepped closer. "I want to know why someone felt it was necessary to tell you to leave Cameron. I want to know what hornet's nest you've stirred up. And I'm not going to stop until I find out."

"Then we both want the same thing." She shouldered her backpack again and moved toward the door. "It appears I touched a nerve when I asked about that boy's murder. I'm going to continue my investigation, and I'll let you get on with yours."

"Don't you think it's just as likely someone doesn't want Cameron made into a tourist destination?" he demanded.

Carly shrugged. "I have no idea. But I guess we'll find out."

She turned and hurried down the stairs before Devlin could tempt her to linger. In spite of her words about traveling light, she wanted to spend more time with Cameron's intriguing sheriff. She wanted to find out why he, also, traveled light through life. And, God help her, one part of her wanted to try and make him change his mind.

By the time she finished another cup of coffee at Heaven on Seventh, most of the breakfast crowd had dissipated. When a small, slender woman with curly red-gold hair pulled back ruthlessly into a braid stopped by her table with a pot of coffee, she looked up from her notes in confusion.

"What happened to Phyllis?" she asked.

The woman nodded at the clock. "Her shift is finished." She watched Carly with unsmiling eyes. "Do you want more coffee?"

"No, thanks." Carly looked around the restaurant and found it nearly empty. "Are you the lunch waitress?"

The other woman shook her head. "I'm the owner."

"You must be Janie, then." Carly looked at her more carefully. "I'm glad to meet you."

Janie nodded once. "Welcome to Cameron. Just be careful what you say about us in your article."

Carly leaned back against the vinyl of the booth. "You agree with Sheriff McAllister, then? You don't want to see Cameron become a tourist town?"

Janie watched her coolly. "I like Cameron just the way it is. I don't want it to change."

Carly nodded. "I'll keep that in mind."

"You do that." Janie slipped the check on the table, then hurried away. She carefully avoided the back booth, where Ben Jackson sat with a couple of the other deputies. Carly watched as Ben stared at Janie, almost as if he couldn't help himself. Janie didn't return the look, but tension swirled in the air between them. Then Janie fled into the kitchen, and Carly knew the owner wouldn't be back in front until Ben had left the restaurant.

Wondering idly why Heaven on Seventh's owner was so skittish, and what was going on between her and the deputy, Carly paid her bill and walked out into the sunshine. Even though it was autumn, the sun was merciless. Heat rose up from the sidewalk in waves, and by the time she reached the newspaper office she was looking forward to the cool dampness in the basement.

Ralph Hanson was sitting at the desk when she walked in, and she saw his face tense at the sight of her. "Morning, Ms. Fitzpatrick. What can I do for you today?"

"I'm back to look at your old newspapers again, Mr. Hanson. If that's all right with you."

She saw him hesitate, and knew that he was searching for an

excuse to forbid her access. She jumped in to reassure him before he could tell her no. "Mr. Hanson, I want to assure you that I have no intention of writing about anyone's personal problems. That's not why I came to Cameron." She hesitated, unsure of how much to say. "I don't know why Sheriff McAllister was here talking to you the other day, and I don't care to know. I'm interested in the town, and that's why I want to look at your papers. That's the only reason."

"June said you were asking about what happened to that Whitmore boy. That was twenty years ago." His expression hardened. "That sounds like you're interested in raking up the past. What does that have to do with making Cameron into a tourist attraction?"

"Nothing, really. It's just an interesting bit of local history." She smiled at him. "People like knowing a place's history. It makes them feel connected to the town. That's why I was interested in the story. Plus it sounds like something out of the Old West." She shrugged. "You know how it is in the news business. The lurid is what draws people every time." Again she silently begged her brother's forgiveness for trivializing his death.

Some of the wariness left Ralph's eyes, but not all of it. "Go ahead, then, and use the papers. But folks around here aren't going to appreciate it if you dredge up old scandals and splash them across the pages of your magazine."

"I don't think you're going to have to worry about that, Mr. Hanson."

He nodded, but watched her as she descended the stairs. She wondered again what had made Ralph and June so nervous. Could they have been involved somehow in Edmund's death?

Dropping her backpack on the table in the basement, she uncovered the newspapers she'd hidden the day before. She was determined to read every one of them, if necessary, to get to the truth.

When Carly emerged into the sunlight again, she squinted at the brightness of the Utah sun and took a deep breath of the fresh air. She was stiff and cold from spending too long in the newspaper office's basement, but she didn't care. She'd found some information, and she was anxious to ask Devlin about it.

But when she arrived at the sheriff's office, she found only Ben Jackson. He looked up when she walked in, and nodded at her gravely.

"Dev told me you'd be by."

For a moment Carly was confused. How could Devlin have known that she'd seek him out? Then she remembered the fingerprints. "Right. You wanted a set of my fingerprints."

Ben stood up and led her over to a table. "It'll just take a minute. Then I can eliminate your fingerprints from the ones we've found in your room." For a moment, a ghost of a smile flitted across his face. "Ms. Corboy was in earlier."

"Did she give you a hard time?"

Ben gave her an actual smile. "She loved every minute of it. Said that it reminded her of one of her favorite television programs. She even asked me for a second set that she could keep." He reached for her hand and expertly rolled each finger in ink, then onto a card.

"Melba seems to be taking it real well."

Ben's smile faded. "She's a tough old bird. But she's still old. I don't like the fact that this happened to her. And neither does Dev."

"Speaking of Dev, is he around?" Carly hoped her question was casual enough.

Ben shook his head. "He had some business out on one of the ranches." He handed her a towel to clean her fingers, then turned around. "He asked me to give you this when you stopped in."

Carly took the note and thanked Ben, then hurried out the door. When she was standing on the sidewalk, alone, she took a deep breath and opened the note.

I'll pick you up at five. Wear comfortable shoes.

He'd scrawled his name and nothing more in a bold, masculine line. So he hadn't forgotten his dinner invitation. She looked down at the note again and a smile curled her lips. Wear comfortable shoes. She wondered what he had in mind.

She found out when he came to Melba's door promptly at five o'clock. He'd changed his khaki uniform shirt for a soft flannel, but he certainly hadn't dressed for dinner. She was glad she'd worn a pair of jeans and a blouse. And her new hiking boots.

"Thanks for taking my advice," he said, his eyes softening.

"It sounded more like a command." Her voice was teasing as she pulled the door of Melba's house closed behind her, then checked to make sure it locked.

He shrugged. "I just wanted to make sure you were comfortable. City-girl shoes would be a definite liability."

"At Heaven on Seventh?" She raised her eyebrows.

"We're not going to Heaven for dinner," he said, opening the door of his truck. She noticed that it was his police Blazer. "I had a better idea."

He didn't say anything more until he stopped in front of the restaurant. "I'll be right out."

He emerged a few minutes later with a large box, which he stowed in the back of the truck. When they were headed out of town, he said, "I thought you might enjoy a picnic. You haven't seen much of the area."

"You showed me a lot of the area the other day."

He shot her a look. "You never even got out of the car. How can you say you know an area if you haven't stepped foot on the ground?"

"Where are we going?" She settled back as a sizzle of excitement raced through her. A picnic. She couldn't remember the last time she'd been on a picnic.

"We're going to the Red Rock Ranch. We have a lot of land up in the mountains, land that isn't much good for grazing. We use it mostly for recreation. You'll be able to see what this part of the country is really like."

"That sounds wonderful."

His eyes softened as he glanced over at her. "I thought it would be a good idea. You've spent almost all your time in Cameron since you've been here."

"Is this supposed to be a propaganda trip?" Her voice was light. "Show me the great, unspoiled land and convince me not to force it to become a tourist haven?"

He shrugged, but didn't seem to take offense. "Look at it any way you like. I haven't had time lately to get up into the mountains, and I miss it." He paused. "I wanted to share it with you."

She thought the last sentence had been dragged out of him unwillingly, but she was still moved. "Thank you, Devlin. I can't think of anyone I'd rather share a picnic with, either."

He slowed the truck and turned into a long driveway that curved around a cliff. When the road straightened out again, she saw a white house and several other, smaller buildings in front of her. A red barn stood off to her left. Behind the buildings, green pastures undulated into the distance, and red cliffs rose up to tower over pastures and buildings.

"This is lovely," she said, and meant every word.

"I think so."

He was driving past the house when a blond woman jumped off the porch and hurried toward them. Braking, he lowered the window as she crossed in front of the truck.

"Hey, Shea."

"Hey yourself, Dev." The woman peered into the window. "You must be Carly." She reached across Devlin to shake Carly's hand. "I'm Shea McAllister, Dev's sister. Welcome to Cameron."

Shea's grip was firm and her hand felt hard and callused. Carly smiled at her. "Thank you. It's nice to meet you." She hesitated. "I'm sure Dev's told you why I'm in Cameron. Are your feelings about my job as strong as your brother's?"

Shea grinned at her. "The only thing I feel strongly about right now is getting a bunch of calves branded." She looked back at Dev. "When will you have some time?"

Dev ran his fingers through his hair. "I can probably spare a half day tomorrow or the next day. I'll let you know in the morning."

"Great." She stepped away from the truck. "Have a good time

up there.'' She shot a grin at Carly. ''Make him show you his hiding place.''

Dev waited until Shea had run into the house again, then he started the truck. Carly turned to him. ''What hiding place is she talking about?''

His face softened. ''When I was a kid, I hated doing ranch work. I understood that we all had to do chores, and I did mine without complaining, but I wasn't interested in anything extra. Unlike Shea.'' His mouth curled into a smile, and Carly saw his love for his sister shining out of his eyes. ''She followed my father and the hands around from sunup until sundown. She couldn't get enough of the Red Rock. I couldn't wait to grow up and get away from the place.''

''So you found a place to hide?''

He grinned again. ''I found a dandy place to spend my extra hours and dream about what I would be when I grew up. Shea found it, of course, but she never told anyone else.''

The truck bumped up a rutted path, steering around rocks. The trees were very close to the edge of the road, and at one point she looked out over the edge of a cliff. The bottom seemed a long way down.

''This doesn't make you nervous, does it?'' Devlin asked.

''Not at all.'' She answered too quickly, and he shot her an amused glance.

''No one's fallen off the road yet,'' he said.

''Thank you for pointing that out.''

''Any time.'' He grinned at her, then swung onto another road, this one even more rutted and full of rocks. At least they were driving away from the cliff's edge.

A few minutes later, Devlin stopped the truck next to a deep blue lake. On the other side of the lake she saw what looked like a tiny cabin tucked into a thicket of dark green trees. The rest of the lake was surrounded by red rock, the remains of once-steep cliffs eroded into fantastic formations and shapes.

''This is my favorite part of the ranch,'' Devlin said, getting out of the truck. ''When I was a kid, I thought you could see forever from up here.''

"It looks like you still can," she said softly, gazing at the vista in front of them. Range after range of mountains fell away in front of them, the rocks a wild palette of colors. Purple, pink, red and orange stood out against the blue sky and the occasional patch of green pasture below them. "This is breathtaking."

"It's home." He spoke without looking at her, still staring out at the magnificent vista, but his reverent voice told her how deeply he felt about this land.

His words hung between them, and Carly knew that if she had really been in Cameron to write a story to attract tourists, she would have turned around and gone home. Standing here, in the late afternoon sun, staring out at this awe-inspiring sight, she understood exactly how Devlin felt about Cameron. And why he didn't want it to change.

But she wasn't here to write about Cameron as a tourist destination, she reminded herself. So she moved away, clambering over the rocks, determined to get away from the feelings bubbling too close to the surface.

"Was your hiding place around here?" she asked.

Devlin turned to look at her, then stepped back from the edge of the rock. "No, it's on the other side of the lake, closer to the house. I'll show you later."

He reached into the truck for the box and a large blanket, and when they had settled on the ground he opened the box and removed the picnic food. "It looks like Janie outdid herself," he said with a smile as he handed her smaller boxes of food.

Carly leaned back against a rock and watched Dev as they ate. She had never seen him so relaxed. The watchful tension that was so much a part of him had disappeared.

"Is this where you go to get away from your job?" she finally asked.

Smile lines around his eyes crinkled as he answered her. "Yeah, I can hide up here. No one will bother to come this far to get me unless it's really important. As much as I didn't want to be in charge of a working ranch, I love the Red Rock. It's a part of me, and it always will be."

"You're lucky," she murmured, almost against her will.

"Where's home for you, Carly?" Dev set his food down and leaned toward her.

She stared at the cliffs in the distance, cliffs that had been part of Devlin's home for his whole life. Then she thought about the nomadic existence she and her mother had followed after they left Cameron. "A condo in New York is home for me," she finally said.

"No, I mean where did you grow up? Where are your roots?"

"I guess I don't have any." She shrugged and tried to make her voice light. "It was just my mother and I, and we moved around a lot when I was growing up."

"I'm sorry," he said after a moment.

"Don't be." She gave him a bright smile. "We did just fine."

Sympathy and understanding filled his eyes, then Dev scrambled to his feet. Apparently he was no more eager than she was to explore the bonds that seemed to be forming between them. "Are you ready to explore my hiding place?"

"Lead on." She took the hand he'd extended, then let him go as soon as she was standing. She didn't need any more connections to Devlin. She was afraid there were too many already.

He loaded the remains of their picnic into the truck, then drove around the lake, stopping at what looked like a sheer wall of red rock. "Here we are."

Carly eyed the rock dubiously. "It doesn't look like a rabbit could find a place to hide in that. Are you sure we're in the right place?"

He grinned at her. "Come and see."

Taking her hand, he scrambled up a short slope and stopped in front of a boulder. It looked like the rock had tumbled down the cliff and come to a precarious rest in front of them. Devlin dropped her hand, ducked down and disappeared.

A moment later he reappeared, grinning at her. "Care to join me?"

Carly edged closer to the boulder, then saw where Devlin had gone. The huge rock wasn't sitting against the cliff, as it appeared from a distance. There was a small opening between the boulder and the cliff. Devlin reached for her hand.

"Come on in."

The opening was plenty big for her to slip through, although it must be a tight fit for Devlin. Once she'd gotten through the opening in the rock, she found herself in a small cave. It extended back into the darkness, but it was tall enough for her to stand upright. Devlin had to keep his head bowed.

"What a great hiding place!" When she looked back at the opening, she could see the boulder, outlined by the blue sky. The light illuminated the front of the cave, but the back was still in darkness. "How did you ever find this cave?"

"Luck, I think." He squatted down on the floor and reached into the darkness. Pulling a old, battered pair of saddlebags into the light, he reached into one of them and drew out a blanket, then spread it on the ground. "I was climbing these rocks one day when I saw the opening." He grinned at her, and his smile seemed to brighten the dimly lit cave. "What kid can resist a cave?"

"So you would come up here and hide from the world?" she asked.

His smile dimmed as he sat down on the blanket, then pulled her down next to him. "My father, mostly. He wanted me to take over the ranch when he retired, and that was the last thing I wanted to do. Shea was far better for the job than I was, but he wouldn't hear of it. Said it wasn't a job for a woman." He stared out at the brilliant blue of the sky. "We had a lot of fights about it when I was a teenager, and this place was a haven for me."

Carly pictured Devlin as a lonely teen, escaping up into the mountains to recover from yet another fight with his father, and her heart stirred in sympathy. She knew something about problems with parents. She touched his arm. "I'm sorry."

He gave her a smile. "It's okay. I'm all grown up now."

There was no question about that. His skin was warm, the coarse hairs surprisingly silky under her fingers. As her fingers lingered, she felt him tense. Slowly he turned to look at her.

"Carly?" he whispered. He looked down at her hand, still resting on his arm, and her heart began to pound. The dry, aromatic desert air filled her head, swirling together with Devlin's scent, and suddenly she forgot about why she was in Cameron, forgot about her suspicion that Dev's father had killed her brother. Her whole world shrunk to the man sitting next to her, and when he leaned toward her, she closed her eyes and reached for him.

Chapter 7

"This isn't why I brought you up here into the mountains," he whispered, his mouth hovering over hers.

"I know." Carly searched his eyes and found the truth in their gray depths. He didn't want this to happen, any more than she did, but he was just as powerless to stop it. "I swore I wasn't going to get involved with you."

"It would be stupid," he agreed.

"I'm leaving Cameron in a couple of weeks," she murmured as his lips skimmed over hers.

"I'm not interested in getting involved with anyone." He leaned around to nip at her earlobe.

"Neither am I."

His mouth lingered on her neck, nuzzling the velvet cord out of his way. "I'm glad we're both realistic."

"There's no future for us." She touched her tongue to his lip, and felt him shudder.

"You're right about that." His hands tightened on her shoulders.

"We can't agree on anything." She skimmed the plane of his cheek, let her hand linger.

Devlin leaned back, his eyes gleaming. "I can think of one thing we seem to agree on."

"That's just hormones."

He drew her closer, until her chest was pressing against his. "Works for me."

And, heaven help her, it worked for her, too. He'd done no more than touch her, and her whole body cried out for him. She knew it was foolish, knew it was only lust tormenting her, but a part of her deep inside, a place that had been empty all her life, needed Devlin. He completed her in a way that was profoundly frightening. She wanted to run, to get away from the threat he posed to her peace of mind, but she was unable to move.

Her breasts ached where they pressed against his chest, throbbing and needy. She wanted to feel his hands on her, on all of her, taking, caressing, touching her. And she wanted to feel him. Wanted to shape the muscles of his back, wanted to let his hair trickle through her fingers, wanted to know the strength of him.

He pressed her down onto the floor of the cave, the rough blanket beneath her. His shoulders blocked out the light, but she didn't care as her eyes drifted closed. His name was a chant pounding through her blood, and his hands trailed fire wherever they touched.

Slowly he pulled the tails of her shirt out of her jeans, then began to unbutton it. A breath of air caressed her as her shirt fell open, then he bent down and took her mouth. Desire crashed through her, a need to be joined to him. When he cupped one breast and slowly drew his finger across her nipple, she arched up to meet the slash of sensation. He repeated the caress on her other breast, and she moaned into his mouth.

Desperately her hands scrabbled at his shirt. She needed to touch him, to feel his skin against hers. Her hands trembled as she tried to unbutton the impossibly small buttons, and suddenly the clasp on her bra was freed and her breasts spilled into his hands.

Clutching his shirt, she couldn't move, couldn't think as he bent his head to her breasts. As his tongue circled first one nipple, then the other, she could only moan his name as sensation crashed through her. The throbbing between her legs became all-consuming, and she felt herself begin to shake.

"I need to touch you," he whispered, and he unfastened her jeans. She reached for him, needing to touch him, too, but he moved away. "Not yet. If you touch me now, I won't be responsible for what happens."

As he eased her jeans down her legs, she felt exposed and vulnerable. She tensed, and Devlin moved back up to kiss her again. "It's all right," he murmured, touching her face. "It's all right."

He swept his hand down her chest, touching her nipples, then drifted down to the juncture of her thighs. Cupping her through her panties, he murmured her name as he bent to kiss her again.

Shocks of pleasure and need ricocheted through her, and she couldn't stop herself from moving against his hand. He slipped his fingers inside the thin silk barrier and touched her again. When he took one nipple into his mouth at the same time, a shattering climax rocketed through her.

"Devlin," she cried, shocked and embarrassed.

He scooped her up and held her against him until the sensations subsided. When she stopped trembling, he kissed her one more time, then deliberately moved away from her.

"What are you doing?" she asked. Her loss of control, and the knowledge that she'd bared her soul and her vulnerability to him, disturbed her deeply. Especially since he was apparently unwilling to do the same.

Desire still filled his face, and when he reached out to touch her, she saw that his hand was trembling. "I didn't mean for this to go so far," he said. His hand slipped down and pulled her shirt together, then he clumsily tried to button it. "I don't have any protection. And I won't take any chances with you."

She knelt in front of him, her shirt gaping open. "So this was a one-sided affair?"

His face tensed, then he pulled her against him. "I didn't mean for it to be an affair of any kind. You're not a one-night-stand kind of woman, and I'm not a long-term kind of guy." He bent his head and brushed his lips along her neck, and she shivered. Desire curled inside her again.

His hands were warm where they rested against her back, then he reached for her shirt and began buttoning it together. "I'll dream about you for a long time, Carly. I won't forget how you tasted and how you felt." His hands grazed her breasts as he snapped her bra together, and she couldn't control the ripple of need that sliced through her. "And I won't forget that you wanted me."

He drew her closer for a moment, and the hard length of his erection burned into her. Then he slipped away and stood up. "I guess it's time we got back to town."

She stood up slowly and faced him. "That's it? You can just say, fun's over, it's time to go home?"

"What do you want me to say?"

"I don't know," she muttered. But she did. She wanted Devlin to say that he wanted her as much as she wanted him, that he would help her find the truth about her brother and they would all live happily ever after.

None of that was going to happen. So she straightened her spine and said, "I want to say that I apologize for letting things go too far. I should have stopped it long before I..." She cleared her throat and added, "It won't happen again."

"I think that would be best," he said gravely. But she saw a flash of regret and sadness in his eyes.

She hurried to the opening of the cave and slipped through the small fissure. Devlin stepped into the sunlight behind her, then said, "Let me go first. It's harder to go down than up, and that way I can give you a hand."

"I can do it myself," she retorted, her words too sharp.

"I'm sure you can. But I still want to go first."

He edged around her on the slippery rock, and even the accidental brushing of his body against hers made her heart pound.

"Get a grip," she muttered to herself as she started down the side of the cliff. Rocks slithered down in front of her, and pieces of the soft stone broke away as she stepped carefully from one rock to another. Finally she was at the bottom of the cliff.

She looked up at where they'd come from. "I can't see a thing. It's like that cave isn't even there."

"That's why it made such a good hiding place." The tourist-guide Devlin was firmly back in place, and Carly told herself it was probably for the best. The physical attraction between them was unexpected and too volatile. It would only hinder her from her objective in Cameron, she reminded herself harshly. From now on, she needed to remember to maintain a safe distance from Devlin.

Devlin watched as Carly stared back up the cliff at the cave, then turned and walked to the car. He wished like hell he knew what she was thinking. What had happened between them in the cave had stunned and shocked him. He'd thought he was in control. He'd figured he could handle it. He'd only wanted to kiss her, but he'd come too damn close to making love with her.

And what scared him the most, and made him want to run the fastest, was that it had taken all of his strength to pull back, to let her go, even after he realized that he didn't have any condoms with him. Even without protection, he'd wanted her so badly that he'd been willing to risk everything to make love with her.

It was definitely time to put some distance between himself and Carly Fitzpatrick.

The sun was fading from the sky as he headed the Blazer back down the rutted road toward the house. Carly was silent, but the air inside the truck was heavy with tension. Memories of the passion they'd shared back in the cave swirled around the truck. Desperately he searched for a topic of conversation. He didn't want to think about the way she'd felt, or the way she'd tasted, or the way she'd come apart when he'd touched her. He was too afraid that he wouldn't be able to stop himself from repeating it.

"Did you go back to the newspaper office today?" He grabbed at the first thing he thought of.

"I did, as a matter of fact. And I found out some interesting things."

He wasn't sure he wanted to hear what they were, but whatever she'd found would be a hell of a lot safer than the lingering memories of the cave. "What did you find?"

"I was looking at copies of the papers from six months or so before that boy died. And I saw that your father and Phil Hilbert had been in a fight over water rights for your ranches."

His tension eased a little. "Yeah, they were."

"Do you remember anything about it?"

He shrugged. "A little. It was a major topic of conversation around the house. But I was a kid, and kids see things from a different perspective. I remember I couldn't figure out how someone could own water."

"Apparently your father and Phil Hilbert didn't have the same problem." Her voice was dry.

"They wouldn't. Water is important around here, because there isn't much of it. So the fight over rights to that river was crucial."

"Who won?"

He shot her a quick look. "You mean you don't know?"

She shook her head. "I didn't get that far in the papers. I had to leave to, ah, get ready to..."

"To have dinner with me." A quick spurt of pleasure filled him. "I'm glad to know that dinner with me was more important than getting the rest of the story."

"Melba would have nagged me forever if I hadn't been ready to go when you got to her house," she said primly. "She's very old-fashioned."

"So Melba knows we had dinner together."

He thought a faint pink stain crept up her neck. "I had to give her a reason I wouldn't be at her house for dinner."

"Melba's okay," he said. "She won't run down to Heaven to spread the word."

"Would you care if she did?" Carly had half-turned in her seat, and he could feel her eyes on his face.

"Hell, no. What I do in my time off is no one's business but mine. I just thought you'd want to know that the whole town wasn't talking about you."

"I'm sure they already are," she said, and her voice was dry again. "So having dinner with their sheriff isn't going to make things a lot worse."

"I'm just another one of your sources, is that it?" He glanced over at her, and she looked away.

"I don't generally kiss my sources, Sheriff." Her voice was strained. "But as long as we're on the subject of sources, you never answered my question."

"Which one?"

"Who won the water rights fight, your father or Phil Hilbert?"

"My father won," he said, slowing down as they passed the house, then speeding up when they turned onto the road that led to Cameron. "It was clear that the river was on Red Rock property. My father offered to sell some of the water to Phil, but he wasn't interested. Phil always was a damned contrary, stubborn fool."

"So what happened to Phil? Where did he get the water for his ranch?"

He shrugged. "You saw the stream that ran through his property. He managed with that, I guess. For a while it was running real well, but several months after the court fight, it seemed to dry up to almost a trickle. He had a hard time for a while, but I think he finally got someone to come in and drill some wells for him. They helped, but he's never really had a good supply of water."

"You said he tried to buy your ranch after your father died. Was he after the water?"

"I'm sure that was part of it. But mostly he just wanted to win. He wanted to wipe the McAllisters off the map of Cameron. I know enough about Phil now to know he holds a grudge. And he has a long memory."

"It must be unpleasant, living so close to him."

He shrugged again. "I don't worry about it, one way or the other. Our cowboys work together, just like the rest of the ranches in the area, when we have a big project to do. The rest of the time I don't see much of Phil. I think he stays out of my way." He slanted her a glance. "Are you going to read the rest of the newspapers tomorrow? About the big water fight?"

"Of course. It's clear that was a big story around here." Her voice was light. "It sounds just like the Old West."

"What about the Whitmore boy who was shot?"

"What about him?"

"Are you going to include him in your story?"

"Why do you ask?"

Her voice had sharpened, and he pulled over to the side of the road. "I'm just curious, that's all."

"Because your family was involved?"

"My family wasn't involved. He just happened to be shot on our property."

"With a gun your father might have owned," she pointed out. "I think that makes you involved."

"The sheriff investigated that shooting thoroughly. If there had been any evidence that my father was involved, it would have come out. The sheriff decided that it was a drifter, and when a drifter was found dead, that was the end of it."

"That was convenient, wasn't it?" she murmured.

The guilt he thought he'd buried rose from his memory, overwhelming him again. It wasn't his fault that Edmund Whitmore was killed, even though it had been his fault that the gun was stolen. Both his father and the sheriff had reassured him of that. But it didn't make any difference. Some childhood memories were more lasting than others.

As they barreled down the asphalt toward Cameron, he felt the tension swirling in the air again.

"You're not going to find any more information on Edmund Whitmore's death than you already have, because there is no more to know. End of story. But if you want to waste your time asking questions, be my guest."

"Thank you. Although I wasn't aware that I needed your permission to ask questions."

"Damn it, Carly, write your story about Cameron, and forget about ancient history. No one wants to rehash a murder from twenty years ago."

"I'm sure that whoever murdered that boy doesn't want me

rehashing the story," she said coolly. "Isn't that a good reason for doing just that?"

He was angry with her, he told himself. She was stirring things up in his town—hell, she was stirring things up inside of him. Things he wanted no part of. But he had to admire her guts. Someone had left her a pointed message on her mirror yesterday, and it hadn't even slowed her down.

"Just be careful," he finally said. "Don't forget about that warning you had last night."

"I wouldn't dream of forgetting about it. Obviously, I've stepped on someone's toes. I intend to find out whose foot they belong to."

He rolled to a stop in front of Melba Corboy's house, and turned to face her in the darkness of the truck. "You are a piece of work," he said, shaking his head."

Before she could answer, he slid out of the truck and opened her door. He was careful not to touch her as he walked her up the sidewalk to the porch. Remembering what had happened the last time he'd seen her home, he kept a good two feet between them.

Carly fumbled in her purse for a key, then slid it into the lock. Before she opened the door, she turned around.

"Thank you for the picnic," she said softly. "Your ranch is a beautiful place. You're very lucky to have it for your home."

"I know."

And because a look of wistfulness passed over her face, he disobeyed his orders to himself and leaned forward to brush her mouth with his. "I had a wonderful time," he murmured. "I wouldn't have changed a thing."

For just a moment, her mouth clung to his, then she backed away. "Good night, Devlin. I'll see you around."

"Good night."

The door closed behind her with a quiet, final whoosh, and he stood in front of it for a long moment. Then, with a silent oath, he turned around and strode back to his truck. "What were you waiting for, fool?" he asked himself. "Were you waiting for her to throw herself into your arms, tell you that all she wants from you is hot sex until she leaves town?''

That was all he was willing to give, he reminded himself. Getting into his truck, he stared out at the dark street for a moment. A treacherous need crept up on him, a need for love, for a family, for someone to be there for him, forever. He was just getting maudlin, he told himself as he turned the key in the Blazer. Watching Becca and Grady find each other, then seeing Abby and Damien do the same, had made him sentimental. He'd be fine in the morning. His job as sheriff gave him plenty of doses of reality.

But as he drove away from Melba's boarding house, he couldn't stop himself from looking up at the window to Carly's room. Light gleamed yellow in the darkness, beckoning him closer. Suddenly he wanted, more than anything, to stand in that light.

When he walked into Heaven on Seventh the next morning, he knew immediately that Carly was in the restaurant. Uneasily, he told himself he must have heard her voice. He couldn't possibly have known any other way. He damned himself for looking, but it only took a moment to spot her. She sat in one of the booths with Bert Pickens, smiling at him and scribbling in the little notebook she carried with her.

He could just imagine the kinds of questions she was asking the ex-sheriff. Scowling, he headed for the corner booth where his deputies waited, avoiding Carly and Bert.

''Morning, Dev.'' Ben Jackson watched him. ''You look like you had an ugly night. Everything all right?''

''Fine,'' he snapped, then he sighed. ''Sorry, Ben. I didn't get much sleep last night.''

''Was there a call?'' Ben sat up straighter. ''I didn't see anything on the log.''

''No, it was trouble at the ranch.'' It wasn't much of a lie, Dev thought sourly. The memories that had kept him awake and restless most of the night had happened on his ranch.

''Do you need to deal with it today? We can probably handle

anything that comes up." Ben looked at the other deputies, who all nodded.

"Thanks, Ben. But it's under control." He wished. "Let's just get to work. What happened last night?"

While the deputy who was on call gave a summary of the calls he'd received, Devlin watched Carly and Bert Pickens out of the corner of his eye. Bert leaned forward in the booth, a charming smile on his face, and smoothed his thinning gray hair back from his face. Dev recognized the look in his eyes, and felt anger curl inside him.

"Hey, Dev, don't mind old Bert. He puts on the dog for all the women." Ben's voice was quiet, and the deputy laid a hand on his arm. "Your Carly is smart enough to see that."

"She's not my Carly," he snarled, then turned around to watch the pair behind him.

"Is that so?" Ben's voice was quiet, barely audible above the drone of the deputy who was speaking. "You can't tell that from where I'm sitting."

Dev finally turned around, shot Ben a killing glance, and tried to focus on what the young deputy was saying. When the meeting was over and all the deputies filed out of the booth, Ben stayed behind.

Dev folded his arms across his chest. "All right, I wasn't paying attention to Matt. So throw me out of office."

Ben shook his head and a ghost of a smile flitted across his face. "When Ms. Fitzpatrick first came to town, I thought she would prove entertaining. Not even in my wildest dreams could I have imagined so many interesting scenes."

Dev narrowed his eyes at his friend. "If you want to talk about interesting scenes, I understand there was one here at this very diner the other day. Between you and Janie."

The smile disappeared from Ben's face. "There was no scene. She merely said asked me how I wanted my eggs cooked."

"Yeah, but she talked to you. And you answered. That's front-page news in Cameron."

"I've spoken to Janie before."

"Name one time."

Ben looked toward the kitchen, then back at him. "We weren't talking about me. We were talking about you." He laid his hand on Dev's arm again. "Is there anything I can do?"

Dev had to admire the way Ben had changed the subject. And he knew there would be no turning him back to the subject of his obsession with Janie Murphy, and his refusal to act on it. "Get her to finish her story and leave," he muttered.

Before Ben could answer, someone slapped Dev on the back. A moment later Bert Perkins slid into the booth with him.

"Mornin', Dev."

"Hello, Bert. Good to see you in town," Dev answered politely.

"Glad I came in to breakfast this morning. That was the best-looking breakfast partner I've had in a long time." He winked, and Dev wanted to smash his fist in the other man's face.

"That girl is determined," Bert continued, shaking his head. "She's got her teeth into this story about Edmund Whitmore, and she won't let go. She's going to shake it until something new falls out, if you want my opinion."

"What did you tell her?" Dev asked.

"Everything I remembered, which wasn't much." The older man grinned again. "But I told her she could take a look at the old reports I filed about the case. She'll be by the office this afternoon."

"Who's supposed to take the time to help her find what she's looking for?" Dev demanded.

Bert winked at him again and leaned forward. "Hell, Dev, you're a red-blooded boy. I figured you'd find plenty of time to help that little gal with her research. She sure is a looker."

"My deputies and I have enough to do, taking care of the problems Cameron has today. We don't need to get involved in a twenty-year-old case you've already solved."

The former sheriff shrugged. "Why would you have to get involved? I didn't say she'd find anything. We found the drifter dead, and that was that. Everyone seemed to be happy about the outcome of that case."

"Everyone except the Whitmores." Dev slid toward the edge

of the booth. "I'll help her find your old reports. And I hope to God you don't regret reopening this can of worms."

He didn't look over at Carly as she sat alone in a booth, drinking coffee and scribbling in her damned notebook. The door slammed behind him as he hurried outside. He'd hoped to avoid Carly today, and for the rest of the time she was in Cameron. He'd decided last night that it was the only smart thing to do. And now she'd be spending God knew how much time with him.

Swearing under his breath, he jammed his hands into his pockets and strode to the sheriff's office. He didn't even look at his deputies as he stormed into the cramped room at the back of the building that served as his office. File cabinets lined the walls, leaving scant room for his desk and the battered couch that leaned against one wall.

He eased the door shut and looked around. Hell, he'd bump into her every time one of them moved in here, he thought with disgust. There was barely room for him, let alone Carly. Throwing himself into his chair, he stared out the window at the red dirt and scrubby bush that stood outside it. And the worst part, he thought grimly, was that he was looking forward to it.

Chapter 8

Carly paused at the door to the sheriff's office and took a deep breath. She hoped that Devlin wasn't inside. It would be much easier if Ben Jackson or one of the other deputies helped her find the reports the ex-sheriff had told her about.

After the emotionally wrenching experience she and Devlin had shared the day before, she'd vowed to keep away from him. It was the only sensible thing to do. She was in Cameron to get to the truth about her brother's death, and Devlin's family was involved somehow. Any good reporter knew better than to become entangled with one of her subjects. And she was a good reporter.

Cool air breathed over her skin as she stepped inside the door. "You must be Ms. Fitzpatrick, the reporter." The friendly voice came from her left. Carly turned and looked at a woman sitting behind a desk. The woman smiled at her. "I'm Marge, the dispatcher. Devlin's in his office." She waved toward the back of the building. "You go right on back."

The door to the office was half-closed, and as Carly raised her hand to knock, she realized her hand was sweating. This is business, she told herself fiercely. *This is about Edmund, not you.*

Swallowing once, she knocked at the door. Dev's deep voice said, "Come on in."

He was sitting in an old wooden desk chair, his booted feet resting on his desk. When he saw her in the doorway, his feet came crashing down to the floor and he sat up straight in the chair.

He scowled. "I didn't think you'd be here so early."

"Would there be a more convenient time?" She prayed her voice sounded impersonal and businesslike.

"There is no convenient time. You might as well get it over with."

"Thank you for being so gracious about helping me," she said sweetly, her temper stirring.

He gave her a hard look. "I have work to do. Digging out reports from twenty years ago isn't real high on my list of priorities. This is as gracious as you're going to get."

Slipping her backpack off her shoulder, she set it on the floor and let her anger go with a sigh. "I know," she said quietly. "I'm imposing on you. I wouldn't do it if I didn't think it was important."

"Why is something that happened so long ago important for your story?" he asked, some of the hardness fading from his eyes.

Her gaze slipped away from his and she studied the file cabinets. Devlin was too good at reading her expression. She didn't want him to see the truth in her eyes, that there was a reason she was pursuing the story of Edmund Whitmore that had nothing to do with an article for her magazine.

"I like to be thorough. And this story caught my interest."

She could feel his eyes on her back. "The file is there on the top of that cabinet," he said after a while. "I found the year, but I didn't have time to go through all the reports."

"Thank you," she said quickly. "I can go through them myself."

When she picked up the file, she found it was several inches thick. "It looks like you had a lot of crimes in Cameron that year," she said, glancing at him.

"It just looks that way." He leaned back in his chair again.

"Every time we go on a call, we have to fill out a report. So if we get a complaint that someone's kid is throwing stones at a neighbor's garage, we have to fill out a form." He sat up straight and looked down at the folder she held. "And that was the year that the Hilberts and my father were having the dispute about the water. I suspect that Bert and his deputy were called out to one ranch or the other a fair number of times."

"Do you want me to take these somewhere else and look through them? I don't want to be in anyone's way."

"No." His face hardened again. "They can't leave the building. You'll have to look at them here."

"Where do you want me to work?"

"You might as well sit on the couch."

As she settled herself on the worn cushions, he swung his chair around to face her. "Were you at the newspaper office again today?"

"Yes. I finished looking at the stories about the water fight between your family and the Hilberts."

"Anything interesting?"

"Pretty much just what you told me—that your father won the court case." She swallowed the sudden lump in her throat and forced herself to meet his eyes. "Did you know the Whitmore boy worked for the paper? I found some stories he'd written about the case."

"I didn't know that." Interest flickered in his eyes. "What kinds of stories did he write?"

She let her gaze slide to the folder on her lap, sorry she had brought the subject up. Seeing her brother's name on the stories had been a series of small stabs to her heart. She'd known her brother wanted to be a reporter, but seeing his name in print made his loss so much more vivid. "Stories about the court case, reporting what had happened. There was an interview he'd done with Phil Hilbert, and one with your dad. It was interesting that he was murdered only a few months after he was involved with that case."

"Are you trying to make a connection between his death and that court case?" he demanded.

"Doesn't it seem coincidental to you?"

He watched her for a moment, then ran his fingers through his hair. Her hands tingled as she remembered the springy softness of it, how it had felt against her skin yesterday. Then she looked away.

"I don't know what to think," he finally said. "But it looks like you're determined to find out."

"It's my job," she said quietly. "It's what I do."

"Fine. You go ahead and do your job, and I'll do mine."

He turned back to the desk, but she suspected he wasn't getting much done. His shoulders were too tense, his back too rigid. Almost as if he was waiting, she thought. Waiting for her to find something he'd rather keep hidden.

An hour later she realized she'd found it. Looking up from the report she was reading, she said, "Devlin?"

"What?"

"Why didn't you tell me about the gun?"

He stared at her for a moment, then looked out the window. "I wondered how long it would take you to find that little piece of information."

"You must have known it was in here."

"I figured it was."

"But you let me go through the reports anyway."

When he turned back to her, his eyes were the color of hard steel. "I was twelve-years-old. I made a mistake and left my father's gun cabinet unlocked. Someone came into the house and stole the Parker shotgun. That's all there is to the story."

"You must have felt very guilty."

For a brief second she saw the pain in his eyes, then it was gone. She was very sure he hadn't meant to share that pain with her. "I was a kid. It was a careless, stupid mistake, but kids do stupid things. The sheriff understood that."

"Anyone could have taken it."

"That's exactly what Bert Pickens realized. Anyone could have taken that gun. The case was unlocked for at least a week before the Whitmore kid was shot. And there were a lot of people in and out of the house back in those days."

She set the file of reports on the couch and rose to stand next to him. "I'm sorry," she said softly.

"What for?"

"I've brought back painful memories. I didn't mean to do that."

"I know. You were just doing your job."

Suddenly her job was tearing her in two. She'd never dreamed that Devlin was involved so intimately in her brother's death. Torn, she stood next to him for a moment, then slowly sat back down. "Aren't there times when your job is hard to do?" she whispered.

"No." His eyes were hard as he watched her. "My job is a matter of right and wrong. Period. I don't bring any other agendas to it. If someone breaks a law, he or she gets arrested. I don't lose sleep at night because of it."

"I wish everything was as black and white as that," she murmured.

He spun around in his chair so he was facing her. "What's going on, Carly? You have another reason for coming to Cameron, don't you? Was this story about making Cameron into a tourist destination just a blind for something else?" Suspicion and mistrust filled his eyes.

She stared at him, appalled. Had she been so transparent? How had he been able to read her so easily? "No," she finally said. "I stumbled on this story and it caught my interest. That's why I'm following it."

The distrust in his eyes told her that he didn't believe her. She raised her head. She didn't care, she told herself fiercely. She couldn't. At least that would take care of the problem of the attraction that sizzled between them. Now she could pursue the truth about Edmund without being distracted by Devlin McAllister.

Her heart was heavy in her chest as she looked down at the pile of reports on the couch. Her vision blurred, but she blinked until the tears were gone. What was more important, she asked herself. Her brother's death, or this wild and futile attraction for the sheriff of Cameron that threatened to spiral out of control?

"I'll get back to work so I can get out of your way," she whispered, not daring to look up at him. Something ached inside her, but she ignored it. Staying focused on her job had never been a problem before, and it wouldn't be a problem now.

He watched her for a long time. She felt his gaze on her, measuring her, but she wouldn't look up. Finally he turned back to his desk.

She was scribbling in her notebook when he turned around to face her again. She gripped her pen more tightly, but continued to write.

Devlin cleared his throat. "It's late, Carly. You need to go get something to eat."

"I'm not finished." She looked up to find him watching her with unreadable eyes.

"I am. I need to get back to the ranch. You can come back tomorrow."

"All right." She was glad of the excuse to get out of the room, she told herself. Setting the folder back on top of the file cabinet, where she'd found it, she turned to Devlin. "Thank you again for letting me read the reports."

"You're welcome." His eyes were distant, and she couldn't tell what he was thinking. "I'll see you tomorrow."

"I'll be back first thing in the morning."

"Fine."

She slipped out the door of the building in front of Devlin and started walking down the street. She knew he stood watching her. When she finally turned the corner, she drew in a shaky breath.

He might suspect that she had another reason for coming to Cameron, but he didn't know why she was really there. There was no way he could know. And if her secrets had opened up a chasm between them, it didn't matter. It was a chasm that needed to be there, anyway.

But as she slipped into Heaven on Seventh and waited to be seated, her heart wasn't sure it agreed.

When Devlin drove through the gates of the Red Rock Ranch that evening, he didn't stop at the house. Instead, he drove up the rutted road that led to the small lake, high on the mountain. The sun was setting behind the mountains, painting the red and pink rocks with glowing color. The sunset touched the lake with fire, and he slid onto a rock next to the shore and stared at the shifting colors in front of him.

His first instinct had been right on the money, he told himself brutally. He should have stayed far away from Carly from the beginning. It was clear that she had another agenda in Cameron, one she wasn't willing to share with him or anyone else. If she had just intended to include the story of the Whitmore boy in her article as background material, surely she'd gotten enough information from the old copies of the *Sentinel*. There should have been no reason to look at the old reports from his office.

And when he'd challenged her on it, he'd seen the truth of his words in her eyes. He grabbed a rock and hurled it into the water, brooding as he watched the ripples spread out. The proof of her deception had hit him squarely in the gut. As had the ease with which he'd read her.

He'd been spending way too much time with the treacherous Ms. Fitzpatrick, he thought grimly. That was going to change. From now on, he was going to stay as far away from her as possible. The last thing he needed or wanted in his life was a woman who wasn't truthful. One of those in a lifetime had been more than enough. He'd learned his lesson in California, and it wasn't going to happen again.

Devlin sat on the rock until darkness embraced him, staring out over the water. He didn't turn around until all the light had disappeared from the sky. When he stood and climbed back into the Blazer, he didn't allow himself to look at the cliff on the other side of him. He wouldn't be going back to his cave for a long, long time.

Slamming the door to his truck, he wrenched the key in the ignition and started the engine with a roar. Maybe if he made enough noise, if he drove fast enough down the dangerous road, he'd be able to rid his memory of the last time he'd driven down this road.

But as he returned to the house, he realized that the faint smell of Carly still lingered in the truck, reminding him of the passion they'd shared. Her scent wouldn't let him forget how much he'd wanted her, and how much he'd been willing to give her.

Cursing himself for a fool, he flew over the rocks in the road, grimly steering the truck along the rutted path. But her ghost stayed with him all evening, taunting him with her smile and tormenting him with her touch. She even followed him into sleep, flitting close to him in his dreams but staying just out of reach.

The next morning, he gave Ben instructions to allow Carly to look at the reports in his office, then he slipped out of the building. He'd make sure he stayed away until she was finished with the papers in the folder. To sit and watch her, knowing that he'd allowed himself to be suckered again by a woman who wasn't telling him the truth, would simply be too painful. And it wasn't as if he didn't have plenty of work to do to keep him busy.

He'd do the work of ten men if it would keep his mind off Carly.

Late that afternoon, as he was talking to one of his neighbors, his radio crackled to life. Reaching into the Blazer, he picked up the hand set and said, "Go ahead, Marge."

"Is that you, Dev?" Marge's voice was filled with relief.

"You got me."

"Where are you?"

There was an urgency in her voice that made him tighten his hand on the radio. "I'm out at the Webber's place. Why?"

"There's been an accident." He heard her swallow. "Thank God you're close. That reporter, Ms. Fitzpatrick, just called in. I couldn't make out all of what she said, but it sounded like her car went off the road, maybe rolled over. There was a lot of static on her phone. I think she's about halfway between town and the Hilbert's place."

"I'll get right on it." His heart pounding, he said a curt goodbye to the man he'd been talking to, then hurried into his truck and slammed the door. A moment later he was speeding down the gravel driveway, his truck skidding as he pushed on the gas pedal.

When he reached the main road, he hesitated only a moment before turning right, praying he'd turned the right way. Flipping on the siren and the lights on the top of his car, he pressed the accelerator to the floor. His blood pounded in his head, echoing her name, and a heavy weight of fear sat on his chest. As the truck screamed down the asphalt, he gripped the steering wheel tightly, his eyes scanning the road for signs of Carly's car.

He'd almost passed the tight curve when he saw a flash of red in the ditch. Stomping on the brakes, he brought the truck to a shuddering halt and was out of the Blazer almost before it had stopped moving. As he ran toward her Jeep, tilted on its side next to a large clump of mesquite, he shouted, "Carly? Can you hear me?"

"Dev?"

Her voice was shaky, but he closed his eyes and muttered a prayer of thanks. "I'm here, Carly. Hold on and I'll get you out of that car."

Only the mesquite bush had prevented the Jeep from rolling completely onto its side. The passenger door was high in the air, and Devlin swung himself up on the running board to look inside.

"My God, Carly! How badly are you hurt?"

She lay sprawled across the driver's seat, blood covering the left side of her face. She'd managed to unhook her seat belt, and had apparently been trying to climb up and out of the passenger side door.

She gave him a weak smile. "I think it looks a lot worse than it really is. Blood can be so messy."

"Can you move?" He yanked open the door and leaned closer to her, forcing himself not to touch her yet. "Do I need to get the evacuation helicopter in here?"

She struggled to sit up. "Don't be silly. I just need some help getting out of the car. The door on my side seems to be jammed."

He looked at the blood on her face and her shirt, noticed the sheet-white pallor of her face and the way her hands were trembling. "I'm not sure you should be moved."

She scowled at him and pushed herself toward the door. "Don't go all squeamish on me. I've been moving ever since the damned car skidded off the road. I just haven't been able reach the door.''

The smell of gasoline drifted past him, and he knew he couldn't wait any longer to get her out of the car. Balancing himself on the edge of the seat, he leaned forward until he grasped her hand. Her fingers curled around him, holding him tightly, as if she never wanted to let go.

Refusing to let his mind wander in that direction, he shifted his grip so he could reach down with his other hand and circle her waist. "I'm going to ease you toward me. Tell me if I'm hurting you.''

"I'm fine," she muttered, but he watched even more color leach out of her face.

When she reached the door, he swung her into his arms, then jumped down from the running board of the Jeep. Holding her gently, trying not to jostle her, he carried her back to his car, where he laid her on the back seat.

"Where are you hurt?" he said, resisting the impulse to run his hands over her.

"I bumped my head when the car tipped over.'' She touched a spot underneath her hair and winced. "And my side hurts.'' Her hand fluttered over her left side. "Probably bruised a few ribs. I'll be fine in a couple of days.''

"Are you sure that's all? Your arms and legs are all right? Your back and neck don't hurt?''

"That's it. I'm pretty tough. I don't break easily.''

He could believe that, he thought, rocking back on his heels as he watched her. She had to be in pain and shaken up, but she was determined not to give in to it. A reluctant stab of admiration went through him. Carly was a strong woman.

But when her eyelids fluttered closed, he gave into the need to touch her. Easing into the back of the Blazer, he gently pushed her hair out of her face. "You took ten years off my life," he whispered.

Her hand groped for his, then held it tightly. "I knew you would come.'' She didn't open her eyes as she spoke. "I told myself to hold on, that you would get me out of that car. You were there almost before I'd finished talking to Marge.''

He shifted her hand in his and bent down to brush his mouth over their joined fingers. "I was close by. But it still seemed like it took forever to get here." He studied her pale face and her drawn mouth. "What happened? Do you remember?"

At that her eyes fluttered open. He saw a spark of indignation in them. "I think I had a blowout. I heard a loud pop, then the car started swerving all over the road. The next thing I knew, I was upside down in that bush."

"I'll get the mechanic to tow it in. He'll be able to tell. Was it your car?"

"It was a rental." A tiny smile curved her lips. "I guess it's a good thing I took the accident insurance."

"I'll call the rental company for you and have them get another car out here."

"Thanks." Her hand stirred in his, then gripped his more tightly. "I'm glad you were close."

"So am I."

She smiled up at him, her mouth trembling. "I've been nothing but trouble for you since the minute I hit town, haven't I?"

Yes, his heart shouted. She was the most trouble he'd seen in a long, long time. Instead he said lightly, "You do have a way of attracting attention."

"I guess it goes along with my job," she answered, equally lightly.

"We need to get you to the doc's," he said, stepping away from her before he could do something stupid. He wanted to gather her close, hold her tightly and reassure himself that she was all right. Instead he eased the seat belt around her and found a blanket in the back of the truck that he wadded up and put under her head for a pillow. "I'll radio ahead, have Marge tell him we're on our way."

He drove carefully, trying not to stop too suddenly or accelerate too quickly. Every once in a while he turned around to look at her. Carly lay too still on the seat, her eyes closed, her face white.

"Are you okay?" he finally said.

At the sound of his voice she opened her eyes and gave him a wan smile. "I'm fine. I'm just conserving my energy."

"Hold on. We're almost at the doc's."

He eased the truck into a parking space outside of the doctor's small office, then killed the ignition. When he saw Carly struggling to sit up, he hurried to stop her.

"What do you think you're doing?"

"Aren't we at the doctor's office?" she said, twisting her neck to look out the window.

"Yeah. But you're going to relax and let me carry you into the exam room."

She scowled at him. "There's nothing wrong with me that a good night's sleep won't cure," she said, staring at him with a mutinous expression. "There's no reason you have to do something as dramatic as carry me into the office."

"Who's going to stop me?"

He slid his arm beneath her knees and lifted her out of the car. His heart stuttered as she stiffened, then relaxed against him. Slowly she twined one arm around his neck and leaned her head against his shoulder. "I don't think anyone's going to stop you," she sighed. "Thank you, Devlin."

"You're welcome," he said gruffly, trying not to notice how right she felt, curled up against him.

A tall man with a gaunt face opened the door. "Bring her right in, Sheriff." Doctor Ellis held the door open, then directed him to a small exam room. Dev set Carly down on the table, then the doctor motioned him out of the room.

"Can't I stay with her?" Dev asked.

"Please don't make him leave," Carly said at the same time.

The doctor's face softened. "You have to step out of the room while I examine her. I'll call you back in as soon as I've finished."

Devlin paced the hallway for what seemed like a long time. Finally the door opened and Doctor Ellis stepped into the hall. "She's going to be fine," he said abruptly. "There's a cut on her scalp that needs to be sutured, and I'm afraid she might have a mild concussion. She's bruised her ribs, but I'm pretty sure none of them are broken. There are some ugly bruises, but they'll fade. All in all, she was damned lucky.''

"Can I go back in the room?"

The doctor watched him carefully. "Do you need to get a statement from her?"

"No, damn it. I want to make sure she's all right."

Doctor Daniel Ellis's face softened. "Go ahead, then. If you just wanted a statement from her, I would have told you to go to hell."

Pushing past the doctor, he found Carly clutching a hospital gown to herself, looking lost and alone in the middle of the exam table. He couldn't stop himself from reaching for her hand. She twined her fingers with his and held on tight.

"The doc says you're going to be fine."

She gave him a weak smile. "I told you so."

"Yeah, you did, tough guy. Are you going to take the stitches without any anesthetic, too?" He reached out and brushed her hair away from the small spot the doctor had shaved.

"I'm not that tough." She looked up at him, and suddenly her eyes swam with tears. "I was scared, Dev. I wasn't sure if Marge could hear me on the phone, and I was afraid no one would find me out there."

"I would have found you." He scooped her up into his arms and held her as close as he could without jostling her ribs. "I'm not finished fighting with you yet."

She gave a hiccup of laughter and snuggled closer to him. "I'm glad you're here, but I don't want to keep you. Ben said you had a lot of work to do today."

He thought about how he'd run out of the office that morning rather than face her, and the reason why. It didn't matter that he'd sworn to stay away from her. This changed the equation, he told himself. Carly was injured and alone in Cameron. Someone had to take care of her. This wasn't personal. He could put aside his feelings long enough to do that. He was the sheriff, after all. It was his job to take care of the people of Cameron. And that included visitors who wouldn't be staying. "I'll stay until Doc is finished with you. Then I'm taking you home."

Chapter 9

"I beg your pardon?" Carly froze, then slowly pushed away from him.

"We have plenty of room out at the ranch. You need to come home with me tonight."

"No, I don't."

She couldn't do it. She could not go and stay at Red Rock Ranch. Carly watched Devlin pace around Doctor Ellis's small exam room and waited for him to stop and face her again. She didn't have to wait for long.

"Dammit, Carly, someone has to take care of you tonight."

"I'm perfectly capable of taking care of myself." She shifted on the hard vinyl of the table and wrapped the hospital gown more tightly around herself. "And Melba will be home if I need anything. I'm not going to stay at your house."

Doctor Ellis came into the room, and Dev stood by her side, holding her hand, as the doctor sutured her head. He told her how to take care of the wound, glanced at Dev, then back to her.

"Let me know if you need help getting dressed," he murmured.

When he was out of the room, Dev stood and looked down at her. She saw clearly that the discussion about moving to her house wasn't finished.

She needed to visit his house, talk to his sister and his mother, but she refused to use her injuries as a way to get her foot in the door. She didn't want to be carried into his house, weak and wobbly, and ask for their help. She didn't want to be obligated to them. She'd never been obligated to anyone. She'd wait until she was feeling better, then go out to the Red Rock and talk to them. On her own.

She felt Devlin's gaze on her face, and she lifted her head to meet his eyes. She softened her voice when she saw the concern in his eyes. "I'll be fine by myself."

He shook his head. "You are one stubborn, illogical woman."

"Just because I know what I need?" She lifted her chin higher.

A reluctant smile played around the corners of his mouth. "Geez, Carly, are you always this tough?"

"Always," she said firmly. "You might as well give up now."

"I can't force you to do the obviously intelligent thing," he said, scowling again. "I suppose you're going to insist that you can walk home to Melba's from here, too."

"If that was an offer of a ride, thank you." Her side ached and her head throbbed, and the cut that had been sutured was beginning to sting as the anesthetic wore off. "I may be stubborn, but I'm not stupid."

"Thank God for small favors," he muttered.

His gaze rested on her again, and she held the flaps of the skimpy gown together in a tight fist. "If you don't mind leaving, I'll get my clothes on."

"I'll get Doc Ellis in here to help you."

"I think he has another patient," she said quickly. "I'll do it myself."

"You can barely stand up. How are you going to get yourself dressed?"

"I'll manage."

Devlin turned around so that she was looking at his back. "Go ahead,'' he said gruffly. "I'll just stay here to make sure you don't need any help."

She didn't want him in the room, but short of pushing him out physically, she knew she wasn't going to get rid of him. Even from across the room, she was too aware of him, too aware of the power he held over her. Devlin had been all business since he'd found her in the Jeep, but still her heart had fluttered every time he'd touched her. And when he'd brushed his mouth over their joined hands, something had moved inside her.

He didn't want to care about her. She'd see it yesterday afternoon, in his office, when he'd figured out that she had another reason for being in Cameron. But he'd treated her like fragile, precious glass when he'd found her that afternoon.

Ignore him, her mind told her. *You agreed it would be better if there was nothing between you.*

Trying to pretend he wasn't in the room, she reached over and tried to pick up her clothes from the chair where Doctor Ellis had laid them. Her side shrieked in pain, and she tried to bite back the involuntary gasp.

He spun around. "What's wrong?"

"Nothing," she managed to say. "I'm just having a little trouble reaching my clothes."

Before she could ask him, he scooped them up and set them on the table next to her. Finally, almost as if he couldn't help himself, he reached out and brushed the hair away from her eyes. "Are you sure you don't want me to get someone to help you?"

"There's no one here besides Doctor Ellis. He's already way behind because of my accident. I don't want to make the rest of his patients wait any longer."

"Fine. I'll help you myself."

"You can't do that!" She felt her face and neck heat. "I can get dressed by myself."

"Save your breath," he said, snatching up her shorts. "You can use it to call me all sorts of vile names." He slid one of her feet into the shorts, then the other. "Can you stand up?"

"Of course I can stand up," she snapped, but when she slid off the table she found herself swaying.

He held her steady for a moment, his gray eyes darkening as he watched her. "Okay now?"

"Fine," she muttered. Someone was trying to crack her head open from the inside, and the room shifted and spun around her. Vaguely she was aware that he had pulled her shorts to her waist and was buttoning them.

He cradled her carefully as he settled her back onto the table. "Let's get your shirt on," he murmured.

She wanted to protest, to tell him to stop, that she could do it herself, but his hands smoothed down her back, soothing and gentle, as he settled her blouse around her. When he eased one of her arms out of the hospital gown, he bunched the material close to her chest as he quickly pulled one sleeve of her shirt over that arm. He repeated the maneuver with the other sleeve, then let the gown fall to the ground as he buttoned her blouse.

Tears prickled her eyes again as she realized how careful he'd been to preserve her modesty. The material of the blouse rubbed against her bare breasts as she looked up at him. "Thank you."

One side of his mouth quirked up in a grin. "Don't mention it, Slick. I figured I'd wait until you were back in fighting form before I ravish you in the doctor's office."

He knelt down and put on her shoes and socks, then stood up again. "All set?"

Before she could answer, he spotted her bra lying on the exam table. He picked up the scrap of lace and stuffed it into his pocket. "Let's not leave this as a souvenir for Doc Ellis."

Carly forced herself to slide off the exam table and stand up. Her side screamed in protest, but she managed not to gasp. "I'm ready." She tried to make her voice bright.

"I can see that." He stared at her for a moment, then shook his head. "If you think for a minute that I'm going to let you walk out of here, that accident must have really scrambled your brains. Let me ask Doc for a wheelchair."

"I don't need a wheelchair."

"Fine." He slid his hands beneath her legs and eased her into his arms. "I'd rather carry you, anyway."

She wanted to protest, tell him to put her down, but her head throbbed and her ribs ached and it seemed easier to rest her head against his shoulder. In a minute he'd carried her past the interested faces of other patients in the waiting room and swung her into the front seat of the Blazer. He snapped her seat belt into place and slid into the seat next to her, but he didn't start the engine.

"Is there anything you need before I take you back to Melba's?" he asked.

She started to shake her head, but stopped abruptly when pain tore through her. "No," she said in a low voice. "I can't think of anything."

He started the truck and drove slowly to Melba's house. Even through her pain, Carly could tell that he drove carefully, trying not to jostle her. A treacherous warmth bloomed and spread inside her. Devlin had every reason to mistrust her, every reason to be angry with her. But it didn't seem to matter to him now.

"Here we are." He paused before getting out of the truck. "I know you're not going to want me to carry you into the house, but I'm going to do it anyway." A smile curved his mouth. "You can bet half the town knows about the accident already, anyway. Knowing Marge, she was on the phone before you were at Doc Ellis's."

"I'm glad I can give the people of Cameron some free entertainment," she said tartly as he opened her door.

"I guess I don't have to worry too much about you," he said as he swung her into his arms. "You're beginning to sound more like yourself."

A minute later he stepped into her room and eased the door closed. His arms tightened around her briefly, then he set her on the bed. "Don't move. I'm going to tell Melba what's going on. I'll be right back."

He left the door open, and she could hear the murmur of his voice and Melba's at the bottom of the stairs. Carly looked around her room. She would be fine here, alone, she told herself firmly. She didn't want anyone fussing over her, checking on her, taking care of her. There was no way she wanted to go to Devlin's family home.

Devlin stepped back into the room and squatted down in front of her. "Melba's going to bring you some chamomile tea and toast." His eyes twinkled at her. "Even Melba should be able to boil water and put bread in the toaster."

"You're too hard on her." Carly's protest was automatic, and Devlin's smile faded.

"One day we're going to have a long talk. About Melba Corboy, and a lot of other things. But not today." He looked around the room. "Do you have a nightgown?"

In spite of her injuries, his words strummed nerves inside her, making them hum. Pictures of Devlin helping her with her nightgown burned into her mind. "What would Melba think if she found you helping me with my nightgown?" she asked.

"She'd say I was being a Good Samaritan, giving a hand to someone who needed help."

Carly gave him a tiny smile. "I think she'd say that the innocent look doesn't become you."

His eyes darkened, and for a moment it looked as if he was going to lean closer to her. Then he pushed away from the bed and stood up. "I hear Melba on the stairs."

He opened her door and took a tray, then shut it firmly again. Dropping the tea bag in the hot water, he watched it for a few moments, then took it out. He dumped a heaping spoonful of sugar into the tea, then handed it to her.

"Thank you."

Devlin stood by the window for a while, waiting while she drank the tea and ate the toast. Finally he turned to face her again. "Let me help you get ready for bed," he said quietly.

Remembering the considerate way he'd helped her get dressed at the doctor's office, she knew there was no reason to refuse. But sudden awareness of him prickled against her skin. They weren't in a busy doctor's office, with the doctor and another patient in the room next door. They weren't surrounded by the smell of disinfectants and the sounds of human illness and injury. They were alone in her room, the door closed, with complete privacy. And allowing him to help her change into her nightgown seemed far too intimate.

Swallowing once, she said, "I can get it. But thanks for offering."

"Scared, Carly?" His voice was barely a breath of sound in the silent room.

"Of course not." She licked her lips and tried to avoid his gaze. "But you've spent far too much time already taking care of me. I'm sure you have a lot of work waiting for you."

He moved over to the dresser that stood on the other side of the bed. "You want to tell me which drawer, or should I just begin looking?"

"The top drawer on the right," she muttered.

"You shouldn't frown like that," he said as he turned away to open the drawer. "It'll make your head hurt even more."

Finally he pulled a long sleep shirt decorated with a picture of Tweety out of the drawer. His mouth twitched as he held it up. "I can see why you wouldn't want me to find this. Your sexy sleepwear has me all atwitter, Ms. Fitzpatrick. It's destined to haunt my dreams."

"It so happens that I'm very fond of Tweety," she retorted, but she couldn't resist his teasing smile. He was trying to make her forget about what had happened, she knew, and he was succeeding.

His eyes darkened as he watched her. "I have a feeling that I'm going to be fond of him, too," he murmured.

Kneeling in front of her again, he dropped the soft folds of the shirt over her head. "I think this will work." The shirt drifted over her chest and pooled around her waist as he slipped his hands beneath it and began to unbutton her shirt.

When the last button gave way, he eased the shirt off her shoulders. In the process, the backs of his hands brushed her bare breasts, and fire shuddered through her. His hands stilled and his eyes turned to molten silver. A muscle quivered in his jaw, then he carefully drew her shirt down her arms and tossed it onto the floor.

"Can you get your arms through the sleeves by yourself?" His voice was a low, husky growl.

Her ribs protested, but she managed to slide her arms through the sleeves. Devlin knelt in front of her, watching, and her hands began to tremble as she unbuttoned her shorts.

"What about this?" He fingered the velvet cord around her neck.

"I don't take that off," she said.

It looked like he wanted to ask her more, but instead he drew her gently to her feet. "Let me help you with the rest of your clothes." He held her against him as he reached down to pull her shorts off. When the shorts had been pulled away and tossed into a pile with the shirt, he held her for a moment before he let her go.

The moment was only as long as a heartbeat, but the soft material of her night shirt was no barrier against the heat and hardness of his body. Desire curled inside her, shocking her with its intensity. Devlin stepped quickly away from her, pulling back the quilt and blanket from her bed.

"Here you go."

He eased her between the sheets, then pulled the blanket back over her. The air-conditioned room suddenly felt far too hot and Devlin was far too close. Mortified that she would respond to his touch when he was only being kind, she closed her eyes.

"Thank you for all your help," she whispered.

"You're welcome."

She could feel him studying her, but she refused to open her eyes. With any luck, he'd assume she was simply tired.

"Is there anything else you need?"

"Nothing, thanks."

The silence in the room was far too loud. Finally she forced herself to look at him. He stood over her, watching, a brooding look in his eyes. "I'll be by to see how you're doing later," he said.

"All right."

He hesitated, as if he wanted to say something else, then turned and walked out of the room.

Carly listened to his footsteps descend the stairs, listened to him talking in a low voice to Melba. Then the front door opened and closed. Devlin was gone.

She should have agreed to go back to his ranch with him, her traitorous heart murmured. Trying to banish the thought, she rolled onto her uninjured side and closed her eyes again. The daylight outside her window was fading to darkness before she finally fell asleep. And when she dreamed, it wasn't of a car skidding off the road and rolling onto its side. She dreamed of a man with strong hands and a gentle touch who cradled her against his chest.

Devlin eased into Carly's room and looked down at her, sleeping in the moonlight. Faint bruises were beginning to show on the left side of her face, and the bandage over the cut on her scalp was a stark white in the darkness. He pulled a chair close to the bed and sat down.

Melba walked up the stairs and stopped at the door. Sticking her head into the room, she whispered, "How is she?"

Devlin stepped out into the hall. "Still sleeping. I'll keep an eye on her."

The older woman studied him, then finally gave a small smile. "You do that, Sheriff. I'm an old woman. I need my sleep."

He nodded gravely. "She's part of an accident investigation. I need to make sure she's all right."

Melba's sharp eyes softened for a moment, then she nodded once. "I'll see you in the morning." She turned and rounded the corner. A moment later he heard the sound of her door clicking firmly shut.

He settled back into the chair, content to watch Carly's slow, even breathing. As the night quieted and the old house creaked its way into slumber, Devlin shifted on the hard chair. Carly hadn't moved. Finally, his eyes burning with fatigue and his muscles cramping, he stood up and opened the closet door. Pulling out a blanket and pillow from the shelf, he stretched out on the floor, next to the bed. His last thought before drifting off to sleep was that he'd better wake up before Carly did in the morning.

The sound of blankets shifting next to him dragged Devlin out of the depths of sleep. He sat up quickly, relieved to find that Carly wasn't awake yet. But she was stirring. Hastily folding the

The Silhouette Reader Service® — Here's how it works:

Accepting your 2 free books and mystery gift places you under no obligation to buy anything. You may keep the books and gift and return the shipping statement marked "cancel." If you do not cancel, about a month later we'll send you 6 additional novels and bill you just $3.57 each in the U.S., or $3.96 in Canada, plus 25¢ delivery per book and applicable taxes if any.* That's the complete price and — compared to the cover price of $4.25 in the U.S. and $4.75 in Canada — it's quite a bargain! You may cancel at any time, but if you choose to continue, every month we'll send you 6 more books, which you may either purchase at the discount price or return to us and cancel your subscription.

*Terms and prices subject to change without notice. Sales tax applicable in N.Y. Canadian residents will be charged applicable provincial taxes and GST.

If offer card is missing write to: Silhouette Reader Service, 3010 Walden Ave., P.O. Box 1867, Buffalo NY 14240-1867

NO POSTAGE
NECESSARY
IF MAILED
IN THE
UNITED STATES

BUSINESS REPLY MAIL

FIRST-CLASS MAIL   PERMIT NO. 717   BUFFALO, NY

POSTAGE WILL BE PAID BY ADDRESSEE

SILHOUETTE READER SERVICE
3010 WALDEN AVE
PO BOX 1867
BUFFALO NY 14240-9952

Play The Lucky Hearts Game

and get...
FREE BOOKS, a FREE GIFT... and MUCH more!

Yes! I have scratched off the silver card. Please send me my **2 FREE BOOKS** and **FREE MYSTERY GIFT**. I understand that I am under no obligation to purchase any books as explained on the back of this card.

Scratch Here! then look below to see what your cards get you...

345 SDL CNGJ   **245 SDL CNGH**

Name _____
(PLEASE PRINT)

Address _____ Apt.# _____

City _____ State/Prov. _____ Zip/Postal Code _____

Twenty-one gets you **2 FREE BOOKS** and a **FREE MYSTERY GIFT!**

Twenty gets you **2 FREE BOOKS!**

Nineteen gets you **1 FREE BOOK!**

TRY AGAIN!

Offer limited to one per household and not valid to current Silhouette Intimate Moments® subscribers. All orders subject to approval.

PRINTED IN U.S.A.

blanket, he replaced it and the pillow in the closet, then moved to stand next to her bed. The sunrise outside her window painted the sky over the mountains with spectacular pinks and reds, and the rosy light that seeped into the room kissed her face with color.

Curls of her dark red hair hid her bruises, and he brushed the hair away from her face and stared down at the ugly marks. They were a little darker this morning, but no additional bruises had appeared. He watched her sleep for a while longer, then slipped out of the room.

Melba was moving around in the kitchen, and he poked his head in the door. "I'll be back in a while," he told her. "Carly is still sleeping, and I have some things to take care of. Call the office if she wakes up and have Marge radio me."

Melba turned around to face him. "I'll do that, Sheriff." She watched him carefully. "I hope that what happened to her isn't connected to that message someone left in her room."

"I hope so, too. That's one of the things I'm going to check on."

Melba turned back to the stove. "If she wakes up, I'll tell her you'll be back."

With one last glance up the stairs, he strode out of the house and climbed into his truck, already thinking about what he needed to do. It might be early, but everyone he needed to talk to would already be up and busy. And the first stop would be the service station where they'd towed Carly's Jeep.

A few hours later he knocked at Melba's door again. The older woman opened the door, and nodded toward the dining room. "She's up and having breakfast."

Carly turned to face him as he walked into the dining room, her movements slow and deliberate. "Good morning, Devlin," she said.

He pulled out the chair next to her and sat down. "How are you feeling?"

She shrugged, and he saw a flicker of pain in her eyes at the movement. "About how you'd expect. Like I got the worst of an encounter with a truck. But I took some aspirin, and I'm sure it'll kick in soon."

"Didn't Doc Ellis give you some pain pills?"

"He did, but I have no intention of taking them. They make me too groggy. Aspirin will work just fine."

"Just not as well."

"Well enough. I have a lot to do today. I have to arrange to get the car towed, and call the rental company and have them deliver another one, for starters."

"I took care of that. Jam Peters has already taken a look at your car. The rental company said they probably wouldn't be able to get another Jeep here until the day after tomorrow."

"Well. Thank you." She set the piece of toast carefully on her plate. "You've been busy. You didn't have to do any of that, you know."

"I know." He watched the struggle in her face between being glad for the help and being mortified that she'd needed it. "It was an easy thing to do, Carly," he said gently. "It wasn't a problem at all."

"Thanks," she muttered again. "So I'm stuck in town for the next two days?"

"What were you planning? A hike into the mountains? Maybe an overnight camp-out?" He felt his temper rise and struggled to control himself. "You're staying in bed, at least today."

"I'm afraid not. I don't have the time to stay in bed. And I'm a lot better." She gave him a bright smile. "Really."

"Carly, you were injured in a car accident yesterday. You've got to hurt like hell today. There's nothing so important that you have to run out and get back to work today."

"It's important to me." She turned back to her toast.

"Well, think about this. That accident of yours wasn't any accident. Someone meant for you to get hurt." He watched the shock fill her face with grim satisfaction. "How important is your precious story now?"

He hadn't meant to tell her so baldly, but she'd made him angry and he'd blurted out the truth. And maybe it was better that she was shocked. She needed to think about what she was doing.

"What?" she whispered. "What are you talking about?"

"There were bolts driven into the sides of all four of your tires.

Jam Peters told me that someone could have done it in a few seconds. And once you started driving, it was only a matter of time before one of them blew out. With the curving roads and mountains around Cameron, your accident could have been a hell of a lot worse than it was." His voice was grim. "It's gone beyond the message-on-the-mirror stage. Thank God you weren't hurt too badly, but what's going to happen next time?"

She'd dropped her toast onto her plate and was staring at him. Her face was pale but her eyes were filled with determination. "I think it must mean that I'm touching a nerve somewhere. Someone obviously doesn't like what I'm doing."

"There's an insight," he said with disgust. "Carly, you need to forget about this story and leave Cameron. I don't know if it's because of what you're doing, or if someone just has a grudge against reporters, but you're obviously in danger here." His heart ached at the idea, but he told himself firmly that it would be best for everyone. Including his heart.

She stared at him, disbelief in her eyes. "You're not serious, are you?"

"Of course I'm serious. Someone tried to kill you." His voice was stiff.

"And you think I should leave, just forget about it?" Her voice rose. "What kind of law enforcement officer are you? Instead of sweeping it under the covers, you should be investigating what happened."

"What do you think I've been doing all morning? I'm not trying to ignore what happened to you. I'll get to the bottom of it, and the person responsible will be arrested. But in the meantime, it would be safer for you to be out of harm's way."

"I don't want to be out of harm's way. I want to do my job." She lifted her chin, a mulish look in her eyes. "And that's what I'm going to do."

"You're going to pursue this story, even though it could get you killed?" He heard the anger in his voice and struggled to control it.

Carly looked back down at the plate on the table. "Yes. And it's not going to get me killed. I'll be more careful."

"How can you be more careful when you have no idea who's behind your accident?" he demanded. "It could be anyone in Cameron."

When she looked back up at him, her eyes were filled with determination. And something more. Something painfully, achingly vulnerable. "I can't stop, Dev."

He could resist the reporter, the bright, self-confident professional who knew exactly what she wanted. He wouldn't concede her an inch. But he had no defense against the vulnerable woman.

"What are you going to do next?" he asked, his voice filled with resignation.

"I was on my way out to Phil Hilbert's ranch when I had the accident. I'd like to talk to him. But until my car is delivered, I'll do more research at the newspaper office."

"I'll drive you out to Hilbert's place. Tomorrow," he said firmly. "You need to take it easy today."

"Thank you." Her gaze searched his face for a moment. "Why are you doing this, Dev? I thought you wanted me to stop."

"I do want you to stop. But it's pretty obvious that you're not going to listen to reason. It's my job to make sure you're safe while you're in Cameron, and the best way to keep an eye on you is to take you where you want to go."

"So this is business for you." Her green eyes dared him to deny it.

"Do you want to make it personal?" He leaned closer, watching her. "If so, let's get real personal. Why are you pursuing this story? You've got all the details you need for your article. So why do you want to talk to Phil Hilbert? And I'll bet you're planning on talking to my family too, aren't you?"

He smiled in grim satisfaction at the look of shocked surprise in her eyes. "Believe me, Carly, it didn't take a rocket scientist to figure that out. So yeah, this is business. It's going to stay that way until you make it personal."

Her green gaze held his for a moment, then dropped down to the plate of crumbs in front of her again. "Thank you for the offer," she said, her voice low. "I would appreciate a ride out to the Hilbert's ranch."

A sharp stab of disappointment surged through him, and he struggled to suppress it. *This was what he wanted,* he told himself. A business relationship. He didn't need to get involved with a woman who kept secrets, a woman who didn't tell the truth.

"I'll come by later to see how you're doing," he muttered.

She gave him a bright smile. "Thanks, but I'm sure I'll be fine. I feel much better already. I'll see you tomorrow."

"I'll see you later this afternoon."

"Fine. I'll be around." She angled her chin higher. "I wouldn't want you to neglect your business obligations."

"I wouldn't dream of it."

He stood up and headed for the door. Once outside, he hurried down the walk. And if he was running away, so be it.

Because he wanted to make it personal. Very personal.

Chapter 10

Carly stared down at the toast on her plate as she listened to the click of the front door closing. This was exactly what she wanted, she told herself. An impersonal, professional relationship with Devlin was the only kind she was interested in.

Right. Her body still burned with memories of the passion they'd shared in the cave. And every time he was near, her whole body quivered with awareness.

Straightening her shoulders, she took another gulp of coffee and pushed away from the table. It didn't matter. Her body might betray her, but it wasn't going to stop her from finding the truth about her brother. Even if she had to alienate Devlin in the process.

She walked up the stairs slowly, her ribs aching. She wanted nothing more than to crawl beneath the covers of her bed and let the oblivion of sleep wash over her. But she couldn't allow herself to do that. Someone clearly didn't want her to pursue the story of Edmund Whitmore. And that meant she was getting close to the truth.

When she opened her closet to retrieve her backpack, the blanket and pillow stored on the top shelf came tumbling to the floor. The blanket had been folded together carelessly, and she automatically refolded it before she replaced it.

As she lifted the pillow to the shelf, a whiff of a subtle, masculine fragrance made her freeze. The pillow smelled like Devlin. Holding it closer, she inhaled deeply, only to find herself engulfed in his scent.

She held the pillow a moment longer than necessary as she resisted the impulse to bury her face in it, then she carefully set it on top of the blanket. Had Devlin spent the night in her room, then left before she woke up?

Her chest swelled as she stared at the pillow and blanket. For just a moment, her treacherous heart wanted to think he had, wanted to think he'd stayed and watched her, even though she'd told him she would be fine alone.

Then she stepped back and gently closed the closet door. It was foolish to think that way, dangerous to want what she couldn't have. Lifting her backpack onto her uninjured side, she walked out of her bedroom without looking back.

The next morning, Carly slipped out of the house to sit on the porch swing and wait for Devlin. He'd stopped by the night before, just as he'd promised, but they hadn't had much to say to one another. His questions about her reasons for pursuing Edmund's story hung in the air, unspoken but potent. She couldn't bring herself to tell him the truth. Her heart told her she could trust Devlin, but her brain insisted he was a McAllister. And the McAllisters had been involved, somehow, in Edmund's death.

He'd told her, stiffly, that he would pick her up early in the morning, then left. Now she waited for him, wondering what they would say to each other on the drive out to the Hilbert ranch.

A few minutes later his white police Blazer stopped at the curb. She stood up to walk out to the truck, but Devlin climbed out and came up the walk to escort her to the car.

Because her heart had begun to pound at the sight of him, Carly scrambled for some way to deflect her feelings. "You didn't have to walk me to the car. I could have made it on my own."

"I was taught that a gentleman doesn't sit in his car and wait for a lady to hop in." He slanted her a look that was impossible to read. "I guess that's another difference between Cameron and New York."

She flushed. "That's not what I meant. I meant you didn't have to walk with me because you think I'm an invalid. I'm fine."

"I'm glad to hear that." His hand on her back didn't budge. "Melba said you managed just fine this morning."

Carly stopped and looked over at him. "Were you checking up on me?" she demanded.

"I called to see if you were ready. She said you were sitting on the porch, so I told her not to disturb you." His voice was as smooth and emotionless as his eyes.

"Sorry," she muttered. "I don't like anyone fussing over me."

They'd reached the truck, but before he opened the door he turned her to face him. "You're here in our town by yourself, and you've had an accident. Someone is going to check on you. This isn't New York. People in Cameron care about their neighbors, and when someone needs help, everyone pitches it. So get used to it." His face hardened. "Unless it bothers you so much that you decide to leave."

"I'm not going anywhere." She hesitated, then put her hand on his arm. It was as tense as a coiled spring. "I'm sorry, Devlin," she said again. "I'm not ungrateful, and it's very sweet of you to bother. Really it is." Swallowing hard, she forced herself to add, "I've never relied on anyone. If I seem ungrateful, it's because I'm not sure what I'm supposed to do."

A thaw crept into his eyes. "I know. I'd already figured that out." His voice was low and husky.

They stood inches apart. Her hand was still on his arm, and she could feel the heat and strength of him through the khaki shirt he wore. His breath fanned her face, and as she watched, his eyes darkened.

It felt as though they hung suspended in time. Drowning in his gaze, allowing herself to get lost in the desire that flared in his eyes, she couldn't look away.

Suddenly he jerked open the car door. "Get in," he said, his voice taut. "I'm not about to provide a show for Melba or her neighbors."

Her heart beating a jagged rhythm, Carly settled herself on the vinyl seat and waited for Devlin to slide behind the steering wheel. He sat for a moment, staring out the windshield, then turned to her. "Have you had breakfast, or do you want to stop at Heaven on Seventh?"

"Thanks, but I had some cereal." Her mouth curved upward. "Since it doesn't have to be cooked, there's not much Melba can do to ruin it."

"Then let's get over to Phil's." He glanced at her as he pulled away from the curb. "Does he know you're coming?"

"I called him yesterday and asked if I could talk to him. He said he'd be around all day yesterday and today."

"Does he know what you want to talk to him about?" Devlin's gaze was shrewd as he glanced at her again.

"I didn't give him any details." She looked down at her clasped hands. "I didn't want to give him a chance to think about his answers."

"In other words, he thinks you're going to ask him some innocuous questions about Cameron and you're going to spring this murder thing on him."

She lifted her chin. "I'm sure he's heard by now that I'm looking into Edmund Whitmore's murder. You said yourself this was a small town and everyone gossips. So I doubt it will be a complete surprise to him."

When he glanced over at her again, there was genuine amusement in his eyes. "I'm looking forward to seeing you handle Phil."

"I don't 'handle' anyone," she said. "I simply ask questions."

At that he laughed. "Slick, I may be a small-town sheriff, but I'm not a complete hick. I'd say you were a world champ when it comes to handling people."

"Except you," she muttered, under her breath.

But he heard her. "You don't think you've been handling me?" His voice was suddenly husky again.

"I don't think anyone handles you." Her voice throbbed in the suddenly quiet car.

"You're wrong." She saw his hands tighten on the steering wheel. "You've been handling me since the moment you drove into town, going too fast in that flashy red Jeep."

Desire curled deep inside her, and she realized she wanted desperately to believe him. But she couldn't allow herself to feel that way. "I'm just different, that's all. I'm not a small-town person like the rest of the people in Cameron."

"No, you're not, are you?" he murmured.

"I'm strictly New York."

But as the Blazer hummed over the asphalt, around the curves and through the magnificent canyons, she wondered if that was still true. She'd felt at peace in Cameron, and oddly, in spite of her accident, safe. She liked the feeling of having a whole community of people to count on. Heck, she didn't even mind knowing that the town of Cameron was gossiping about her.

Devlin must really be getting to her, she thought as she stared out the window. She'd have to be careful not to let it show.

"Here we are at the Hilbert place." His voice interrupted as he turned onto a crushed gravel driveway. "The house is about a quarter mile into his spread."

Carly sat up and reached for her notebook. Before they arrived at the house, she had already made some notes on the Hilbert ranch.

"It's not as well kept up as your ranch," she said, after watching the fence drooping in spots, and the patches of bare earth in the pastures.

"Shea takes good care of the Red Rock," he replied. "She'd work twenty-four hours a day if she thought that would make it a better ranch."

"Doesn't Phil care as much about his ranch?"

Devlin shrugged. "You'd have to ask Phil. We don't spend a lot of time together."

They stopped in front of a house that needed a coat of paint. The shutters were faded, too, and one of them tilted slightly. The barn sagged in the middle, and its roof was missing a few shingles. All in all, the Hilbert ranch looked tired.

She said as much to Devlin before they got out of the truck, and he looked over at her. "That's very astute. Phil is getting older, and it's probably getting harder for him to do everything that needs doing."

"Does he have any children to help him run the place?"

"He has one son. But Bobby was a troublemaker, and didn't find life in Cameron to his liking. He took off several years ago, and now he's probably causing trouble for some big-city police officer."

"That's too bad," she murmured.

"Don't feel too sorry for Phil," he warned. "He'll use your sympathy against you when you're interviewing him."

Her heart warmed and she couldn't resist smiling at him. "Thank you," she said quietly. "I think I like it when you're on my side."

"I wasn't ever on the other side. And I still don't want to see anyone get hurt because of what you're doing."

Her smile faded. "I try never to hurt the innocent."

He studied her for a moment, then nodded. "All right. Let's go find Phil."

Devlin stayed close to her side as they walked over to the two-story house. She wondered if he intended to stay with her during her interview with Phil. She hoped not. She had a feeling that Phil Hilbert would be a lot more forthcoming if the neighbor he hated wasn't close by.

Phil opened the door a moment later. "Hello, Carly. Welcome to the Tall T Ranch." He noticed Devlin standing next to her, and his gaze sharpened. "You too, Dev. Are you providing an escort service out to the dangerous Tall T?"

"Carly's car was damaged in an accident a couple of days ago," he answered evenly. "Her new rental hasn't arrived, and she didn't have any way out to your place. She didn't want to keep you waiting on her convenience, so I offered to give her a lift."

He looked over at Carly. "I have a lot of paperwork to do, so I'll wait in the car."

"That's fine," she murmured, but her heart softened. His glance was plainly asking her if she was all right. She knew if she asked, he wouldn't budge from her side.

She couldn't help watching as Dev strode back to the Blazer. The sun glinted off the burnished gold of his hair, and he looked strong and vital.

"Good-looking young man." Phil Hilbert's voice held a trace of malice, just enough to whet her curiosity. She turned to face him.

"Is he a good sheriff?"

He shrugged. "Good enough, I guess. He's left me alone. I was a big backer of Bert Pickens, the sheriff before McAllister. I told him not to retire. He had a lot of good years left in him."

Carly asked Hilbert some general questions about Cameron, then brought up the subject she was really interested in. "I understand there was a murder in Cameron about twenty years ago."

For just a moment, Hilbert's eyes flattened, and he had the wary look of a cornered animal. Then he blinked, and slowly shook his head. "I'd forgotten all about that. A kid was murdered, wasn't he? By a drifter?"

"Yes, it was a kid." Carly swallowed hard. "And the drifter story seems to be the popular one."

"You don't believe it." Hilbert's eyes were shrewd.

"It does seem very convenient," she said carefully.

Hilbert let his gaze settle on the Blazer. "The body was found on the McAllister ranch," he finally said. "Way up in the mountains." He shrugged. "Hard to imagine that a kid would wander all that way. Or a drifter. But the sheriff was satisfied."

"Are you implying that the McAllisters were responsible?" Carly's hand tightened on her notebook as she watched Phil Hilbert.

"I'm not implying anything." Again he looked at the truck, and his gaze hardened. "It just seems mighty coincidental. Especially since the McAllisters had a gun go missing before the murder."

"For someone who'd forgotten all about the incident, you seem to remember a lot." Her voice was perfectly expressionless.

"Talking to you about it brings it back."

"Do you have any idea why the boy was killed?"

Phil shrugged carelessly. "None at all. Maybe the kid got into a fight with the drifter. Maybe he tried to rob him. He was a teenager, after all."

His careless dismissal of her brother stirred Carly's temper, but she forced herself to clamp it down. "Can you tell me anything else about your local history?" She made herself change the subject. "Anything else that our readers would find interesting?"

Phil steered the conversation into safe waters, and they talked for a while longer. Finally she reached out and shook his hand. "Thank you for your help, Mr. Hilbert. May I quote you in my article?"

"Of course." He held her hand a moment longer than necessary. "And call me Phil."

"Thanks, Phil. I appreciate your time." She gently extricated her hand from the older man's grasp.

"Always glad to help the media."

She felt his eyes on her as she walked down the stairs toward Devlin's Blazer. She had to resist the urge to run to the truck and Devlin.

Devlin watched through the rearview mirror as Carly shook hands with Phil, then turned and walked toward him. Her dark red hair curled around her shoulders, shining in the sunlight, and her long legs in trim jeans seemed to go on forever.

His mouth dry, his heart pounding, he waited until she was halfway across the yard, then he jumped out of the truck to open the door for her. She flashed him a grateful smile, and scrambled into the truck more quickly than she needed to.

When he'd settled himself back behind the steering wheel, he looked over at her. "You seemed in a hurry to get back in the truck."

She gave him a small smile. "Just anxious to get back and write down my notes."

He studied her for a moment, then he started the truck and

drove back toward the road. But instead of heading back toward Cameron, he continued down the road toward the Red Rock Ranch.

When they had pulled into the driveway of his ranch, out of sight of the road, he stopped the truck and turned to her. "What did Phil say that upset you?"

She shot him a startled look. "How did you know I was upset?"

He didn't want to tell her that he seemed to know a lot of things about her. He didn't want to be this aware of her, but that didn't seem to matter.

"Don't ever take up poker, Slick. You'd lose your shirt in no time. It's written all over your face."

For a moment, she stared out the windshield. Then she sighed. "I didn't like him," she said quietly. "And that's not supposed to happen. I should be able to talk to him and write my story without letting my emotions get in the way."

"Why didn't you like him?" He tried to keep his voice casual, but his hands tightened on the steering wheel. If Phil had done or said anything out of line, he'd take him apart, piece by piece.

"I don't know for sure." Carly turned on the seat of the car to face him. "He didn't say anything wrong to me, or do anything out of the ordinary. But I still didn't care for him."

"What kinds of things were you asking him?"

Carly shrugged. "The usual. I asked him about the town, about the people who live here." She slanted him a look. "I asked him if you were doing a good job as sheriff."

"And what did he say?"

She smiled for the first time since getting back in the truck. "He gave you a rather lukewarm endorsement. Then he told me he hadn't wanted Bert Pickens to retire."

Dev snorted. "Of course he didn't want Bert to retire. They were poker buddies, and he figured he had a nice little 'in' with the sheriff's department." He glanced in the direction of the Hilbert ranch, and felt his anger stirring. "But I've never treated Phil any different than any other citizen of Cameron."

"I know that. And I think Phil knows it, too."

She laid a hand on his arm, and he looked down as her fingers curled gently around him. A fire started burning, deep in his gut, and he wasn't sure if he wanted her to move her hand or hold on forever.

When she drew her hand away, he shifted on the seat. "What other insights did Phil give you?"

She met his gaze, and she wasn't smiling anymore. "He implied that your family was responsible for the death of Edmund Whitmore."

Anger stirred again, and this time he didn't try to restrain it. "What did he say?"

"He told me that the boy's body was found on your ranch, way back in the mountains. His implication was that it was too far off the beaten path for anyone but a McAllister to have killed him. And he mentioned the gun that was missing from your house."

Devlin stared at the red cliffs that rose above the green pastures, the symbol of this land and his home. Phil had cast a shadow over his land, over his family. He hadn't wanted to reopen the case, but now he had no choice. "Phil was wrong," he said softly.

"What do you mean?"

"The McAllisters weren't responsible for that boy's death. My father wasn't a murderer. Why would he have wanted to kill a child? They never did find a motive for the murder. It was a senseless crime, with no explanation." He stared at his land again, land that had been in his family for three generations. "Phil must hate us more than Shea and I realized."

"I don't intend to write about innuendo and suggestion in my article," she said quietly.

"Then what do you intend to write?" He turned to face her.

"The truth. And I'll find it, believe me."

Her eyes were hard and determined, and her chin was tilted defiantly. He sighed.

"Apparently someone else thinks you'll find it, too. I'm going to reopen the Whitmore boy's case. I'll get to the bottom of this murder, once and for all." He watched her carefully. "Are you satisfied now?"

Slowly she nodded, although he thought he saw fear in her eyes. "If anyone can find out the truth, it would be you." She hesitated, then added, "But what about the gun that was missing from your father's collection?"

"What about it?"

"People will find out that you were the one responsible for its being stolen."

"What if they do? It was twenty years ago. I was a child. I don't think anyone believes that I was the person who killed the Whitmore boy."

Carly looked away from him then. Staring out the window, she murmured, "I feel like I'm responsible. I started digging into this case, and now your role in it is going to come out. I don't want anyone to think less of you, and now I'm afraid that they will."

His heart tightened in his chest as he watched her staring out the window. Her shoulders were hunched and her back was tense. Slowly he reached out a hand and smoothed it down her back. She shuddered at his touch, and he couldn't suppress the memories of the passion they'd shared just a few days ago.

He couldn't stop himself from reaching for her, from drawing her back against him. Still she hadn't turned around to look at him. "It's all right, Carly. No one will think less of me. No one will care, one way or another." He bent his head to kiss the back of her neck, and she shuddered again. "But I appreciate your concern."

She twisted in his arms, so that she was facing him. "I never meant to hurt you, Dev."

"I didn't think you had."

She swallowed once. "I don't want to hurt your family, either."

"You won't."

"How can you be sure? If you reopen the investigation, you don't know what you'll find."

"I know I won't find that my father was a murderer, if that's what you mean."

She watched him, her eyes troubled. "Are you certain?"

"As certain as one person can be about anything." He leaned

back so he could see her better. "I would have thought you'd be delighted. I thought this was exactly what you wanted, to find out who killed Edmund Whitmore."

"It is." She licked her lips. "I do want to find out who killed him."

"But," he prompted as she hesitated.

"But I don't want you to be hurt." Her whisper was so low that it was barely more than a breath. It sounded as if the words had been torn out of her.

He was unbearably moved by her concern for him, but when she wouldn't meet his gaze, he knew she was still hiding something from him.

Tell me the truth, he wanted to beg. *Trust me.*

But she didn't. And trust wasn't something that could be forced. He tightened his hold on her for a moment, pulled her close enough to make his already taut body even harder, then he set her gently back on her own end of the seat.

"We'd better get back to town," he said. "It's been a long day for you, and you're still recovering."

She looked down to fasten her seat belt, and he saw a pulse pounding in her throat. When she looked up at him, he saw desire in her eyes, a desire she tried desperately to hide. His hands started to shake and his heart began to pound.

"I'm a lot better," she said brightly. "I hardly notice my ribs anymore, and my head is fine."

"I could have told you it would be," he said, deliberately putting the truck in gear and turning it around on the gravel driveway. "It's too hard for a little thing like a car accident to slow you down." He kept his voice as light as hers. He didn't want to stir the passion that lay just below the surface.

To his surprise, she laughed, a gurgle of delight that wrapped itself around him and tried to worm its way into his soul.

"I guess my hard head is good for something, then."

"I guess so."

Neither of them said anything for a few minutes, then he casually asked, "What's on your agenda for tomorrow?"

"Do you think my replacement car will be here then?"

"Probably. The car rental office said it should take a couple of days to get it to Cameron. They're going to truck it in, and then take the wrecked one back with them."

"I thought I'd go out and spend some time driving around the area. Other than the time you showed me the area ranches, I haven't really explored this part of Utah."

"Are you telling me that you're going to take some time off from your story and just be a tourist?" He raised one eyebrow as he looked over at her.

It was impossible to miss the guilty look that flashed across her face. "Is there something wrong with that?"

"Not at all," he said dryly. "And I'd be glad to think that's what you're doing. But I know better."

"You have an awfully suspicious mind, Sheriff." Her voice was light and teasing.

"Like I said earlier, don't take up poker. It's not tough to figure out that you're not going to drive around and admire the scenery."

"I won't deny that if I find myself someplace interesting, I'll take a look."

"By interesting I take it to mean someplace that's connected to the Whitmore murder."

"Interesting can be defined a number of ways," she said, grinning at him. "That's one of them."

He shook his head. "You are a dangerous woman, Carly. I pity anyone who tries to keep up with you."

They kept the conversation light as they headed back into Cameron. Devlin figured that she was no more eager than he was to explore the desire and passion that simmered just beneath the surface. He told himself that was the way he wanted it. He reminded himself of what had happened the last time he got involved in a relationship with a woman who had a hidden agenda. But his heart didn't seem to agree.

Chapter 11

The next morning, Devlin led the truck from the rental company over to Melba Corboy's. A black Jeep Cherokee sat on the truck bed, and it only took a few minutes for the driver of the truck to deliver it to Carly, get her signature on the paperwork, and drive away. It would stop at Jam Peters's garage and pick up the damaged Jeep before heading back to Las Vegas.

"Thank you," Carly said to him as the truck disappeared around the corner. "For making all the arrangements, then making sure he found me."

"You're welcome," he said. He glanced at her new vehicle. "Have you decided where you're going to take it today?"

"Just around," she said. "Nowhere in particular. I'm going to stop at the *Weekly Sentinel* office first, then drive around the area."

"Is there a phone in this Jeep?"

"There should be. I requested one with a phone."

He checked, just to make sure, then stood on the curb, scowling at her. "You're going to go and get yourself into trouble, aren't you?"

"Of course not! I'm just doing a little sightseeing."

"Right. And I'm the Easter Bunny." In spite of himself, he felt his heart softening. "Take it easy, Carly. You're still recovering from your accident. I'll be happy to take you anywhere you'd like to go."

"You have a job to do, Dev," she said, but he thought he saw disappointment in her eyes. "I can't take up all your time."

"Just make sure you don't end up as part of my job," he said. "I don't like these accident investigations. And the accident you had the other day was a little too close for comfort."

"I'll be careful. I won't go anywhere unsafe."

"I wish I could believe that."

"Really, Dev, I'm not going anywhere you need to worry about."

"Those are famous last words if I ever heard them," he muttered. Shaking his head, he said, "Use that phone if you need anything. Even if you just get lost."

"Don't worry. I will."

He didn't want to leave, but he couldn't stand in front of Melba's all day. "I'll talk to you later. Stop by the office when you get back to town."

"I will."

As he slid into the truck and drove away, he felt her eyes following him. Just before he turned the corner, he looked back and saw her standing on the curb, watching him.

Carly watched Devlin drive away, then went back into the house. Grabbing her backpack and some bottles of water, she threw them into the new Jeep and headed for the newspaper office. After scanning a few more issues of the *Weekly Sentinel* and finding nothing about her brother or his murder, she replaced the papers and headed out of Cameron.

She'd been telling Devlin the truth. She wasn't heading for anywhere in particular. She wanted to visit the place where they'd found Edmund's body, but she would need permission from Devlin to do that. Edmund had been found on McAllister property.

So today she would just get out of town by herself and do some thinking. She had a decision to make, and she was terrified of making the wrong one. It was time to tell Devlin the truth. He had a right to know she was Edmund's sister, especially since he was reopening the investigation. But although her heart told her she could trust Devlin, her stubborn mind was still wary.

It had been a long time since she'd trusted anyone with the private Carly. No one really knew her, bone deep. If she told Devlin the truth, she would be trusting him with part of her soul.

And that scared her. It would give him a power over her that she didn't want to relinquish.

Her mind twisted and turned, making an argument, rejecting it, then thinking of something else. Finally, a few miles after she'd passed the entrance to the Red Rock Ranch, she saw a small road that seemed to lead up into the mountains. There was no ranch close to it, and she knew that behind the Red Rock was a national forest. Assuming that this road led onto federal land, she turned her Jeep off the asphalt and headed up the rutted dirt road.

As she drove uphill, over the winding, twisting road, she thought she saw puffs of dust on the road behind her. Each time, they were hidden when the road turned once again. For a moment she wondered if Devlin had followed her, but she quickly discarded the thought. He would have been up front if he wanted to accompany her. *It was probably the dust she had stirred up herself,* she told herself.

Ten minutes later she emerged from a grove of aspen trees, magnificent in their autumn yellow leaves, into a small clearing. Rock jutted out on her left and the road passed in front of the cliff, mere feet away from a steep drop-off. She forgot all about the dust behind her as she caught her breath at the view. Purple mountains seemed to stretch forever in every direction. The road continued past the cliff, heading into more trees, but Carly pulled the Jeep to the side of the road and stepped outside.

Careful to stay close to the rock, she walked behind the Jeep, then stopped, staring at the magnificent view. Pressing her palm against the cliff on her left side, she stood drinking in the scenery. She was high in the mountains and the air was noticeably cooler than down in Cameron, but the rock held the warmth of the sunlight and she leaned against it, letting its heat seep into her bones.

She wasn't sure how long she stood there, soaking up the heat of the rocks, thinking about what she should do. The endless vista of mountains stretching out in front of her was oddly calming to a woman who'd spent her entire adult life in a large city. She would never have imagined that she'd find so much comfort in such a wild, untamed place. But she couldn't tear herself away.

The first pebbles skittering down the cliff didn't alarm her. The rock was soft and crumbly, breaking away in her hand as she flattened her palm against the cliff and peered up at the shower of small stones bouncing toward the ground. The rock debris that lay along the road was evidence that the cliff was slowly eroding away, pebble by pebble.

As she stared up the cliff, narrowing her eyes against the sunlight and the bright blue of the sky, she saw a much larger rock teetering on the edge of the cliff. She watched in horror as it slowly toppled over the edge, hurtling toward her.

She managed to leap out of the way just in time. The rock smashed into the place she'd been standing moments earlier. As she stood staring at it, she heard an ominous rumbling above her.

Dozens of rocks, large and small, were crashing down the cliff, bouncing off the surface, dislodging more pieces of jagged stone as they fell. The roaring avalanche was headed directly toward her. There was no place to run—the road fell away into space only a few feet in front of her.

Pressing herself into a tiny seam in the rock, Carly crouched down and covered her head with her arms. In moments, the first of the falling rock hit her. Tiny rocks with razor-sharp edges sliced into her arms. She ignored the pain, bracing herself for the impact of the larger stones. The crashing of rocks around her filled her ears, blocking out everything else.

One bounced off her knee with a glancing blow, hard enough to make her cry out involuntarily. Another skimmed her arm and made her eyes water with the pain. She heard the dull thud of boulders slamming into the ground, only inches away.

Finally the barrage dwindled away to a few small pebbles that bounced against the rock and rolled to a stop. Then there was silence again. From far away, she heard a bird call. The wind rustled the leaves of the aspen trees. But the ordinary, everyday sounds were drowned out by the pounding of her heart, beating frantically against her chest.

"Sheriff, there's a call for you."

Devlin looked up from the stack of reports he'd been reading and frowned at his dispatcher. "Could someone else take it, Marge? I need to get through this paperwork."

"She asked for you specifically." The dispatcher paused delicately. "I think it's that reporter."

Devlin snatched up the phone. "Carly? Are you all right?"

"I think so." She drew in a shaky breath, and his fingers curled tightly around the phone. "The thing is, I've had another accident. I can't drive back to town."

"What happened?" he shouted into the phone. "Are you hurt?"

"No, I'm fine. There was an avalanche, or whatever you call it, and there's a pile of rocks behind the Jeep. They're completely blocking the road. I'll need some help clearing them away."

"Can you tell me where you are?"

"I'm not sure. In the mountains." He heard her take another shaky breath, and his heart started to pound.

"Do you remember where you left the main road?" He tried to keep his voice calm.

"I took a trail that left the main road about three or four miles from the driveway to your ranch. I figured it was national forest property and I wanted to see where it led."

Her voice was definitely quavery now, and he wanted to fly to her, to wrap his arms around her and tell her that nothing was going to hurt her. Instead, he asked carefully, "Was it on the same side of the road as the Red Rock?"

"Yes. I wasn't paying real close attention, but I don't think it was more than a few miles past your driveway."

Slowly he exhaled. "I know just where you are. You're on Red Rock property. Stay right where you are, and I'll be there as quickly as I can."

"Believe me, I'm not going anywhere."

Even over the phone he could hear the bubble of hysteria in her voice. "You'll be fine, Carly. Stay in your Jeep until I get there, in case there's another rock fall. And lock the doors."

"I already did." Her voice quavered again.

"Good. I'm on my way."

He disconnected the phone and almost ran out the door. "Trouble, Sheriff?" he heard Marge call behind him.

"Get Ben Jackson on the radio and have him meet me back here in about an hour." The door slammed behind him, and he jumped into his truck. He threw on the lights and sirens, and floored the accelerator as soon as he hit the edge of town.

Ten minutes later he bumped his way cautiously up the rutted trail that was the back road out of the Red Rock Ranch. The road was dry and dusty. There was no way of telling how many vehicles had driven over it lately, but he continuously scanned the area, looking for anything out of the ordinary, anything out of place.

He didn't see anything that alarmed him until he reached the place where the road curved around the cliff. A huge pile of debris blocked the road behind Carly's Jeep. Barely waiting for his truck to stop, he leaped out the door and ran to Carly, slipping and stumbling on the rocks in the road.

Her face relaxed when she saw him, and she reached to unlock the door. He didn't miss the way her hand shook.

And he didn't miss the shocking smears of blood on both of her arms, either.

"My God! I thought you told me you weren't hurt."

He reached for her, running his hands down her arms, smoothing the hair away from her face.

Instead of pulling away from him, she buried her face in his shoulder and wrapped her arms around him. "It's nothing," she said, her voice muffled by his shirt. "They're just scratches."

He held her close, angry he hadn't been able to protect her, to keep her safe. Her heart fluttered against his and he tightened his arms around her.

"Are you hurt anywhere else?" he asked.

"I'm sure I have a couple of bruises on my arms and legs, but

that's it.'' She didn't lift her head as she spoke. "I think I was
lucky.''

"You were damned lucky." He looked at the pile of rocks
behind her Jeep and tightened his arms again. "Let's get you out
of here."

At that she raised her head. "What about my car?"

"The hell with your car. It's not going anywhere. We'll worry
about it later. Right now, we need to get you back to Doc Ellis."

She swallowed once, but didn't look away from him. And she
didn't let him go. "I don't think that avalanche was an accident,
Devlin."

Fear twisted in his gut, but he tried to keep his face impassive.
"What do you mean?"

"I didn't move for a long time after the rocks stopped falling."
She swallowed again. "I was afraid that if I did, it would set off
another avalanche. So everything was very quiet. I thought I heard
a car engine start up, not too far away. And that's not all."

She looked toward the trail, where his Blazer sat. "When I was
driving up here, I kept seeing puffs of dust behind me, the kind
that you get as you drive along. I never saw another car, so I just
assumed that they were from me. But when I heard the car, after
the avalanche, I wondered. So I locked the door to the Jeep and
called you."

"Thank God you did," he muttered. He pulled her closer,
touching her hair, her back, her face, just to assure himself that
she was all right. "Let's get you to Doc Ellis."

"I don't need to take up more of his time. I'm fine."

"I'm sure you are, but we're going to get Doc's opinion on
that."

He let her go reluctantly, keeping one arm wrapped around her
waist to help her across the pile of rocks in the road. When they
got to his truck, he eased her onto the seat, then climbed in and
began backing up. As soon as they reached a place where he could
turn around, he headed the truck down the mountain, picking up
speed as they went.

"I'm really all right," she finally said. "You don't have to
drive so fast. I'm not going to bleed to death or anything."

"Sorry," he muttered as he slowed down. He reached for the radio. "Marge? Is Ben back at the office yet?"

When she answered in the affirmative, he said, "Have him meet me over at Doc Ellis's place. I'll be there in about ten minutes."

Ignoring his dispatcher's flood of questions, he replaced the radio in its holder and turned back to Carly. "Did any of the rocks hit you in the head?"

"No. I covered it with my arms." She looked at the scratches and bruises that seemed to cover her from shoulder to fingers, then tried to smile. "I may be hard-headed, but I didn't want to go up against a bunch of boulders."

"Who knew you were heading up into the mountains?"

"No one. I didn't even know myself that I was going to take that road until I saw it."

"Who besides me knew you were driving out of town today?"

"Melba did." She paused, then said uneasily, "I stopped at the *Weekly Sentinel* office before I took off. I probably mentioned it to the Hansons, but they would hardly know where I was going. And I can't see either Ralph or June climbing rocks."

"I'll check and see if anyone saw either of them leave the office." He glanced over at her. "Did you notice any cars behind you this morning?"

She shrugged. "No, but I wasn't looking." She paused, then looked out the window of the truck. "For the first time since I came to Cameron, I wasn't thinking about my story. I was enjoying the scenery and thinking about...other things."

What had she been thinking about? Did it have something to do with him? He ached to ask, but wasn't sure if he wanted to hear the answer. Clearing his throat, he said, "Here's the clinic again. Let's get you looked at."

An hour later they emerged into the sunlight again. Carly squinted at its brightness, and almost stumbled as Devlin steered her toward his truck. But he held onto her, and she didn't fall.

He hadn't let go of her since he'd found her up on the mountain. Even in the exam room, Doctor Ellis had had to order him to leave. And she'd felt bereft without the comfort of his hand on her side, or on her arm. He'd hovered outside of the door, returning the moment Doc had walked out of the room.

"I told you I wasn't badly hurt," she said brightly as he settled her into the Blazer again.

His eyes were brooding as they settled on her. "That depends on your definition of hurt. I saw that bruise on your knee."

She'd be sore tomorrow, she knew, but she plastered a smile on her face. "A good soak in a hot bathtub, a couple of aspirin, and I'll be as good as new."

Instead of starting the truck and pulling out of the tiny parking lot next to the clinic, he leaned back against the door and watched her. "Carly, we need to talk about what's been going on."

"Maybe the avalanche was an accident," she said, speaking too quickly. "I was probably just seeing my own dust in the road, and you told me yourself that sound carries a long way in the mountains. I probably heard a truck from your ranch."

"We'll see. I talked to Ben Jackson while Doc was examining you, and I sent him up to take a look. If there's anything to see, he'll find it. He's a tracker, and he knows what he's doing out there. He's going to call me as soon as he's finished."

She shrugged and smiled again. "I was just in the wrong place at the wrong time."

"I'd like to think that's all it was."

She felt her smile fading. "But you don't think so."

"I think it was pretty damned coincidental that the rock fall happened exactly where you were standing. What do you think the odds are of that?"

He sat up and leaned toward her. "I doubt that this 'accident' was very accidental. I think it was deliberate, and I think it's time to do something about it."

"I'm not going to leave." She angled her chin at him. "So don't even say it."

A ghost of a smile flickered across his face. "I wouldn't dare. I think I know you well enough by now to know it wouldn't work." The smile disappeared and his eyes hardened. "I want you to move to the Red Rock. Right now. Nothing against Melba, but you're essentially alone in that boarding house. There's no one else staying there. Out at the Red Rock, there are always people around. Shea and my mother are in and out of the house all day, and our housekeeper Maria is always there. And our three hands, Dusty, Joe and Levi, are around, too. You won't be alone.''

She wanted to agree immediately, and that scared her. She had come here for a reason, and her resolve was slowly being eroded away. Clearing her throat, she stared blindly out the windshield. ''I'm not sure I can do that,'' she said quietly.

''Why the hell not?''

She turned to face him then. ''I can't take advantage of you that way, Devlin. I intend to talk to your mother and your sister for my story about the Whitmore boy's murder. It would make it awkward for all of us when I had to ask questions.''

''The hell with your story.'' He grabbed her shoulders and pulled her closer to him. ''It's your safety I'm concerned about. And what difference does it make to your story if you stay at the Red Rock? You can still talk to my mother and my sister.''

''I'll feel like I'm taking advantage of their hospitality.'' Her voice was stiff. ''Like I was there under false pretenses.''

His eyes were dark with anger as he stared at her, but gradually they softened. Smoothing his hands down her arms, he picked up her hands and absently rubbed her scraped knuckles. ''I think I understand,'' he said, and his voice became low-pitched and husky. ''I understand a lot more about you than you think. You want to feel like you've gotten your story because you earned it, not because someone felt obliged to talk to you. I respect that.''

His eyes turned into molten silver. ''But it doesn't change anything. Your safety is more important than your sense of honor. It's more important to me, and it should be more important to you.''

She couldn't look away. His grip on her hands tightened, and he held her gaze locked with his. She was drowning in him, in the strength that seemed to pour out of him, in the caring she saw in his eyes.

When he leaned forward, she found herself swaying toward him. She'd yearned for him, needed his kiss, his touch. Even though she knew it wouldn't last, couldn't last, he filled a place deep inside her that had been empty her whole life.

His lips touched hers, and she was on fire. She moaned his name, but the sound was swallowed by his mouth. When he pulled her toward him, she slid into his arms and felt like she was home.

She tasted his desperation, felt his desire in his kiss, in his touch, in the way his hands held her. She answered with passion, pouring herself into the kiss, molding herself against him.

Nothing existed but Devlin. Need clawed at her, a need that only he could satisfy. When he shifted on the seat, pushing her back against the cushions, she clutched his shoulders and pulled him closer.

Suddenly he broke the kiss and drew back. His eyes were hot and wild, and the planes of his face were taut with desire. With a shaking hand he pushed her hair away from her face, smoothing down her cheek. Then he sat up and gently set her away from him.

"I'm sorry, Carly."

She couldn't look away from him. The wildness was fading from his eyes, but they were still full of need. For her. "There's nothing to be sorry about."

His mouth thinned. "I've never gone in for public displays. And this is about as public as we could get."

The air was too heavy in the truck, still throbbing with need and desire. A desire she knew was doomed. Deliberately she smiled at him. "Oh, I don't know about that. We could have been kissing in Heaven on Seventh. That would have been a little more public."

Reluctantly, he smiled back. "That would have set the town to talking."

"It's all right," she said gently. "I was scared and you comforted me. That's all there was to it."

His gaze turned smoky again. "It didn't feel like comfort to me."

Nor to her. It felt frighteningly, overwhelmingly real. "I doubt anyone saw us, Devlin. We're on a side street here, and there isn't a lot of traffic in Cameron. You're reputation is intact.''

He looked like he wanted to say something, but he nodded and started the car. "I'll take you over to Melba's so you can pick up your things and explain to her what's going on. Then I'll drive you out to the Red Rock."

"Are you sure that's a good idea, Dev?" She couldn't imagine living in the same house with him, seeing him every morning and every night, knowing he slept in a room under the same roof. Both of them would explode with the tension.

From the way his jaw worked, she knew he was thinking the same thing. "It's the only answer," he finally said. "I can't spend every minute of every day with you. This is the next best thing."

"I don't want to put your family at risk." She scrambled to think of a reason to persuade him it wasn't a good idea.

"I don't either. I'll spend as much time as possible with you. But when I can't be there, I don't want you to be alone." He looked over at her. "Please, Carly. Do this for me."

She knew she should tell him no. She knew she had no business going to live at his ranch. But when he asked her like that, there was simply no way she could refuse. "All right."

Devlin waited in the truck while she collected her bags and talked to Melba. She was surprised when the older woman smiled at her. "The sheriff is a good man, Carly. He'll take care of you."

"I know," she whispered. Impulsively she reached out and hugged her landlady. "I'll be back before I leave town."

And she would. She had things to say to Melba before she left Cameron. The thought of leaving this town and the people she'd gotten to know brought a lump to her throat, but she ignored it. Turning around, she hurried out the door without looking back.

She and Devlin were both silent as they drove out of town and toward the ranch. Finally she said, "Shouldn't you have at least called and let them know I was coming?"

"I did. While you were getting your things from Melba's."

She waited for him to continue. When he didn't, she finally

said, "What did they say? Is it okay with your mother and your sister?"

"Of course it's okay." He glanced over at her, his eyebrows lifted in surprise. "Why wouldn't it be?"

"Not everyone would want their life disrupted by an unexpected guest," she muttered.

One side of his mouth quirked up in a smile. "Are you going to disrupt their lives, Carly?"

"You know what I mean." She scowled at him. "Most people like a little warning when they have guests."

He glanced over at her again, and his eyes softened. "It's all right. They're happy they can help. And you won't be any trouble. There are plenty of extra bedrooms, and Maria always cooks for a crowd. One more at the table won't make any difference to her."

His eyes softened even more. "I know you're not used to taking from people, Carly. You're self-sufficient and proud of it. But it's something we all have to do once in a while. There's no shame in needing someone."

She felt as if he'd looked directly into her soul and seen all her secrets. It disturbed her, but it didn't terrify her as it would have done just a couple of weeks ago. And that's what scared her the most. It was time to counterattack.

"What about you, Dev? Do you ever allow yourself to need anyone?"

His mouth tightened and his hands gripped the steering wheel more tightly. Then he deliberately relaxed them. When he looked over at her, his eyes were shuttered. "I did, once. Not anymore."

Before she could ask him what he meant, he wrenched the steering wheel to the left and turned into the driveway of his ranch. "Here we are," he said. "Welcome to the Red Rock Ranch."

Chapter 12

Devlin kept his eyes on the drive, refusing to look over at Carly. He should have known that she would take his remarks about needing people and turn them back on him. It was dangerous to underestimate her.

Which is what he should have been thinking of earlier, when he'd been kissing her within an inch of her life in front of the doctor's office, he told himself savagely. He couldn't allow himself to forget that Carly was a woman who wasn't being truthful with him. He didn't know the truth yet, but he knew there was more to her story than she'd told him.

And that should have been the perfect reason for staying away from her. The fact that he hadn't been able to stay away from her frightened him. Trying to create some distance, he said, "I'm sure that Shea or one of the hands will give you a tour of the ranch. Feel free to go anywhere."

"Thank you," she said, after pausing a moment too long. Her voice was cool. "Will you show me where Edmund Whitmore was found?"

So she had gotten his unspoken message. He felt a pang of

disappointment that she hadn't put up a fight, hadn't refused to allow him to distance himself. But it was better this way, he told himself. Better that they both knew where they stood. "Yes, I can take you there."

"Good."

When they rounded the last corner and the house came into view, Devlin saw that Shea was sitting on the porch swing. She jumped up when she saw them.

She was at Carly's door almost before the truck stopped moving. "Welcome to the Red Rock," she said, opening the door. "I'm so glad my brother convinced you to stay with us."

Devlin could see Carly's hesitation. "I appreciate you having me. I didn't want to barge in on you like this, but he insisted."

Shea reached into the back of the truck and grabbed one of Carly's bags. "And we're glad he did. We've got plenty of room, and I know you'll be safe out here. Come on in. Maria's just about got dinner on the table." She flashed him a grin. "Dev knows how Maria feels about people who are late for dinner."

Devlin watched his sister disappear into the house, then turned to Carly, who looked stunned. He struggled to suppress a grin. "Shea can be a little overwhelming. But she's right. Maria doesn't like stragglers. Let's go have dinner."

Carly smiled weakly. "I don't think I've ever met anyone quite like your sister. She really doesn't seem to mind having a total stranger foisted on her."

"I told you she wouldn't." Finally he did smile. "Shea's one of a kind. She's opinionated, but if she's on your side, she'll fight for you to the death. Come on in."

An hour later he sat back in his chair at the table and watched Carly talking to one of the cowboys. She had been quiet in the beginning, thanking his mother for letting her stay and answering Shea's questions in a low voice. But then Joe, Dusty and Levi had joined them at the table, and Dusty had begun to tease her about her city clothes. Before he knew it, Carly had been joking and smiling like everyone else, her reluctance to stay at the Red Rock apparently forgotten.

He didn't want to leave. He wanted to stay and listen to Carly trade banter with his family, to watch her bloom. The realization made him surly. Pushing his chair away from the table, he said, ''I don't know about the rest of you, but I've got work to do this afternoon. I'll see you later.''

There was silence as he left the room. As the screen door banged shut behind him, he heard Shea say something in a low voice, and Levi cackled in response. Scowling, telling himself he didn't care what they said about him, he gunned the engine of the Blazer and twisted the steering wheel to head back to Cameron.

Carly was only staying at his house because she was in trouble. That was all there was to it. And if it felt right, if it felt like coming home to see her sitting at his table, laughing with his family, it didn't matter. Because she wasn't the kind of woman he was interested in. She wasn't the kind of woman to build a life with. He'd known that the minute he'd realized she wasn't telling him the truth.

As the truck shot down the driveway, spraying gravel in all directions, he wished he could convince his heart.

Carly listened to Devlin's truck roaring away, then turned to Shea. ''Your brother is right. I've kept you from your chores for too long. If you'll show me where to put my things, I'll let you get back to work.''

Shea grinned at her, but her eyes held a thoughtful look. ''He was in a bad mood, wasn't he?'' She watched Carly carefully. ''I wonder why that would be?''

''I have no idea.'' Carly was afraid her cheeks were turning pink. ''I think he was just irritated because he's had to spend so much time on my accidents lately.''

''Mmm, that's probably it.'' Shea watched her with laughing eyes. ''Why don't I show you your room? Then I'll take you around the Red Rock, if you like.''

''I'd love that. But I really don't want to keep you from your work. I've taken up too much McAllister time lately.''

''Don't worry about it. I can check on the cattle at the same time, so I really won't be goofing off.'' Shea hesitated, then asked, "Can you ride a horse, or would you prefer to take the truck?"

"I've never learned to ride a horse." Carly was appalled at the wistful note in her voice. "So I guess it better be the truck."

Shea's blue eyes assessed her, then she nodded. "The truck it is. But then I'll give you a riding lesson."

"That's not necessary," Carly said, in spite of the rush of pleasure at the idea. "There aren't many places to ride horses in New York City."

"You never know when you'll need to know how to ride," Shea said, and her mouth quirked up in a grin as she studied Carly. "Who knows? You may not live in New York for the rest of your life."

"That's where my job is," Carly said, wondering why the thought of returning to the city she loved felt so unappealing.

"You never know." Shea grabbed a set of keys, then headed for the door. "Come on, Carly. We're burning daylight."

Several hours later, Carly staggered into the house and headed up the stairs to take a bath. The bruises on her legs ached, as well as muscles she didn't even know she had. Shea had given her a riding lesson, and although she'd enjoyed it thoroughly, her body was reminding her that she'd overdone it.

Sinking into a tub of hot water, she closed her eyes and thought about Devlin's family. Devlin's mother had been quietly concerned about her and had assured her that she would be safe at the Red Rock. She had even told Carly that she would delay her yearly winter trip to Arizona to make sure there was always someone around the house.

And Shea had treated her like she was a member of the family.

Carly let the hot water relax her muscles as the memories warmed her heart. She couldn't remember ever feeling such a sense of family. It was as if everyone on the Red Rock had symbolically linked arms, including Carly in the chain, and turned to face the threat together.

It was a feeling she'd never had before in her life. She wondered if her family might have turned out to be like the

McAllisters, if it hadn't been for the tragedies they'd had to face. But the McAllister family had faced tragedy, too, she realized. Devlin's father had been suspected of murder, but it had apparently only made them stronger.

And now she was going to reopen all their wounds.

She sat up slowly, letting the water sluice off her body. Her heart ached. What was she doing? In finding justice for her brother, was she going to destroy the McAllister family?

Carly slid back down into the water, telling herself it didn't have to be that way. The truth couldn't hurt. It was only lies and innuendos that were painful. The McAllisters would be just as happy as she was to get to the truth.

As she closed her eyes and tried to relax again, she worked on convincing herself that it was true.

"Hey, city slicker, it's almost time for dinner." A knock on the door and Shea's laughing voice roused her from the warm water. "Hurry up in there, or I'll send Dev up to shag you along."

Carly scrambled out of the cooling water and dried off, then stuck her head out the door to make sure no one was around before she hurried into her bedroom. Telling herself that no one would care what she wore to dinner, she picked out a pair of khaki pants and a flattering, feminine blouse in a dark green. When she arrived downstairs, Shea and her mother were standing with Devlin and the three older cowboys. It sounded like all of them were trying to talk at once.

In spite of the way they'd treated her that afternoon, the realization of what she might do to this family made Carly feel like an outsider again. She stood hesitantly in the doorway, reluctant to intrude.

Then Devlin turned and spotted her. A flare of need flashed into his eyes and he stilled, then he set down the glass he was holding and walked over to her. By the time he'd reached her, his eyes held nothing but polite inquiry.

"How are you feeling? Shea told me about your riding lesson."

"I'm fine." She tightened her leg muscles experimentally. "A hot bath worked miracles."

"I told her she should have taken it easy on you after your accident this morning, but Shea always acts first and thinks later."

She angled her chin at him. "I'm perfectly capable of deciding for myself whether or not to ride a horse."

He smiled, making his dimple flash, and she felt herself melting. "She told me that was exactly what you would say."

She looked over at the rest of them, talking in the other corner of the room, and had to fight to keep her eyes from misting. "Everyone has been so nice to me. Thank you."

"You don't have to thank me," he said, his voice somehow intimate in the crowded room. "I didn't tell them to be nice to you. I didn't have to."

"Cameron isn't anything like I expected it to be," she whispered.

"I imagine it isn't. This is a different world than New York, Carly."

"I know." She looked up at him. "I think I like your world, Dev."

Something moved in his eyes. "I'm glad." He looked away. "Now we'd better go in to dinner, or Maria will make us wish we were back in your world."

Although Devlin sat next to her at dinner, he made it clear that the personal discussion was over. He talked to Shea and the cowboys about what they had done during the day, and he asked her what she had thought about the Red Rock.

She told him about her riding lesson, and when she tried to give it a humorous spin, Shea jumped to her defense and told Devlin that she was a natural. Once again, Carly felt included in the family, felt the ranks closing around her. She wanted to savor the feeling, even though she told herself it would only last as long as she stayed at the ranch.

After dinner, Joe, Dusty and Levi, the three cowboys, disappeared toward their cabin. Shea watched them go, grinning, then turned to Carly and Devlin.

"God forbid they start their poker game late." She pushed away from the table. "I have a bunch of paperwork to do. I'll see you tomorrow." She cocked her head at Carly. "Do you want to come with me in the morning?"

"I'd love to," Carly answered.

Shea nodded. "I'll see you bright and early, then."

They watched her walk out of the room, then Devlin leaned back in his chair. "It sounds like Shea has taken you under her wing."

"She's made me feel very welcome." She felt her mouth curl into a smile. "I couldn't resist going with her to check on the cattle in the back pasture. She made it sound like the best treat there is."

"To Shea, it is. She can't imagine doing anything but work this ranch."

"I know." She smiled. "A few weeks ago, I wouldn't have understood that. Now I think I do."

"Do you, Carly?" He tilted his head and watched her.

She nodded slowly. "Yes. There's something special about this land, this part of the country. I thought I would miss the city, miss all the plays, the stores, the excitement. But I haven't missed it at all."

"You've only been here a little more than a week."

"That's true." She watched him steadily. "It sounds like you think I'm pretty shallow. That I'll miss the city eventually."

"Don't you think you will?" he asked carefully. "That is your home, after all."

"I don't know. Maybe. I don't miss it now, though."

He looked as if he wanted to challenge her, as if he didn't want to believe her. He studied her for a moment, then looked as if he'd made a decision. "Come on outside with me for a while," he said. "The ranch is beautiful at dusk."

As they were walking out of the house, he snagged a couple of jackets from the rack by the door and handed her one. "Here, take this. It gets chilly once the sun goes down."

It was one of his coats. The sleeves were ridiculously long, hanging past the ends of her fingers, and she could have wrapped the coat around herself twice. She put it on and snuggled into it. Dev's scent permeated the material, rising up and surrounding her as she walked out of the house. It left a sharp ache inside her, an ache she didn't want to acknowledge.

As they walked down the steps, she stopped abruptly and gasped. The sky shimmered above them, painted with too many shades of pink and purple to count. The mountains glowed with the reflected light, the reds and purples of the rock blending into the sunset, until the air felt alive with color, throbbing with it.

"Pretty amazing, isn't it?" Devlin said softly.

"I've never seen anything like it," she answered, unable to tear her gaze away from the sight. "It looks so different, and we're not that far from Cameron."

"It's the mountains. Or maybe it's just the Red Rock." Even in the semidarkness, she saw his mouth soften. "This is a special place."

"You're very fortunate," she said quietly.

Finally he looked at her. "I know that, and so does Shea. The Red Rock will always be our home."

"I envy you your home, your family."

"We make our own homes. And you have a family, too."

"Not anymore. And I never had a family like yours. I never knew what it felt like to be loved unconditionally."

"I'm sorry."

She saw the sympathy in his eyes and immediately regretted letting the words slip past her guard. "It was a long time ago." Her voice was light. "I'm a big girl now, and I get along just fine on my own."

"Maybe that's the problem, Carly."

"What do you mean, the problem?"

"Maybe you need to learn that you can't always get along on your own."

"It's worked for me for a long time."

"And are you happy?"

She tossed her hair over her shoulder and tucked her hands into her pockets. "My work is very satisfying, and I love what I'm doing. I'm respected in my profession." She shrugged her shoulders. "What more can I ask?"

She felt him studying her, but refused to meet his gaze. "A lot more, I think."

Instead of continuing to speak, he took her elbow and walked her over to the fence around the pasture closest to the house. "What you do for a living is important. Hell, you'd better enjoy it, because you're going to be doing it for a long time. But it's not the most important thing in life."

He turned to face her. "Your family is what's important, the people you're tied to by blood and by birth. Because when the chips are down, those are the people who are going to be there for you, no questions asked. Those are the people who will stand by you and stand up for you. Those are the people you can trust, the people you can count on, no matter what. And I'm sorry you don't have that in your life."

But she did, she realized suddenly. Edmund wasn't alive, but she was doing for him exactly what Devlin was talking about. She was the only person he had left who could stand up for him, who could get to the truth of his murder. She was the only person Edmund could count on.

And by standing up for Edmund, she was endangering Devlin's family.

She turned and leaned on the fence, her heart heavy. Sooner or later, she would be forced to choose. And she knew that was something she didn't want to do.

"What are you thinking about?"

Devlin's voice tickled the hair on the side of her head. He was too close, so close that she could smell the after-dinner coffee on his breath, smell the faint aftershave he'd probably applied that morning. Her heart rolled in her chest, slow, tumbling movements that made her breathless.

But she had to remember what she was doing here, why she was on the Red Rock Ranch. So she said lightly, "I'm thinking that I wish I was a photographer, instead of a writer. It's the only way to do justice to this magnificent sunset."

She felt Devlin settle his arms on the top rail of the fence. "I tried to take pictures of it when I was younger. It never looked the same on a piece of paper. The colors were there, but not the feeling. It was like someone had taken the soul out of the scenery. It was flat, just a series of pretty colors. I stopped taking the photographs after a while. I decided to make it a point to watch the sunset itself every night.''

''You're lucky you can come home every night to watch the sunset.''

''I don't make it every night. Lately I've been making it home less and less. Eventually I'll probably move into Cameron.''

''How come? You're not that far away.''

She saw his mouth curl up in a half smile. ''One of these days, Shea is going to get married. She and her husband will want the house to themselves.''

She noticed he didn't say anything about getting married himself. ''Is Shea seeing someone? She didn't mention it to me.''

He grinned at that. ''Shea doesn't have time to think about anything but this ranch. Or so she says. But one of these days, a man is going to come along who's going to change that for her. Or at least I hope so.''

''What about you?'' she asked lightly. ''Maybe you'll want to live here with a wife.''

The smile disappeared from his face. ''Not likely. I told you before, I'm not a marrying kind of guy.''

She studied him for a moment, watched his hard eyes, his tight mouth. ''Someday you'll have to tell me about that.''

Slowly he looked over at her. ''Maybe I will. And maybe someday you'll tell me about your family.''

She nodded as her eyes slid away. ''Maybe so.''

They looked out over the pasture again as the color dimmed above them and the sky began to darken to navy blue. ''I've got good news,'' he said finally, his light voice declaring that the time for exchanging confidences was over. ''You'll be getting your Jeep back tomorrow.''

''Are you going to help me move the stones behind it?'' she asked eagerly.

''It's already been done. I had Ben Jackson and one of the other deputies do it this afternoon.''

"Thank you, but I wanted to help. You didn't have to ask your deputies to do that."

"We weren't doing you a favor, Carly. It was a police job."

She felt chilled suddenly, even though she'd been warm a moment earlier. "Why is that?"

"Ben found some evidence, up on the cliff, that the rock slide wasn't accidental. They were faint, but there were some footprints that didn't belong there."

"You mean there was actually someone up there, pushing those rocks down on me?"

"You've made at least one enemy here in Cameron," he said.

She stared out at the pasture. The moon was beginning to rise, and it cast a ghostly white light over the cattle, off in the distance. "I tried to tell myself that the message on the mirror was just a crank who didn't like reporters, and that the bolts in the tires were the trick of a kid, someone who didn't know what would happen to the car. I didn't want it to be personal." She turned to him and tried to smile. "I guess it is now, though."

He gripped her shoulders through the jacket, and even through the material, she felt the urgency of his hands. "It's been personal all along, Carly. You know that. I've got to find out who killed that Whitmore boy, because I have a feeling that when we know that, we'll know who's been trying to kill you."

"You don't believe it was a drifter?"

"No drifter from twenty years ago put those bolts in your tires, or pushed those rocks down on top of you." His voice was grim.

"If you publicize what's happening, everyone will find out about your father's missing gun. They'll suspect he was involved."

"What difference does that make?"

Her heart ached for him. "I don't want to hurt your family, Dev. And it looks as if that's just what I'm doing."

His eyes softened. "You can't hurt my family, because none of us were involved."

She felt as if she'd started a boulder rolling down a hill. Now it was picking up speed, and she had no control over it anymore.

And she had no control over where it would stop, or what it would flatten on its way down. "I'm sorry, Dev," she whispered.

"You have nothing to be sorry for," he said.

But she did. Before she could tell him so, his hands tightened on her shoulders and he pulled her closer. "Don't look like that, Carly," he muttered. "Don't look like you've lost your last friend in the world. I'll take care of you. No one's going to hurt you."

She wanted to tell him that wasn't what she was afraid of. She wanted to tell him she was afraid *she* would hurt *him*. But suddenly his eyes flared hot, and he speared his fingers through her hair.

"I swore I wouldn't do this, Carly. I promised myself I wouldn't touch you while you were on my ranch. But I'm going to have to break my promise."

His head dipped down and captured her mouth. His kiss wasn't tentative, didn't ask permission. It seared her soul, branded her. No other man had ever kissed her before, and no one would ever kiss her again. Not like Devlin.

She leaned into him, and he wrapped his arms around her and drew her close. They fit together perfectly, the softness of her body molding to the hardness of his. Once again, Carly felt like she'd come home. But instead of frightening her, she gloried in the rightness.

He trailed his hands down her back, beneath the jacket, and her pulse quickened. She felt the urgency of his touch, the need he could barely suppress. And her body responded. When she brought one hand around and touched his chest, she felt him tense. And when she reached for his shirt, bunching it in her hand at his belt, he trembled beneath her fingers.

The muscles of his abdomen were rock hard beneath her palm. He quivered when she moved her fingers, tangling them in the silky-soft hair on his chest. Slowly she touched one of his flat male nipples, and when it hardened immediately, she felt an answering tightening, deep in her abdomen.

He groaned into her mouth, his hands tightening on her hip. But he didn't move to stop her, didn't move to touch her. He allowed her to continue her exploration. She lingered on the tight nub for a moment, then slid over and touched its mate. It, too, hardened immediately. When she slipped her other hand under his shirt so she could touch both his nipples at once, she felt his legs trembling against hers.

Suddenly he cupped his hands on her hips and pulled her against him, cradling her in the V of his legs. He was huge and hard against her, and she could feel his heat, even through their layers of clothes. He fumbled with the waistband of her slacks, then slid his hands down over her hips.

The calluses on his hands scraped against her skin, sending sparks of desire shooting through her. One of his hands dipped close to her intimate heat, making her throb with need. When she felt his other hand fumbling with the buttons on her blouse, she felt her breasts tighten, anticipating his touch.

As her blouse and bra fell open, she felt the night breeze brush her skin. "You're so beautiful," he whispered. "More beautiful than I remembered." He bent down and brushed his lips over one breast, not touching the aching peak.

"Please," she begged.

He smoothed his hand between her breasts, touching the small key that hung at the end of the velvet cord, but again carefully avoiding her nipples. "What do you want, Carly?" he whispered.

"Touch me. Please."

His hand tightened on her, then he bent down and took one peak in his mouth. He suckled it, then smoothed his tongue over it with gentle swirls. By the time he moved to her other breast, she was writhing beneath his hands, unable to stop herself from moaning his name.

She ached for him. Her body trembled in his hands, until she wasn't sure where she ended and he began. She hadn't known that desire was a living thing, twisting and growing inside you until it possessed you completely.

She reached for him blindly, trying to press closer at the same time as she fumbled with the buckle on his belt, determined that their loving would not be one-sided this time. He stilled when she touched him, then began to tremble when she cupped her hand around the hard ridge of his erection that strained against the front of his jeans.

By the time she'd freed him from his jeans and briefs, he was shaking against her. He was hot and heavy in her hands, hard and smooth as velvet. When she touched the tip of him with one finger, he surged against her, pinning her against one of the fence posts.

He pulled at her slacks, trying to push them over her hips, when his hands stilled suddenly on her. The next moment he pulled her against him and stepped into the shadow of a huge pine that stood next to the pasture.

Then she heard it, too. Voices that she recognized as belonging to Levi and Joe drifted over to her. She tried frantically to pull up her slacks, to button her shirt, but Devlin stilled her hands.

"It's okay. They can't see us," he breathed into her ear.

He stood holding her for a long minute, until the voices faded away, then he stepped back. He pulled the edges of her blouse together, then repaired his own clothing. When he looked at her again, his face was grim.

"I'm sorry, Carly. I'd promised myself I wouldn't do that again."

Chapter 13

Carly leaned against the fence in the moonlight, and Devlin shoved his hands into his pockets to stop himself from reaching for her. Her mouth was swollen, her lips dark red and puffy. Her blouse was crooked and her hair was mussed. Her eyes looked dreamy and unfocused—just like a woman who'd been making love.

Which they would have been doing in another moment, he told himself grimly. Thank God that Levi and Joe had come along when they did. The cowboys had saved him from himself.

Because making love with Carly wouldn't be a casual roll in the hay. He knew that now. If he didn't touch her, didn't make love with her, he could pretend that she didn't matter. He could tell himself that she just caused an itch that needed scratching, and he would be fine once she left town.

But if he let down the barriers enough to make love to her, he would never be the same. She'd take a part of his heart with her when she left Cameron, and he'd never get it back. He didn't intend for that to happen.

"Let's get you back to the house," he said, his voice gruff. "You must be getting chilly."

"Actually, I was too warm." Her husky voice sounded like she'd just gotten out of bed, and arousal flashed through him again.

"I'm ready to call it a night," he said, and he damned the desperation he heard in his voice.

She studied him for a moment, then pulled the jacket more closely around herself. "You're right. It is getting chilly out here."

She pushed past him, heading for the house. He caught up with her just before she reached the porch.

"Wait, Carly."

Her back was ramrod stiff, but she turned around slowly. "What?"

"Are you angry because we didn't jump in the sack?"

She flinched at the crude language, but didn't look away from him. "No. I never wanted to 'jump into the sack' with you. I'm not interested in casual sex, with you or anyone else. I *am* interested in why you push me away every time we get close."

"Can you tell me that any relationship we might have would be more than casual sex?" he demanded. "How long are you planning on staying in Cameron, anyway? Or are you going to give up your job in New York and move out to Utah? I'm sure as hell not planning on moving to New York. So exactly where does that leave us?"

Her eyes never wavered. "I have no idea, Devlin. But I guess we'll never know, because you don't seem willing to even try and find out." She looked over toward the bunkhouse where the three hands lived. "Instead of being angry at the interruption, I should be thanking Levi and Joe for coming by when they did. They saved me from making a huge mistake."

Something twisted inside him at her words, something raw and painful. But she was right. It was nothing more than he'd been telling himself. He didn't have anything to give her, and it was a good thing she'd finally realized it. Now maybe she would finish her story and get the hell out of Cameron, before he forgot that he wasn't interested in a relationship with her.

"I'll see you in the morning, Carly." He looked at her face in the moonlight. Her eyes were huge and dark, and full of pain. It was better that way, he told himself. Better that she should hurt now. It would hurt far worse if she let herself hope for anything more from him.

"Good night, Devlin." Her words were so soft they were barely more than a breath of air on the night breeze. She stood for a moment more, then turned and ran silently up the stairs and into the house.

He stayed outside for a long time. He wanted to make sure she was in bed and asleep before he passed her room on his way to bed. If he heard her moving around, if he knew she was awake, he might do something they both would regret.

He felt like hell in the morning. It had taken him hours to fall asleep, and when sleep had finally come, someone had turned up the heat in his room so that his dreams were hot and restless. Now his eyes felt like they'd been rubbed with sandpaper during the night, and the coffee he'd gulped made his nerves jump and twitch.

The only thing that made him feel better was that Carly didn't look as if she'd slept any better than he had. She was subdued at breakfast, although she made an effort to talk to Shea.

His sister was quiet, watching both of them. Finally, when they were finished with the stacks of pancakes that Maria had made, Shea pushed away from the table.

"Are you coming with me, Carly?" she asked, her voice too casual. "Or do you and Dev have plans for the morning?"

Dev scowled. "I'm going to take her to pick up her Jeep," he said. "Then I have to get back to town."

"Fine." Shea looked down at her plate, trying to hide a small smile. "I'll see you later this morning, then, or maybe this afternoon." She gave both of them an innocent grin as she strolled out of the room.

He and Carly were the only two people left in the dining room, and silence hung thick and heavy in the air. "You don't have to take me to get the Jeep," Carly finally said. "I know you have things to do in town. If you tell Shea where the Jeep is, someone else can take me to get it."

"I said I'd take you, and I will." He pushed away from the table. "Ben can run the office for a while by himself."

"Fine. I just didn't want to take you away from your work."

"This is my work. Whoever tried to hurt you yesterday is connected with this case."

"I see. In that case, I won't apologize." Her cool voice couldn't completely disguise the hurt beneath it, and he felt like a total jerk. "I'll get my keys and be ready to go in a minute."

He listened to her footsteps retreat up the stairs and told himself this was the way he wanted it.

"Smooth, Dev. Real smooth."

He spun around to find Shea leaning against the door frame. She rolled her eyes at him. "It doesn't sound like you have the sense that God gave to a sheep. And we both know that sheep were out of town when God was passing out brains."

"Stay out of this, Shea," he warned.

She raised her hands. "Hey, I'm just trying to give you a little sisterly help here. What good does it do for me to talk you up to Carly if you're going to make a complete ass of yourself when you're with her?"

"Carly and I don't need any help from you."

"You need someone to knock some sense into you, that's what you need."

"And I suppose you're such an expert at relationships?"

She stuck her chin out at him. "I know a good thing when I see it. And you and Carly are a good thing."

"Carly is a city girl," he said quietly. "Her job and her life are a million miles away from Cameron. And on top of that, she's not telling me the truth about why she's here. Now do you see why it won't work?"

"I see what you think you know." She shifted away from the door frame and walked over to him, giving him a hug. "Don't give up, bro. Give her a chance. She might surprise you."

"I doubt it." He forced a smile onto his face. "But thanks for trying, Shea."

She smiled at him, but a shadow of sadness passed over her face. "Don't hold Carly responsible for what Judy did to you, Dev. Carly isn't anything like Judy."

"We'll see, won't we?"

He heard footsteps coming down the stairs, so he waved Shea out of the house and turned to wait for Carly. When she stepped into the room, her face was tight and closed. She'd slung her backpack over one shoulder, and she held her car keys in her hand.

"Ready to go?" she said brightly. Her voice was completely impersonal, and for a moment he ached inside. He wanted to see her eyes soften and glow when she looked at him.

But it was better this way, he told himself. "All set."

When they'd started to climb the road that led into the mountains, he looked over at her. "Where did you plan to go this morning?"

"I was hoping you could tell me where they found Edmund Whitmore's body. I'd like to take a look at the spot for my story." She stared out the windshield.

"I'll take you there."

Her gaze flew over to him. "That's not necessary. If you give me directions, I can find it myself."

"It's not easy to find. And besides, I'd like to take another look at it myself."

"You don't need to watch over me like I was a child," she said in a low voice. "I'm sure I'll be fine here on your ranch."

"First of all, I'm not going with you because I think you need a keeper. I want to get a look at the place myself. And second, you seem to have forgotten that you were on my ranch yesterday. That didn't stop someone from trying to kill you."

"Yesterday I ignored the signs that someone was following me. You can be sure I won't make that mistake again."

"I'll take you to the spot," he said, swinging his truck around a corner. "It doesn't make sense for both of us to drive there separately."

"I suppose not."

She sounded reluctant to spend time with him, and he told himself that he was happy. He'd accomplished just what he'd set out to do yesterday evening. Swinging onto the track that led back into the mountains, to the place where the Whitmore boy was found, he glanced over at her. But all he saw was her cloud of dark red hair. She was staring out the window, her back toward him.

"I was looking over the police reports from the year the Whitmore boy was killed," he said. He was just sharing information with her, he told himself. He wasn't trying to get her attention focused on him again.

She swung around to face him, and he felt a momentary flush of victory. "Did you find anything interesting?"

"Just that Phil Hilbert was desperate to get water, and my father was just as determined to keep it from him. Apparently there were a number of confrontations before Phil took my father to court."

"What kind of confrontations?"

"My father accused Phil of illegally diverting water onto his property. Phil denied it, of course, and the sheriff never found any evidence. But my father was apparently convinced that Phil was stealing water. He just couldn't prove it."

"What did the sheriff say?"

"How did you know I asked Bert Pickens about it?"

She gave him a tight smile. "I think I know you well enough to have an idea how you work. You're thorough. I figure that's the first thing you would have done."

"You're right." He glanced over at her with approval. "I did ask him." He shrugged. "Bert said that Phil and my dad were always fighting. And neither he nor my father ever found proof that Phil was stealing water. Bert just assumed it was one of those neighborhood fights that got out of hand, with my dad making wild accusations."

"Didn't he think it might have been connected when the Whitmore boy was killed, then found on your property?"

"He claims not. He didn't see any connection."

"The Whitmore boy was writing articles in the town newspaper about the court fight. Didn't he think that was enough of a connection?"

"No. There's no evidence that the kid was doing anything more than reporting on the court case. There was never an article in the *Sentinel* that implied more."

"I still think it was connected," she said stubbornly.

"Maybe it was. But we're going to have to find more proof."

"I'll find something," she vowed.

"Haven't you looked through all the old copies of the *Weekly Sentinel* already?"

"Yes, but I haven't started looking at the courthouse. Maybe there's some information there."

"You'll have to go to Garfield, then. That's the county seat."

"I'll keep that in mind." She was silent for a moment, then she shifted so she was facing him. "Why are you doing this, Devlin? Why did you reopen this case? Aren't you afraid of what you'll find?"

"You mean that my father was involved?" His voice was blunt.

She nodded. "Don't you think there's a possibility? The gun that's missing was from your collection. The body was found on your property. And you said yourself that your father and Phil Hilbert had been fighting a lot. What if the Whitmore boy found something that incriminated your father, and he shot the boy in a moment of passion?"

"First of all, I don't think that's what happened. I might not always have gotten along with my father, but he wasn't a murderer." He looked over at her. "But even if he was, it's my job to find out. And since whatever happened twenty years ago seems to be a part of what's been happening to you, I can't ignore it. Even if my family is involved."

She was silent for a long time. Then she said, "You're an honorable man, Devlin."

He shrugged, uncomfortable. "I'm just doing my job."

"Even at the risk of your family."

"I told you, I don't think there's any risk to my family. But even if there was, even if my father did kill that boy, Shea and my mother and I would survive."

"I feel like I've put you into an impossible position," she said, and her voice was so low he could barely hear her. "I'm forcing you to choose between your job and your family."

"I'm not making a choice. I'm doing my job, but my family will survive, no matter what. I know that. It makes doing my job a whole lot easier."

Carly looked out the window again, seemingly concentrating on the scenery. "I never knew families could be like that. Supportive of one another. Always there for each other. I always thought your family was what held you back, what kept you from doing what you wanted to do. You have a special family, Devlin."

He couldn't miss the wistfulness in her voice, the longing that he wasn't sure she was even aware of. "My family is very special. But there are a lot of others like mine around Cameron. People have to rely on their families out here. It builds strong bonds."

"Maybe I should leave the Red Rock. I don't want to disrupt your family."

"You couldn't do that. Believe me, Carly, the McAllisters have handled tougher things than this. I want you to stay here. This is the safest place for you to be right now."

"I'll stay for a while," she finally said.

He wasn't sure why her words brought him so much satisfaction. He wanted her gone. He wanted her to leave Cameron and never look back. But his heart soared with the knowledge that she would be staying.

Wrestling with his heart, it took him a moment to realize they'd arrived. Braking the Blazer, he said, "We're here."

Carly looked around, forcing herself to ignore Devlin and concentrate on the place where her brother was found. They were high in the mountains, and the vegetation was sparse. The rocks thrust up from the earth in eerie shapes, and boulders littered the base of the cliffs. It felt like a place that had been untouched for years.

She said the first thing that came to mind. "What would the

Whitmore boy have been doing up here? It's miles away from anything.''

"Nobody knows." He shifted in his seat so he was facing her, but she didn't look over at him. She was memorizing the landscape. "That was one of the things that puzzled Bert." He paused, then added, "I'm still not sure whether the boy was killed here or whether his body was just dumped here after the fact."

At that she looked over at him. "Wouldn't that have been in the police and autopsy reports?"

He rubbed his hand over the back of his neck. "Bert Pickens wasn't the most sophisticated law enforcement officer around. That wasn't the kind of thing he'd have thought to ask. So we'll never know."

"You mean no one ever thought it was important to know that?" She heard the incredulity in her voice, but couldn't restrain herself.

"Carly, there had never been a murder in Cameron before the Whitmore boy was killed. Bert's strength was breaking up bar fights out at May's and placating neighbors who were squabbling. He wasn't equipped to handle a murder."

"So why didn't he call in someone who was?"

"After they found the body of the drifter, he figured the case was solved. No need to involve anyone else."

Carly stepped out of the truck and looked around. The only sound was the eerie whistle of the wind as it blew relentlessly through the rock formations. It swirled around her in gusts, tearing at her hair and peppering her with gritty dust. Although the sun was shining, the air was cold this high in the mountains.

She barely heard Devlin move to stand next to her. "It's a lonely place to die," he said, and she heard genuine sadness in his voice.

"Yes." She didn't want to think about her brother, seventeen-years-old, dying up here by himself, alone and in pain.

"You look like you're taking it personally."

She was taking it very personally. Swallowing hard, she said, "I don't like to think of anyone dying that way."

"Neither do I. I'm going to do my best to figure out what happened."

And she knew he would. In spite of his reluctance to let anyone close to him, in spite of the fact that he was a McAllister, Devlin was a decent, honorable man. He would do his best to provide justice for her brother, and suddenly she was ashamed of herself. She owed it to him to tell him the truth. It might not make any difference to his investigation, but she didn't want to have any lies and half-truths between them.

Before she could speak, he spun around. "Get in the truck, Carly," he said, his voice clipped.

"I'd like to look around a little more," she started to say, but he interrupted her.

"Get in the truck now. And lock the doors."

When he pulled his gun out of his holster, she scrambled into the Blazer and locked the doors. He headed toward the base of a cliff at a dead run, and she watched as he disappeared around a pile of debris.

Minutes ticked away, and her anxiety ratcheted higher and higher. She found herself holding her breath, listening for any sounds at all. But the keening of the wind was the only thing she heard.

Should she radio into his office, ask Marge to send some of the deputies up here? Her hand hovered over the radio, until she realized she had no idea where they were or how to get here.

She stared at the piles of rocks, watching the place where he'd disappeared. What was going on? What had he thought he'd heard? Her eyes flickered over the shotgun that stood ready next to the dashboard. Would she have to use the huge gun to protect herself or save Dev? Would she be able to?

Suddenly Devlin appeared next to the truck, seemingly out of nowhere. Almost sobbing in relief, she reached over to unlock the door. "What happened?" she asked, almost before he was in the truck.

"I heard something behind us. It sounded like someone slipped on some rocks."

"Did you find anything?"

"Not a damn thing." He scowled at her. "But I think someone was there. Ben would have been able to follow his tracks, but I'm not anywhere as good as Ben when it comes to tracking. Whoever was here could have gone anywhere."

"No one followed us up here, did they?" she asked.

"No. But someone might have been up here before we got here."

"Why?" she whispered.

"It's no secret in town that I've reopened the investigation into the Whitmore boy's murder. Anyone who was involved could have found out about it."

"But why would anyone come back here, twenty years later?"

"What would you do if you'd committed a murder? The sheriff at the time closes the case, and you figure you're safe. Then, twenty years later, you find out that someone is looking into the murder again. You'd want to make sure you hadn't left anything behind."

"What would there be to find after twenty years, though?"

"You wanted to come up here," he countered. "What for? Didn't you think there might be something to find? If you were the murderer, wouldn't you have to make sure you hadn't left anything behind?"

"I suppose so," she said. She scanned the area again, but didn't see anything out of the ordinary. "It gives me the creeps to think someone was standing and watching us."

"Me too." He started the engine with a grim twist of his hand. "I'll get Ben up here to look around. Whoever was up here will be long gone, I'm sure, but if anyone can find traces of him, Ben can."

"If you think it was the murderer up here, that means you don't suspect your father," she said quietly.

"It would be kind of difficult for my father to push a bunch of rocks down on top of you, or poke holes in your tires. He's been dead for several years." There was no inflection in his voice.

"Maybe there's another explanation for my accidents," she said.

"Why are you so determined that my father was the murderer?" He glanced over at her, but she didn't meet his gaze.

"I'm not determined that he's the murderer. He just seems like the most logical suspect."

"Then how do you explain the things that have been happening to you?" he demanded.

"I don't know." She looked down at her hands. "Who do you think is responsible?"

"I'm not sure. But since you seem convinced the Whitmore boy's murder is connected with the water fight between my father and Phil Hilbert, maybe it's Phil."

"Maybe." She remembered the tired old man she'd talked to. "He doesn't seem like he'd have the...energy to try and hurt me or anyone else."

She saw his hands tighten on the steering wheel. "People can do amazing things when they're fighting for survival. Desperation is a powerful motivator."

"I know," she said quietly.

He glanced at her sharply, but when she didn't say anything more, he picked up the radio and asked Marge to have Ben Jackson meet him at the Red Rock. Neither of them said anything more as the truck bumped down the rocky track back to the ranch. He took her to her Jeep, then led her back to the house.

Ben was waiting when Devlin parked the Blazer next to the barn. Carly watched the two men talking, then she climbed out of the Jeep and headed into the house. She hadn't had a chance to tell Devlin who she really was, and she didn't particularly want to make a public announcement. She'd wait until they had some time alone.

But they weren't alone for the rest of the day. Devlin talked to Ben, then he headed back into Cameron. It was almost, she thought, like he was avoiding her. Almost as if the discussion of who could be trying to kill her had reminded him that they were on opposite sides. Or maybe the memories of the passion they had shared the night before had scared him away.

He sat at the opposite end of the table at dinner that night, although she felt his gaze on her whenever she turned to talk to

Levi. And when she helped clear the table and load the dish-washer, he didn't take the opportunity to escape. When she walked back into the dining room, he was still sitting in his chair, staring into his coffee.

Shea pushed back her chair and stood up. "Dev, why don't you and Carly go sit on the porch? You probably want to tell her what Ben found today, don't you?"

Devlin scowled at his sister. "Knock it off, Shea."

"Knock what off?" Shea's face was the picture of innocence. "I figured you wouldn't want to be interrupted."

"Yeah, right." But he stood up and looked at her. "You want to hear what Ben found today?"

"I could hardly refuse such a gracious offer," she answered sweetly.

Carly thought she saw a dull red flush under his tan. "You want some coffee?" he asked.

"No, thanks."

He tossed her a jacket, and she realized it was the same one she'd worn the night before. She almost tossed it back at him, but instead she wrapped it around herself. If he could act completely unaffected by what had happened, so could she.

Settling herself on the porch swing, she watched as he leaned against the railing and looked out over the ranch. Dusk was set-tling, and the last remnants of another spectacular sunset were fading into darkness. "You missed the sunset tonight," she said lightly.

"That's the thing about the Red Rock. There's always tomor-row."

"I'm beginning to see that," she said in a low voice.

Abruptly he straightened and turned to face her. "I love this ranch, Carly. This is my home. Ben found some evidence that we weren't alone up there this morning. Now it's becoming per-sonal."

It was becoming personal because it was affecting his ranch, not because someone was targeting her. A spear of sadness lanced through her, but she told herself to deal with it. She'd known all along that she and Devlin were on opposite sides of the fence. "I've seen how much this ranch means to you," she murmured.

Leaning against the railing, facing her, his eyes became unfocused as he stared into the distance. "It wasn't always that way," he said quietly. "When I was eighteen, I couldn't wait to get away from the Red Rock, away from Cameron."

"Why?"

He smiled, but there was no humor in it. "My father insisted that it was my duty to take over the ranch. I'm not a rancher, but he didn't care. I wanted to go into police work, but he wouldn't even discuss it. That's why I ran away and joined the Air Force. I was an MP, stationed in California."

He turned and stared into the gathering darkness. "That's when I realized how special Cameron really is."

"What happened?" she asked softly.

"Justice wasn't universal in the city. It was only for neat, clean people who lived in neat, clean suburbs. A homeless person was beaten nearly to death near the base, and no one cared. The values I'd been raised with—a person's word is their bond, help your neighbor, protect those weaker than you—were considered signs of weakness where I lived. It was every man for himself. And every woman for herself." Even in the darkness, she saw his mouth tighten.

"Someone hurt you."

His shoulders tightened, then he sighed. "I was a damn fool. Her name was Judy, and she was sophisticated, beautiful, worldly. I was a green kid. I thought she loved me." His mouth tightened again. "It turned out she loved the money she thought I had. Somehow she found out that the Red Rock was the largest ranch in the area. She'd refused to marry me, refused to live in the 'godforsaken wilds of Utah,' as she put it. Then suddenly she changed her mind.

"I was thrilled. I planned a wedding, but just a few days before the big day, I happened to overhear her talking to one of her friends."

She heard the pain his voice as he hesitated. "You don't have to tell me this, Dev."

He turned to face her again. "I want to tell you. I've hurt you, pushing you away, and I want you to understand why."

He came and sat next to her on the swing. "She told her friend that she would marry me, but there was no way in hell she was moving to a stinking ranch in Utah. If I wanted to leave, that would be fine with her. She'd console herself with her generous divorce settlement."

"Oh, Dev," she whispered, covering his hand with hers. "I'm so sorry."

"Don't be. It hurt at the time, but I got over it." He laced his fingers with hers and held on tight.

His eyes glittered in the moonlight, and she saw the pain and the wariness that were Judy's legacy to him. She wanted to tell him the truth about who she was, share herself with him the way he'd shared himself, but first she needed to take away his pain.

"She was a fool," she said fiercely. "An utter fool."

Before he could say anything else, she pulled his face to hers and took his mouth in a kiss.

Chapter 14

She immersed herself in the kiss, determined to take the hurt out of his eyes, vowing to make sure he forgot that Judy existed. Her hands tightened on his face, her fingers rasping against the roughness of his beard. He groaned, deep in his throat, then wrapped his arms around her and pulled her close.

She felt the desperation in his grip, the need that he struggled to subdue. But when she slid her arms around him and trailed her mouth down his neck, he shuddered once, then found her mouth with a fury of passion.

Carly felt like she was drowning in his kiss, drowning in the desire that poured out of him. With an inarticulate murmur, he pressed her down onto the swing and covered her body with his. The swing swayed gently beneath them, rocking as Devlin moved against her.

"I tried to stay away from you." He propped himself on his elbows and stared down at her. His face was pale in the moonlight, the angles and planes sharp with passion. His eyes burned into her, igniting a fire inside her, searing her with the raw desire she found in their depths. "I did my best, Carly. You shouldn't have kissed me.'' He smoothed one hand over her face, his hand trembling but incredibly gentle.

''I needed to kiss you,'' she said, and she gloried in the fierceness in her voice. ''I don't think I've ever needed anything as much.'' Devlin made her feel whole and complete, in a way she'd never felt before. She wanted, more than anything, to make him feel the same way. ''Please don't stop.''

He groaned and buried his face in her neck. ''I don't think I could stop now if my life depended on it.'' But when he moved to kiss her again, his mouth was gentle and light.

She understood what he was doing. He was giving her one last chance to say no, a chance to ease away from him. He was giving her a chance to step back and leave Cameron with a part of her heart intact.

But she didn't want to be safe. She didn't want to stop and think about the consequences. She wanted him, and nothing had ever felt so right.

So she wrapped her arms and legs around him and poured herself into the kiss. He hesitated for only a moment, then he responded. Their bodies strained together, their hands touching, caressing, holding. She burrowed her hands under his shirt, needing to touch his skin, needing to feel his heat. She traced his muscles, hard and trembling with need, and let her fingers play in the coarse, soft hair on his chest.

He growled, low in his throat, and tore her shirt out of the waistband of her jeans. Buttons flew as he pulled it apart and found her breasts. She bucked against him as he tugged on her nipples, then shoved the shirt up and took one peak in his mouth.

His hands replaced his tongue on her breasts as he swallowed her gasps with his mouth. Now his tongue swirled against hers, tasting, taking, possessing her. Wave after wave of sensation crashed over her, and she lifted her hips to his, begging for more.

Cool air caressed the bare skin of her chest as Devlin took his hands away and framed her face. His breath hitched as he rested his forehead against hers, his hands tangling in her hair.

''What's wrong?'' she whispered in a throaty growl.

''We have to stop,'' he said, his voice low and tortured.

Her body was stretched taut beneath his, throbbing with need. "Why do we have to stop?" she asked, struggling to focus on his face.

He brushed the hair away from her face and pressed a kiss to her cheek. "Because we're lying on the front porch swing, in view of everyone."

"Oh." Reality crashed down on her, and she remembered where they were. A light shone out of the house window behind them, and although she and Dev were shrouded in darkness, anyone who stepped onto the porch would see them. The light from the bunkhouse was too close, gleaming through the darkness.

She tried to smile. "Another case of bad timing, I guess."

His eyes were still hot with desire, and suddenly he slid off her, then took her hand and pulled her to her feet. "Come with me."

They slipped in the front door of the house and headed for the stairs. There was no one around. Wrapping his arm around her shoulders, he pulled her close. "Shea will be working late in her office, my mother went to visit a friend in town and Maria has already gone to bed. No one will see or hear us." His breath tickled the hair on her neck, and she shivered again.

When they stopped at what she knew was his bedroom door, he pushed it open and led her inside. Once the door was closed and locked, he turned to her, but didn't touch her.

"Now no one can interrupt us. There won't be any Dusty or Joe or Levi, there won't be any Melba Corboy. There won't be any excuses. This is your last chance to leave."

She stepped closer to him. "I don't want to leave. Unless you want me to go."

Slowly he trailed his hand over her face, touching, caressing. "I haven't wanted you to go since the first day you drove into Cameron. I've been dreaming about this, about you, since the first time I kissed you, on Melba's front porch. I can't fight it any longer."

"I don't want you to fight it," she said, and she wrapped her arms around his neck. "Nothing has ever felt so right. Hold me, Dev. Make love to me."

He groaned again as he pulled her against him. "It's hard enough to fight myself, Carly. I can't fight you, too."

Their mouths met again, and the kiss was a vow and a promise. It started out gentle, an exploration of each other, but the fires burned hotter and hotter. Suddenly they had both waited too long. Devlin pulled at her shirt, and the rest of the buttons flew across the room. He skimmed it down her arms, along with her bra, and she stood in front of him, naked from the waist up.

Even in the dim light she saw his eyes darken. "You are so beautiful," he murmured. His hands shook as he unbuttoned her jeans, then pulled them down her legs.

When she reached out to undress him, he kissed her hands then pushed them away. "Let me, this time." His voice was harsh. "If you touch me, this will all be over too quickly. I want it to last forever."

The moonlight from the window dappled his magnificent body with shadows as he stripped away his clothes. His broad chest was solid, hard with muscle. The hair on his chest gleamed dark gold as it tapered down to a narrow line that disappeared into his white briefs. His legs were dusted with the same dark gold hair that covered his chest. And when he pushed the briefs down, she felt herself swallow.

He followed her down onto the bed, then covered her body with his. It took only one touch, one kiss to stoke the fires even higher. Twining herself around him, she tried to touch him everywhere at once.

He moved his hands and his mouth over her, caressing, arousing and tormenting her. When she arched her back, sobbing his name, he reached for a foil packet, then plunged into her. She exploded in a burst of light and heat, grasping his shoulders, trying to pull him even closer. When he shuddered and emptied himself into her, she wrapped her arms around him and held him tight.

She had no idea how long they lay on the bed, entwined with each other, their hearts pounding. When he tried to move away from her, she tightened her arms. "No," she murmured.

"I'm not going anywhere," he said, kissing her neck. He slid onto his side, then pulled her against him. "Good night," he murmured.

She was almost asleep, but she thought she heard him add "love" in a sound that was barely more than a breath.

Devlin woke up with the sun in his eyes the next morning, and he rolled over to avoid it. His hand brushed against something warm and soft, and suddenly he remembered the night before.

Carly lay sleeping next to him, her arm flung over the side of the bed, her hair spread over his pillow. In spite of the fact that they hadn't done much sleeping the night before, he felt himself harden again as he looked at her.

In spite of all his warnings to himself, he and Carly had made love the night before. Many times. And it had been making love, he told himself. He hadn't mistaken the way she'd touched him, the way she'd opened herself to him. And he hadn't been able to stop his heart from caring about her. Slowly he pulled her closer, nuzzling her neck and sweeping his hand down her thigh.

She opened her eyes and looked at him. For a moment, he saw confusion in her face, then he watched as she remembered. She gave him a slow, sleepy smile, then said, "Good morning."

Her voice was low and husky, a voice made for the bedroom. "Good morning yourself."

She stretched beneath the sheets, then smiled at him again. He saw the exact moment when her eyes changed. Her smile faltered, then faded completely. Slowly she sat up, pulling the sheets up to cover her breasts, and stared at him.

It felt like one of the horses had just kicked him in the gut. "What's wrong?"

She licked her lips. "I have to talk to you, Devlin. I should have told you last night, but..." She looked away. "I guess we got carried away."

His heart began to pound. "What is it, Carly? Are you married?"

At that she looked back at him, shock on her face. "Of course I'm not married. Do you think I would have made love with you if I'd been married?"

"Then what is it?"

She swallowed once, the muscles in her throat rippling. "I think we should get dressed first."

"This sounds serious," he said, trying to joke about it. But his heart was thundering in his ears, and a sick feeling gathered in his stomach.

Carly scrambled out of bed and threw her clothes on. The blouse she had been wearing was missing all its buttons, and her face flushed red as she clutched it together. "I'll meet you downstairs, all right?"

Before he could answer, she bolted from the room. Moments later, he heard the door to her room close.

His hands trembled as he got dressed, but he tried to tell himself it couldn't be anything that serious. As he headed down the stairs, he couldn't stop himself from looking over at her room. The door was still firmly closed.

Thankfully, no one but Maria was around when he walked into the dining room. She stuck her head out of the kitchen. "If you're going to be late for breakfast, you take what's left over."

He couldn't eat a thing. He downed a cup of coffee, waiting for Carly's footsteps on the stairs. Finally he heard her.

"Would you like something to eat?" he asked, but she shook her head.

"Let's go outside, Dev."

What could be wrong? He led her out the door, then steered her toward the pasture where they'd stood two nights ago. "No one will bother us here."

She grasped the top rail of the fence and stared out into the distance for a while, almost as if she was gathering her courage. Finally she turned to him.

"There's something I need to tell you. I should have told you a long time ago, but I was afraid. Afraid you wouldn't help me, afraid that if you knew the truth, I wouldn't be able to find out what had happened to Edmund Whitmore."

She took a deep breath. "My name is Carly Fitzpatrick, but I wasn't born with that name. I do work for *Focus* magazine, but that's not why I came to Cameron. I used to be Caroline Whitmore. My mother changed our names after we moved away from

Cameron. Edmund Whitmore was my brother, and I came back to Cameron to find out who killed him.''

Devlin stared at her, not sure he heard her correctly. He'd done a routine background check on Carly when she'd first come to town, but it hadn't revealed this. ''What?''

She didn't look away. ''I've been lying to you from the beginning, Devlin. I didn't come to Cameron to write an article about the town. I came to find out what had happened to my brother.''

It felt as if someone had reached into his chest and ripped out his heart. ''Why, Carly? Why didn't you tell me who you were from the beginning?''

''Because you were a McAllister. I thought it was your father who killed my brother.''

''Did you think I would try to hide the truth from you, if I knew who you were?'' He couldn't keep the pain out of his voice.

''At the beginning, yes, I did.''

''And last night? Were you still afraid that I wouldn't tell you the truth last night?''

''Of course not,'' she whispered, but she looked away. ''There just wasn't the right time to tell you.''

''So you let me spill my guts to you, tell you all about Judy and how she betrayed me, but you couldn't find the right time to tell me the truth about yourself.'' He welcomed the anger that flared inside him. It was a distraction from the pain that threatened to overwhelm him. ''You played me for a fool. You even got me to reopen the case, but you didn't think it was necessary to tell me your connection to it.''

''I wanted to tell you.'' He heard the pain in her voice, but refused to listen to it. ''I've wanted to tell you for a while.''

''Then why didn't you?''

She stared at him for another moment, then dropped her gaze. ''I was scared. I was afraid that if I told you the truth, you wouldn't let me pursue the story. I was afraid that if you thought I was going to find out something about your family, you'd make sure I didn't have access to any information.''

His heart twisted inside him. ''I thought you knew me better than that.''

"I do, Dev." She reached out to touch him, then fisted her hand and let it drop to her side. "I know you wouldn't do that. But I couldn't get past the fear. I needed to find out the truth about Edmund so badly. And telling you the truth felt like a betrayal of my brother."

"So why tell me now? Why not simply let me figure out what happened to Edmund, say thank you, and go back to New York?" Disgusted with himself, he realized he was fishing for words he would never hear her say.

She paled. "How can you say that?" she whispered. "After last night, how could you even think I would run back to New York when I know what happened to Edmund?"

"It's pretty easy, Ms. Fitzpatrick. You're a user, and you've been using me all along. Why should I think anything's changed because we had great sex last night? You had an itch, we scratched it, and that's that."

He was almost undone by the tears that pooled in her eyes. "That's not all that happened last night, and you know it. We shared a lot more than sex."

"Maybe *I* did," he said, anger making him strike out at her. "But I didn't notice you spilling your guts to me."

"I'm sorry, Dev. I'll leave this morning." She turned away, and he heard her sniffling. His hands ached to reach out and comfort her, and he damned his treacherous heart. He'd been right all along. He was better off alone, better off without anyone in his life.

But he couldn't let her walk away until he knew who was trying to kill her. It was his job, after all. His heart twisted again, and he looked away from her. "No. Stay here. I don't want you to leave the Red Rock. You'll be safe here, and I don't want to have to worry about you while I get to the bottom of your *brother's* murder."

He stormed away, refusing to look back. In another moment, he'd be telling her that it didn't matter, that he loved her anyway. He might have made a fool of himself over Carly, but he wasn't going to compound that mistake.

Carly listened to the sound of Devlin's footsteps fading away, then heard his truck start. He drove away from the house much too quickly, his anger humming in the sound of the tires spitting gravel.

He had every right to be angry, she knew. She should have told him the truth before they made love the night before. But she had been a coward, and had allowed herself to be swept away by passion rather than tell him who she was.

She swallowed again and scrubbed the tears away from her face. He had told her to stay at the ranch, but she couldn't allow herself to sit quietly while Devlin solved the murder. Especially now.

Determined to do something, she headed back to the house to get the keys to her Jeep. Shea was coming out of the house just as she walked in.

"Hey, what's wrong?" Shea touched her arm, forcing her to stop.

"Nothing." She tried to smile.

Shea wrapped her arm around Carly's shoulders and led her to the porch railing. Settling herself on the edge, she said, "What is it, Carly? What has that blockhead brother of mine done?"

Carly felt the tears gathering in her eyes again. "He hasn't done anything. It's me. I've been lying to him since the day I arrived in Cameron."

Shea narrowed her eyes, and the air suddenly felt cooler. "What do you mean?"

Carly poured out the whole story to Shea, and the other woman's face gradually eased as she listened to what Carly had to say. Finally there was silence.

"You've messed up, big-time," Shea said.

"I know." Carly swallowed, determined not to start crying again.

"Do you love him?"

"Of course I do."

"Then show him. He's afraid to take a chance on letting anyone get close. You were the first woman since Judy that he's allowed into his life, and now he feels like you've betrayed him, too. You've got to prove to him that you love him.''

"How do I do that?" she whispered.

Shea shrugged. "You have to figure that out for yourself." She slid off the railing, and her face softened. "You're good for him, Carly. He needs you in his life. Don't let him scare you away."

Carly stood watching as Shea hurried down to the barn. Shea was right, she realized. Devlin had every right to mistrust her. She hadn't shown him that she loved him, but that was going to change. And she'd start by not running away, as he clearly expected her to do.

She'd come to Cameron convinced that the McAllisters were involved in Edmund's death. Now she was equally convinced that they weren't. She hadn't known Devlin's father, but no murderer could have raised children like Dev and Shea. Devlin might never forgive her betrayal, but at least she could clear his family name. If she could give him nothing else, she could stand up in front of everyone in Cameron and tell them that the McAllister family wasn't involved in the death of her brother.

Running into the house, she grabbed her keys and backpack, stopping only long enough to take a couple cans of soda and some candy bars from the kitchen. Whatever was going on had started with the newspaper articles that Edmund had written. She was convinced of that. So she'd go back and talk to the Hansons one more time.

She'd just parked her Jeep in front of the newspaper office and slid out when Devlin strode out of the sheriff's office. For a moment she stood still, wondering if he'd even notice her. She wasn't ready for another confrontation with him.

But his internal radar seemed to be working just fine. He paused before he got into his police Blazer and looked directly at her.

Slamming the door shut, he walked across the street. There was no anger in his face—it was expressionless. Her heart ached. Any expression, even the anger and pain that had been in his eyes this morning, was better than this cold appraisal.

"What the hell are you doing here?" he asked.

"I'm going to take another look at the newspapers."

"You've already looked at all the newspapers about your brother's murder. You told me so. What are you really doing here?"

She wanted to flinch at his implication that she was lying to him again, but she knew he had a right to doubt her. "I want to make sure there isn't anything I've missed."

He made a scoffing sound. "You could have read every back issue of the *Weekly Sentinel* in the amount of time you've spent here. Tell me the truth, Carly."

"I am telling you the truth." She wanted to reach for him, but his eyes were too cold, too harsh. "I'm going to look around one more time, make sure there isn't anything I've missed." She fingered the black velvet cord she wore around her neck and touched the tiny key it held. "This belonged to my brother. I don't know what it opens, but maybe it's something in the newspaper office."

His eyes flickered over the key and dismissed it. "You were supposed to stay at the Red Rock. We agreed it was the safest place for you."

"You decided I was supposed to stay there. I don't remember agreeing with you."

Something hot flared in his eyes, then was ruthlessly subdued. "Carly, I don't have the time to both solve your brother's murder and watch out for you. I want you to stay at the Red Rock so I don't have to worry about you."

"I'm not going to sit quietly at your ranch while you solve my problems for me," she said, her temper rising. "And besides, what's going to happen to me in Cameron? Is someone going to snatch me off the street in broad daylight?"

He shook his head, but she thought she saw a flicker of respect in the gray depths of his eyes. "You are a piece of work, Slick. Fine. Go ahead and harass the Hansons again. Just don't do anything stupid, all right? You've already complicated my life enough. See if you can go right back to the Red Rock when you're finished."

She angled her chin a little higher. She might deserve his cutting words, but she would never let him see how much they hurt. "That's exactly what I was going to do."

"Fine."

"Good." But she was reluctant to let him go. "Where were you going?"

His eyes hardened. "I'm going out to talk to Phil Hilbert. It's time I got a statement from him about this mess."

"Do you think he was involved?"

His eyes glittered like shards of glass. "He's the logical suspect. If you hadn't been so fixated on my father, you would have seen that, too. I can't think of anyone else in the area who hated my father enough to try and frame him for a murder."

"I guess I'll see you later, then," she said.

"You will," he agreed. "Unless you decide you've had enough and leave town."

"I'm not leaving," she said, her voice firm with conviction. "You're not going to chase me away."

He stared at her a minute, then muttered, "You can't blame a man for trying." He spun around and stalked away, and moments later his white Blazer roared down Cameron's Main Street.

She waited until his truck was out of sight, then she took a deep breath and walked into the *Cameron Weekly Sentinel* office. Ralph Hanson was sitting at the desk, and June was staring over his shoulder.

"Good morning," she forced herself to say with a smile. "Do you mind if I look around again?"

Ralph looked up, an expression of sick dismay on his face. Finally she saw a spark of recognition in his eyes. "Good morning, Carly. What did you say?"

Remembering the Hanson's conversations with Devlin when she'd first arrived in town, she wanted to ask what was wrong, and if there was anything she could do to help. But she knew the Hansons were proud people, so she pretended she hadn't noticed anything. "Is it all right if I take another look at your archives?"

"Go ahead." Ralph waved his hand toward the stairs, then looked back down at the papers he held in his hands.

Carly hesitated for a moment, then turned and descended the

stairs. The air was damp and musty, but she was used to it by now. She placed her backpack on the table, then turned and surveyed the room.

She'd looked everywhere in the basement, she knew. She'd found every newspaper from the time before her mother sold the paper, and read every article about her brother's death. There was nowhere else to look.

There *had* to be more, she told herself. Somehow, Edmund's death was related to the fight between the McAllisters and the Hilberts. And somewhere in this office was the proof she needed.

She touched the key that dangled at the end of the velvet cord, and began to search.

She'd been in the basement for two hours when she discovered the crawl space. The door had been hidden by piles of broken furniture, and when she moved the chairs and tables and opened the door, a blast of old, stale air greeted her.

Her heart pounded with excitement as she pulled a flashlight out of her backpack. Boosting herself into the crawl space, she directed the beam of light around the room.

She was disappointed to see that it merely held more debris. Boxes of office records stood stacked against the wall, teetering on the uneven gravel that covered the floor. Several old typewriters lay at crazy angles in front of them. An ancient cash register stood propped against one of the boxes. As she moved the beam of light around the room, all she saw was the normal discards of a place of business.

Edging toward the back of the shallow room, she trained her flashlight on the corners of the crawl space. In the first corner, she saw nothing but cobwebs and spiders. Shuddering, she aimed the light at the other corner.

Almost obscured by the spiderwebs was a small, brown wooden box. Her heart thudded when she saw it, but she didn't know why. Pulling a tissue out of her pocket, she brushed away the webs and pulled the box out of the corner.

Carved onto the lid were the words Property of Edmund Whitmore. Private!

Carly swallowed as she stared down at the box. Her hand shook as she reached for the key she wore around her neck. She would have sworn she'd never seen the box before, but somehow she knew the key would fit. Memories flashed in front of her, pictures of her brother pressing the key into her hand just a few days before he died. ''Keep this for me, Carrie,'' he'd said. ''Keep it safe for me.''

Her hand trembled as she fit the key into the small lock on the box. The lock was stiff and tight, but eventually she heard it click open. When she lifted the lid, she saw a neat stack of typewritten papers. Below those were several small notebooks. Her heart contracted when she realized they were the same kind she herself now used.

Carly slid out of the crawl space, ignoring the spiderwebs, the dust and the mold. She set the box on the table, took a deep breath, and lifted out the first paper.

Chapter 15

Carly gripped the steering wheel of the Jeep and pressed the accelerator a little harder as she sped along the road out of Cameron. It was over. After twenty years, she finally knew the truth about Edmund's murder. She'd meet Dev at the Red Rock and show him the copies of the papers she'd found, and he would handle the rest. Ben Jackson had promised that he would keep the originals safe. Dev trusted him completely, and so would she.

She barely slowed down as she headed into the series of curves in the road before the entrance to the Red Rock. There was an insistent rhythm inside her, urging her home. To the Red Rock and Devlin. Ben had told her that he'd call Dev on the radio and have him meet her there. A few more minutes, and she'd be able to see the entrance to the ranch.

As she drove around a particularly sharp curve, she spotted something in the road ahead of her. Slamming on the brakes, she managed to stop the Jeep just in time to avoid an assortment of rocks spread across the road. Another rock fall, she thought, and shifted into four-wheel drive in order to go onto the shoulder and around the mess.

But before she could start the car again, her door flew open. Phil Hilbert stood in front of her, a deadly looking shotgun held steadily in his hands.

"Get out of the truck, Carly," he said.

"Phil! What are you doing?"

"What does it look like I'm doing? Get out." She saw his finger tighten on the trigger of the gun.

She slid off the seat and onto the rocky shoulder of the road, using one hand to push her backpack onto the floor, hoping he wouldn't notice it. But he gestured into the car with the gun.

"Get your pack, too. Is there anything else in the car?"

"No."

He watched, implacable, as she reached into the car for the backpack. She held it in front of her like a shield. Her hands shook, but she refused to let him see her fright.

"What do you want, Phil?"

He frowned at her. "I thought you were intelligent, Carly. Isn't it obvious?"

"Maybe you should explain it to me."

He gestured impatiently with the gun. "You've apparently found some documents that might implicate me in the unfortunate situation that developed here twenty years ago. We're going to get rid of the documents, and then you."

"I already gave the originals to Devlin," she said. "So you're too late."

He smiled at her. "I know you're lying, Carly. McAllister was at my ranch until just a short time ago. Then he headed for his own place, right before this convenient rock slide. I intercepted you before you got to the Red Rock. He's still there, waiting for you and those interesting documents."

"I left them at his office."

He tilted his head, then shook it. "I don't think so. I know how you journalists operate. You don't trust anyone with your paperwork. You might have copies with you, which I'll make sure I destroy, but I bet you left the originals right where you found them. After all, they'd been safe there for twenty years, hadn't they?"

"How did you know I'd found anything?"

"The Hansons were very helpful." He spoke in a conversational tone, but the shotgun never wavered. "I called them to ask if they'd seen you, and they were eager to be of assistance. They owe me a great deal of money, you see. They told me you'd made copies of some papers, then put the originals back in the basement. Then you got in your truck and headed out toward the Red Rock."

Carly remembered her guilt at the small deception earlier when she'd told the Hansons she was putting the papers back but had hidden them in her backpack instead. Now at least the evidence against Phil would be safe.

She glanced down the road, hoping that someone would come along, praying for Devlin. Phil saw her looking, and shifted the gun in his hand. "Enough of this talking. I have plans for you, and they don't include chitchat. Get into my truck."

She wouldn't get in the truck. She tensed, ready to turn and run, but he cocked the gun. "Don't try it, Carly. There's nowhere to go." He smiled at her. "I picked my spot carefully. You can't climb these cliffs, and I'd have several clear shots at you before you could find cover. Have you ever seen what a shotgun can do to the human body?"

He held the gun on her steadily, and she found herself staring at it. Suddenly Phil grabbed her arm and yanked her toward him. "I don't have all day." He pressed the gun to her back, then shoved her toward his truck. "Get in."

It took only moments for Phil to start the truck. They sped past the entrance to the Red Rock, then turned onto the road she'd taken earlier in the week. With her hand wrapped around the door handle, she watched out of the corner of her eye for a chance to escape as Phil drove up the rutted track. The truck jolted and bumped over the road, but the gun never moved from her chest.

Devlin stood next to Carly's abandoned Jeep, his mouth acrid with fear and his blood roaring in his ears. Footprints and tire tracks told him she'd been taken away in another vehicle, and fury swept over him.

Every instinct screamed at him to run after her, to find her and keep her safe. But he forced himself to stand motionless, to wait for Ben to arrive. Ben was a tracker. He would be able to figure out where they'd gone. It would be useless for him to go charging off, without having any idea where they'd gone.

It seemed like an eternity before he heard the siren on Ben's police Blazer. The other man swung out of the truck almost before it had stopped moving, then crouched down and stared at the pavement in front of Carly's Jeep.

Devlin wanted to scream at the deputy to hurry, to tell him where to find Carly, but he choked the words back. Ben was aware of the urgency. He was working as fast as he could.

"They drove farther down the road," Ben finally said, nodding toward the Red Rock.

"Let's go."

Devlin jumped into his truck and waited for Ben to lead the way. Ben drove slowly, stopping frequently to get out and look at the road. Finally, when they'd stopped at the track that led into the mountains behind the Red Rock, he nodded. "They went off the road here."

"That's Red Rock property." Dev narrowed his eyes. "What's that bastard doing?"

Ben, staring up the rutted trail, paid no attention. "It should be easier to follow him up here. Are you ready?"

Every instinct in Devlin's body screamed at him to go faster, but he forced himself to endure the excruciatingly slow pace. Finally, when they were in a small clearing, Ben stopped his truck and got out.

After what seemed like a long time, he laid his hand on Dev's shoulder. "Something happened here. My guess is that she got away from him, but I can't be positive. There are two tracks of footprints leading away from the area. One doubles back, and the tracks from his truck continue on the road."

Devlin looked around grimly, finally recognizing the place. "We're not far from where that drifter was found at the base of a cliff, his neck broken. I suspect that he had the same thing in store for Carly."

"Probably." Ben's voice held no inflection. "What do you want to do here?"

Dev made a quick decision. "Which way do you think Carly went?"

"Over there, I think." He pointed to the rock-strewn base of a cliff. "I can't be sure, though, without tracking her farther."

"I'll try to find her. You go round up the rest of the deputies and anyone else who's willing to help, and bring them back here. We'll spread out and try to find Carly and the bastard who took her."

Dev waited until Ben had turned his truck around and headed down the trail, then he started for the base of the cliff.

It was getting darker. Carly leaned against the wall of the cave and tried not to think about spending the night out here, alone. She could face the dark, she told herself fiercely. At least she'd gotten away from Phil Hilbert.

The can of soda she'd hit him with had only stunned him momentarily, but it had given her enough time to scramble behind a pile of rocks. Fear and desperation had given her feet wings, and she'd managed to run quite a distance over the uneven ground while he struggled to his feet.

His angry shouts and threats had echoed off the rocks, but she hadn't stopped to listen to them. By the time the shouting stopped, she had managed to climb down a small cliff and she was running across another small canyon.

She'd heard him behind her, huffing on the cliff, but she hadn't slowed down. She'd just kept running, blindly, hauling herself up one cliff and sliding down the next. Her hands were torn and bleeding, and her arms and legs ached with the strain when she finally stopped, her chest burning.

She recognized this place, she realized with a surge of hope. A small, deep blue lake stood in the clearing, and at one end was a tiny cabin. This was the spot where she and Devlin had shared a picnic.

And a whole lot more.

Telling herself not to think about that, she skirted the cabin and headed for Devlin's cave. There would be no protection in the cabin. If Phil managed to follow her this far, it was the first place he would look. But she would be safe in Devlin's cave.

It took a while to find it. All the boulders and red rocks looked the same, but finally she found the entrance and slipped inside. She could see most of the small valley from the opening, and she finally allowed herself to relax as she watched for Phil.

He never arrived, but neither did anyone else. By the time it started to get dark, she knew she would be up here all night. There was no way she could find her way down the mountain in the darkness.

When the darkness was complete and she could no longer see out the door of the cave, she found the old set of saddlebags that Devlin left here and wrapped herself in the blanket. She ate one of the candy bars, but forced herself not to touch the cans of soda. She might need them again. Telling herself to sleep, to save her strength for the next day, she closed her eyes, but sleep wouldn't come.

Too many noises drifted into the cave. At first the squeaks and chirps and low grunts of mountain animals and birds jarred her nerves. Every sound made her jump as she imagined that Phil had found her. But after a while she relaxed against the wall of the cave, her body exhausted. The sounds began to seem normal, simply a part of the night.

Her eyes closed and she was drifting between awareness and sleep when she heard a different sound. A rock rolled down the cliff, bouncing off other rocks on its way. A sound like the scuff of a boot echoed sharply in the sudden silence of the night.

Carly held her breath, and realized that all the other sounds of the night had stopped, too. Her heart began thudding against her chest, almost painful in its intensity. She closed one hand around the can of soda and the other around the pocket knife she'd set out earlier. They were pitiful weapons, but they were all she had.

The moon had not yet risen, and the darkness was almost complete. With nothing but inky blackness in front of her, she strained to hear. In the silence, she thought she heard fingernails scrape against the stone.

She couldn't see the blade of the knife, but she held it stiffly in front of her. Shrugging off the blanket, she crouched in the blackness, waiting for whoever was out there to stick his head above the floor of the cave. She'd only have one chance, and she would make it a good one.

"Carly?"

The voice was a disembodied whisper, floating up into the cave. She tightened her grip on the knife and shifted her feet.

"Carly? Are you up there? It's me, Dev."

His voice was still hushed, but she recognized it. "Dev?" she said, unable to force herself to speak above a whisper. "Devlin?"

The next instant he appeared in the entrance to the cave. Hauling himself over the ledge of rock, he reached for her and pulled her into his arms with rough hands.

"My God, Carly are you all right?" His grip on her tightened almost painfully, then he leaned back and touched her face. "Are you hurt? What happened?"

"I'm fine," she said, but couldn't stop the quiver in her voice. Her hands fisted on his shirt, and she never wanted to let him go. "I'm fine. How did you find me?"

His fingers trailed over her face, as if he was memorizing her with his hands. Finally, he speared his hands through her hair and pulled her close again. "Ben pointed out your trail, and I tried to follow it. It took me a while, though, because I'm not a tracker like Ben. Once I got to this valley, I hoped you'd remember the cave."

"It took me a while to find it." She shivered, and he pulled her closer. "I was afraid to leave, afraid that Phil was waiting for me. When it got dark, I knew I'd never find my way down the mountain at night."

"So it *was* Hilbert."

Even in the darkness, she could feel the anger vibrating off him. "It was Phil," she agreed. "Didn't Ben show you the papers I'd left at the office for you?"

"There wasn't time. Once I found your car, I radioed Ben and we followed you up the mountain. I wasn't interested in a bunch of papers."

"I found them at the newspaper office." The memory brought back a flood of emotion. "Oh, Dev, I was right. Edmund had found proof that Phil Hilbert was stealing water from your father. He'd been investigating the whole time the court fight was going on, and afterward. He wrote a bunch of articles about it, then put them in his special box." She fingered the cord that hung around her neck. "This key was the key to that box. Apparently Edmund wanted to check one more fact before he ran his articles. He knew that if Phil was convicted of stealing water, he'd go to prison and my brother wanted to make sure everything was verified. That's when Phil Hilbert caught him and realized what he was doing."

"Did Phil admit that he'd killed your brother?"

"Yes. He told me he had no intention of going to prison for taking what he needed. He seemed quite proud of the fact that he'd gotten away with murder for so many years," she said bitterly. "He was going to take the copies of Edmund's articles that I had, then kill me. I told him I'd left the originals for you, but he didn't believe me. He figured I'd just put them back where I found them, in the newspaper office. And he didn't think he'd have any trouble getting them away from the Hansons. Apparently they owe him a lot of money.

"I even suspected the Hansons of being involved. They seemed so upset that I was looking at the old newspapers."

"They were, but not because of that." He sighed. "They were afraid you would figure out who they were. They'd been convicted of fraud before they moved to Cameron. Your father knew about it and gave them a second chance, but they've been afraid that you'd find out, then tell everyone in town."

"I would never have done that!"

"I know, but they were scared. And the Hansons would never hurt you."

Devlin eased her against the wall and covered them both with the blanket, but he didn't take his arm away from her shoulders. He held her tightly against him, and Carly thought she felt his mouth brush her hair.

"You're safe now. In the morning, we'll radio Ben to pick us up, then I can arrest Phil. I've been suspicious of him all along and when I interviewed him today, my suspicions grew even stronger. But the papers you've found will go a long way toward proving he killed your brother.''

''He told me he'd done it!''

''There were no witnesses,'' he said, pulling her closer. ''In a trial, it would be his word against yours.''

She wanted to turn to him, to lose herself in his embrace, but she forced herself to sit quietly in the curve of his arm. Devlin was comforting her now, but that was because she'd been cold and frightened. They had parted in anger, and now the harsh words he'd spoken hung between them.

''How did you get away from Phil?'' he asked, shifting his arm slightly.

''I hit him in the head with a soda can,'' she said, shivering at the memory of those terrifying moments.

''What?''

She shrugged. ''It was the only thing I could think of. He was watching me too closely to bend down and pick up a rock. I'd put two cans of soda in my backpack this morning, and I was able to take one out without him noticing. He'd been bragging about what he'd done to my brother, and how he killed a stranger to make it look like the stranger had murdered Edmund. He said that after the first time, killing was easy.'' She shivered. ''He wasn't paying close attention to my hands. Then he noticed that I was edging away. He pulled me closer to him, and I hit him in the head with the can of soda.''

She couldn't see Devlin, but she thought she felt him smile. ''I'd like to have seen that.''

''It didn't really hurt him. He fell down, but it didn't take him long to get back up. But by that time I'd managed to hide behind some rocks, so he couldn't shoot me. After that, it was just a matter of outrunning him.'' She managed a smile of her own. ''I guess all that jogging I do back in the city finally paid off.''

''I think there was a lot more than running involved.'' His hand tightened on her shoulder, then he pulled her closer. ''It took an incredible amount of courage to run through the mountains. You didn't know where you were, and you didn't have any food or water.''

"It wasn't much of a choice," she said. "It was either run or stay and let him kill me."

"I'm proud of you, Carly," he said quietly. "You used your head and managed to escape. You even kept the evidence safe, and now Hilbert is going to pay for what he did. He won't be able to hide behind Bert Pickens this time."

"You don't think Bert deliberately protected him, do you?" she asked, shocked.

"No. Bert might not have been the best sheriff around, but he wasn't dishonest. Hilbert just used his weaknesses against him."

For the first time since Phil had pulled her out of her car that morning, Carly began to relax. Dev was here, and she was safe. That was all that mattered right now. Snuggling closer to him, she longed to wrap herself around him but forced herself to settle for whatever he could give her.

But suddenly he pulled her into his arms. "God, Carly, I was so scared," he muttered into her hair. "When I saw your Jeep on the side of the road, I wanted to kill whoever was responsible for hurting you."

"I knew you would find me," she said, and her voice thickened again. "The whole time I was running away from Phil, I kept telling myself that it would be all right. You wouldn't let anything happen to me."

"I'll keep you safe, Carly. No one will find us in this cave tonight, and tomorrow I'll make sure you get back to the ranch."

"I know, Dev. I know you will. I trust you. Completely."

"You shouldn't," he muttered. "I didn't do a very good job of protecting you from Hilbert in the first place."

"You couldn't have known that he would stop me along the road," she said, tightening her hold on him. "It's not your fault."

"Maybe if I had reopened this investigation earlier, spent more time on it, I would have arrested Phil before he was able to hurt you."

"You don't know that, Devlin. And it doesn't matter. You found me when it counted. You're here when I need you."

"God, Carly, if anything had happened to you..."

His voice trailed off, but Devlin suddenly couldn't bear any separation from her. He pulled her closer, his fear a living thing snarling inside him. He found her mouth in the darkness, and she tasted of life and hope.

Desire shot through him like a burning spear, twining and mingling with the fear that had tormented him earlier. Carly shifted beneath his mouth, opening to him, and he groaned into her mouth.

She murmured something to him, then tightened her arms around his neck, holding him like she would never let go. He felt her desire in the trembling of her arms, in the passion in her kiss, in the touch of her hands on his body.

The fire flared higher inside him, consuming him, completely obliterating all rational thought. It didn't matter that they were in a cave, with nothing but an old blanket between them and the rock and dirt floor. It didn't matter that he'd sworn to stay away from Carly, refused to give her another chance to break his heart. All that mattered was the need that spiraled out of control inside him, the need to claim her, to prove to both of them they were still alive.

He fumbled with the buttons on her shirt, his fingers clumsy in the darkness. Her hands brushed his, trying to help, but she was shaking as hard as he. Finally he pulled the shirt out of her jeans and shoved it to her neck, then cupped her breasts in his hands.

Her breath quivered and broke, and her hips arched up, searching for him. When she slid her hands beneath his shirt and splayed her fingers against his chest, a red haze of desire blotted out everything but his need for her. Taking her mouth in another searing kiss, he pulled apart the buttons on her jeans, yanking them down her legs. He barely managed to unbuckle his belt and his own jeans before she closed her hand around him, guiding him toward her heat.

She cried out when he slid into her, wrapping her legs around him. Her fingers dug into him through his shirt, and she cried out again as he felt the waves of her release caress him. Her name was a chant on his lips as he poured himself into her.

They lay entwined together for a long time, their rapid breathing echoing through the small cave. She held him tightly, her hands clutching at him as if she was afraid to let go. Finally he rolled over, taking her with him, so that she was lying on top of him.

As he stroked down her back, he realized that the wad of material bunched up between them was her shirt, which he'd shoved up around her shoulders. Her jeans were tangled around her knees. He let one hand linger on the smooth skin of her bare derriere as he tried to straighten out her clothes with his other hand.

"I'm sorry," he murmured. "I don't know what happened to me. I took you like a rutting animal."

He felt her smile against his chest. "Did you hear me complain?"

Desire surged back in a huge, crashing wave as she opened his shirt and began to trace circles on his chest. He felt himself harden again. "Carly, don't," he said, but there wasn't much conviction in his voice.

She stilled her hand, and he wanted to beg her to continue. "That doesn't feel like a no," she finally said, letting her hand drift below his waist.

He was responsible for their safety. He had to stop. He needed to pay attention to their surroundings, make sure that no one surprised them. But the night was dark, the noises from outside the cave were all the normal night sounds, and as she caressed him, he felt his resolve dissipate like mist on a cloudless day.

When he was throbbing with need, aching to feel her close around him, he pulled her hand up to his mouth and kissed her palm. "God help me, Carly, I can't stop myself. I want you too much."

He couldn't see her, but he felt her hand touch his face. "I want you, too, Dev," she said in a throaty whisper. "More than I've ever wanted anything." Her hand trembled on his cheek, then trailed down his throat to stop at the pulse pounding at the base of his neck. "Make love with me. Please."

The darkness, the night outside the cave, the danger that still faced them, all faded away. The world shrunk to only Carly, and the need that threatened to consume him. Easing her down onto the blanket, he cupped her face in his hands and lost himself in her kiss.

A cool breeze drifted across his bare skin, and Devlin stirred, reluctant to open his eyes. He didn't want to wake and abandon the dream he was enjoying. Carly slept beside him, curled into him and twined around him. Her leg was wedged between his, and his hand cupped one of her breasts. Her scent filled his head, more intoxicating than reality could ever be.

Then he heard a low, satisfied murmur next to him, a sound saturated with the memory of pleasure. Snapping his eyes open, he saw that he hadn't been dreaming. Carly was snuggled next to him, her naked body only partially covered by a blanket, and a small smile played on her lips.

The night came back to him in a rush, the tender lovemaking they'd shared as well as the heat and passion that had flared out of control. As he looked at her, he felt himself getting hard all over again.

But nothing was going to happen in the light of day. He'd opened himself to her last night, shown her a part of him that no one else had ever seen. He'd needed her. But he was back in control, he told himself, and he eased himself away from her.

He was every kind of a fool for allowing himself to lose control last night. He couldn't think about what had happened between him and Carly. The sun shining into the opening of the cave reminded him that Phil Hilbert was still out there somewhere, undoubtedly searching for Carly. As they'd made love into the morning hours, completely forgetting their situation, they could have allowed Phil to find them.

His lips tightening, he snatched up his clothes that had been scattered carelessly over the floor and began to dress. Carly rolled over and opened her eyes. "Good morning." Her voice, low and sultry, strummed across his nerves, and her smile kindled the embers of desire.

"Good morning," he snapped back, fighting the need that swelled inside him. "Get dressed. I can't believe that we did this. I can't believe I allowed myself to forget what I was supposed to do."

Her smile faded as she sat up. When the blanket slipped off her shoulders, she grabbed for it and pulled it up to cover her breasts. "What's wrong?"

"What's wrong?" The words exploded out of him. "We're hiding in a cave, trying to escape from a murderer, and how did we spend the night? We sure as hell weren't doing what we should have been doing."

"And what was that?" She reached for her clothes, but didn't take her eyes off him.

"We should have been watching, making sure that Phil wasn't out there. We should have been sleeping, so we could start walking as soon as it got light. We should have been out of here hours ago."

"I thought you said no one knew about this cave besides you and Shea."

"It doesn't matter how many people know about this cave. Once we leave here, we have to walk across a lot of open ground before we'll have any cover again. And Phil Hilbert is no fool. He knows that you're up here somewhere. He's probably just waiting for us to show our faces. We've lost the advantage of surprise."

"I'm sorry," she said as she buttoned her blouse and pulled on her jeans. "I'm ready to go."

"Hell, it's not your fault." He rubbed the back of his neck. "I'm the one who should have known better." Anger at himself rose inside him. "I was a damn fool. Let's go."

She followed him out of the cave without saying a thing. The sunlight stabbed at his eyes, and he saw that she was squinting, too. He waited for a few moments to let their eyes adjust to the light, then he started down the side of the cliff. When he got to the bottom, he held up his arms and lifted Carly down. She stepped away as soon as her feet touched the ground.

Slinging her backpack over her shoulder, she gave him a tight nod. "I'm ready."

Chapter 16

Carly didn't say a thing as they walked through the rock debris at the base of the cliffs. Instead of heading directly across the valley, toward the cabin and the road, they stayed in the shadow of the cliffs. There was at least a small chance they would blend into the rocks. Walking across the valley, they would stand out like a pair of elephants in downtown Cameron.

She was being a real trouper, he thought, glancing back over his shoulder at Carly. She was keeping up with him, and not once had she complained about being hungry or thirsty. They'd each drank one of her cans of pop and split her last candy bar, but he was already thirsty again. And he knew that she had to be even more thirsty and hungry. She'd run a couple of miles across rugged mountain terrain with a killer on her heels.

"We'll get to a spring in a few minutes," he said gruffly. "We're high enough in the mountains that the water is safe to drink."

"Good."

Her face was already red, and he watched her with concern. "Do you have any sunblock in that bag of yours?"

She shook her head. "I hadn't planned this little side trip through the mountains." Beneath the simmering anger in her eyes he saw a shadow of pain.

"Carly, what's wrong?"

Her eyes flashed as she finally looked at him. "Does it matter?"

"Of course it matters!"

She opened her mouth to answer, then snapped it shut. "The only thing that matters right now is getting out of here alive," she said wearily. "I thought we were supposed to be paying attention and watching for Phil."

She was right. Cursing himself, he turned around and tried to ignore the hurt on her face. He had been too abrupt this morning, in too much of a hurry to get moving. He wanted to apologize, to explain why he'd been so angry at himself, but they didn't have the time.

There would be plenty of time for talking when they were safely back at the Red Rock, when Phil Hilbert was in custody. Until then, his number one concern was Carly's safety. And if she didn't understand that, he didn't have the time right now to explain it to her.

They walked through a narrow opening in the rock and were finally out of sight of the valley that held the cabin and the cave. He took a deep breath and looked around. There was more cover here, and they were less likely to be surprised. "Wait a minute, Carly. I want to radio Ben and tell him where we are."

She stopped walking and sat down on a rock as he pulled his radio out of his belt. He'd turned it off, afraid that it would crackle to life unexpectedly. Sound carried a long way in the thin mountain air, and he didn't want to broadcast their presence.

"Hey, Marge," he said quietly into the handset. "Is Ben around?"

"He's right here."

"Are you all right?" Ben's first words revealed his concern.

"I'm fine and so is Carly. Phil Hilbert is our man. Send someone out to his ranch to pick him up, although I doubt if he's there. Carly managed to get away from him in the mountains behind the Red Rock, and now we're hiking out. We'll be roughly following the trail that leads up to the cabin. Radio me when you're getting close, and I'll tell you exactly where to find us.''

"Right." Ben paused. "How many men do you want me to bring?"

"Round up as many of the deputies as you can. I think Phil is still somewhere up here, and I want to roust him out."

"Will do. I'll take care of sending someone to his ranch, then I'll be on my way."

"Thanks, Ben." Dev hesitated. "Tell whoever goes to his ranch to be careful and not do anything stupid. It sounds like Phil is on the edge, and I don't want anyone to get hurt."

There was a pause on the other end of the radio, then Ben said, "I'll go there myself on my way to your place."

"Good. I'll expect to hear from you in another couple of hours."

He turned off the radio and replaced it in his belt, then turned to Carly. "We're going to stay close to the road, because that's the quickest way back to the ranch. But there's a stream not too far from here. There isn't a lot of water in it this time of year, but it's clean and it's cold. We both need some water."

She nodded and stood up, slinging her pack over her shoulder again. Her movements looked slow and painful, and for the first time he noticed the dried blood and fresh bruises on her hands and arms.

"My God, Carly, what happened to you?" He grabbed one of her arms and stared at her injuries.

She looked down, then shrugged. "That must have happened when I was trying to get away from Phil. I climbed up and down a bunch of rocks, and I must have scraped myself up."

"You should have washed these last night."

She pulled her arm away from him. "With what? Soda? I didn't even think about first aid for a bunch of minor scratches. Last night I was more concerned about staying alive."

"You should have told me you were hurt."

She lifted her gaze and held his steadily. "At what point would that have been? While we were making love? Or this morning, after we woke up and you wouldn't even look me in the eye? I don't think so, Devlin.''

"Look, Carly, I know you're upset about the way I acted this morning. But I was angry at myself because I hadn't been doing my job. My only thought last night should have been getting us back to the ranch safely. But I wasn't paying any attention to what was going on outside the door of that cave.''

Her chin lifted and her eyes shot sparks of anger at him. "Don't try to make excuses. We shared something in that cave last night, something important. You're angry because you were vulnerable. You let down your barriers, opened yourself to me, and you couldn't stand that. You showed me that you needed me as much as I needed you, and that appalled you in the light of day.''

He opened his mouth, ready to hotly deny her accusations, but something stopped him. Maybe there was a grain of truth in what she said. Maybe he was angry that she'd managed to break down the barriers around his heart. He'd known that the chances of Phil finding them in the cave were remote. But instead of facing the truth about himself, he'd chosen to focus on his job instead.

He couldn't afford to take the time to make it right with Carly now. "We'll talk about it once you're safe," he said, looking around. "I'm not going to stand here and discuss our 'relationship' while there's a murderer looking for you. Let's go.''

"You were right, weren't you?'' she said, her voice almost a whisper in the dry air. "You aren't interested in any relationships. I thought I'd ruined things, by not telling you the truth. But I couldn't ruin what was never there in the first place. If I hadn't lied to you, there would have been some other reason why a relationship between us wouldn't work. I should have listened to you when you told me there could be nothing between us.''

"Dammit, Carly, this isn't the place to be having this discussion.'' He grabbed for his reason, because it felt like his heart was slipping away.

"I suspect that there never will be the right place or time to have this discussion. So we might as well have it now.'' She angled her chin higher. "Don't worry, Dev. I won't make any claims on you. I'll admit that I should have told you sooner who

I was. I wish I had told you sooner. Keeping my identity from you was wrong, but at least I told you what I'd done and asked you to forgive me. And that was the perfect excuse for you, wasn't it? I played right into your hands. I gave you a reason for pushing me away, and you grabbed onto it with both hands. I felt horrible about it, but now I know that if I hadn't told you that lie, you would have found something else.''

''That's not true, Carly.'' But he had a sickening feeling that she had read him perfectly. He'd been trying to push her away from the first day she'd driven into Cameron. And this morning, after they'd made love in the cave, he'd been even more desperate to get away from her. Because he'd felt himself falling more and more deeply in love with her, and it scared the hell out of him.

Her eyes darkened with regret and sorrow. Then she picked up her backpack and shrugged it onto her shoulders. ''You can tell yourself whatever you want, Dev. But you're right. It's time to go. Let's find that water.''

He wanted to stop her, to tell her that she was wrong, but he realized that she wasn't. And they didn't have the time to resolve things now. Phil Hilbert could be anywhere.

''This discussion isn't over,'' he warned her.

She glanced over her shoulder at him. ''It is as far as I'm concerned.''

''Come on,'' he said brusquely. ''We both need water, and your arms need tending.''

Neither of them spoke as they hiked over the loose stone. The morning sun beat down on them, heating the rock cliffs that rose next to them. Carly's face was getting redder, and he wished he had a hat for her to wear. But she didn't say a thing. She just kept walking, even though he saw her stumble once or twice.

Finally they reached the small stream that tumbled down the mountain. Carly threw her pack next to one of the mesquite bushes that lined the stream, then knelt next to the water. She splashed her face repeatedly, then let the cold water run over her arms and hands.

She looked over at him. ''Are you sure it's safe to drink from the stream? I've never done that before.''

"There aren't too many places left where it's safe to drink the water without treating it first. But this is one of them. The water is from snow runoff, high in the mountains. There isn't much of a stream left by this time of year, but it's not polluted. Go ahead and drink."

She cupped her hands and brought the water hesitantly to her mouth. Once she started to drink, she drank for a long time. He drank all he could hold, then filled the two pop cans he'd saved.

"This won't be much, but it'll be something. We'll get thirsty again before we get back to the ranch.

"I don't think you're going to have to worry about being thirsty," a voice said behind them.

He spun around to face Phil Hilbert, who was holding a shotgun steadily on them. The older man smiled, his eyes glittering with triumph. "I figured you'd stop here on your way down the mountain. It's the only water around." His smile twisted into a slash of anger. "I should know. Your father guarded this stream like a miser with a stash of gold."

"It was his property and his stream," Devlin answered, his eyes on the gun. "That was his right."

"Right, hell. I needed that water." Hilbert smiled again, a sly grin this time. "And I got the best of your father in the long run. He had no idea that I was diverting this stream."

"But Edmund Whitmore knew, didn't he?"

Carly's voice was confident behind him, and Devlin moved over to put himself between her and the shotgun.

"Don't move, McAllister," Phil said sharply. "I like you just where you are. I have a nice, clear target in either of you."

"Edmund Whitmore knew, didn't he, Phil?" Carly asked again.

Phil's face turned an ugly red. "I found him up here, snooping around where he didn't belong. He managed to find the place where I was diverting the water, and he was writing in that damned notebook of his. He promised not to tell anyone, but I knew better than that. He was as bad as his damned father, always sticking his nose in where he didn't belong."

"Why did you kill him, Phil? Was water more important than a boy's life?" Carly asked.

"Hell, yes." He gave her a scornful look. "You're from the city. You have no idea what it's like to live out here. If you don't have water, you don't survive."

"You have a stream on your ranch. I saw it."

"That stream is hardly more than a puddle of spit. It couldn't sustain the number of cattle I wanted to raise."

"Then maybe you should have tried to raise fewer cattle."

"You mind your own business, city girl." Phil's face became hard and implacable. "You shouldn't have stuck your nose in here, either."

"You're wrong about that." Carly stepped closer to Phil, and Dev wanted to push her back. But he was afraid that if he made any sudden moves, Phil would fire the gun.

"I have every right to stick my nose into this. Edmund Whitmore was my brother."

She paused, and Devlin watched Phil narrow his eyes. "The hell you are."

"Surely you remember that Edmund had a sister. My mother and I left town after Edmund was killed, but I never forgot my brother."

Out of the corner of his eye, Dev saw Carly close her hand around the velvet cord she wore around her neck. "My brother gave me something right before he died. It was the last thing he ever gave me." Slowly she pulled the key out from beneath her blouse. "This is the key to his special box, the box where he kept his notebooks and his stories. I found it in the basement of the *Weekly Sentinel* office yesterday.

"Do you know what was in it, Phil?" She didn't wait for him to answer. "All the stories he'd written about the water rights fight you had with Dev's father. All the research that he'd done. And all the proof that you'd been diverting water all along."

This time Carly smiled, and Dev reached out to grab her. "Don't, Carly."

She paid no attention to him. "Those papers are now in Dev's office. If we're killed, Dev's deputies are going to know who did it.''

"You're lying," Phil snarled, but Dev thought he looked worried. "You've got the papers with you in that backpack." He gestured to the backpack with the shotgun.

"I have copies in the pack," she said. "Go ahead and look."

"Don't worry. I'll have plenty of time for that later."

A chill passed over Devlin and he tried to distract Phil. "That shotgun looks familiar, Hilbert."

Phil looked over at him and sneered. "It should, McAllister. It's the Parker 28 gauge that you were careless enough to lose for your father.''

"I didn't lose anything. It looks to me like you stole that gun."

"I prefer to think of it as borrowing." He smiled at them. "Actually, I was quite proud of my foresight. One day I arrived at your ranch and there was no one around. I walked into the house and saw the gun case was unlocked. No one but your father had a 28-gauge shotgun around here, so I threw it in my truck. I thought it might come in handy later. And I was right."

His smile grew even wider. "But don't worry, your family will get it back. It'll be found next to your bodies after you use it to kill Ms. Fitzpatrick, then yourself. And everyone will know, then, that it was your family all along who was responsible for the Whitmore boy's murder."

"You're forgetting the papers that are in my office," Devlin said, glancing over at Carly. She was staring at Phil.

"Circumstantial evidence. After you're found with the gun, those papers won't mean diddly."

"We'll see." His voice was noncommittal. He didn't want to make Phil lose his temper. Then any advantage he and Carly had would be lost. "I suppose you killed that drifter who was found at the bottom of a cliff on the Red Rock with his neck broken."

"I thought that was very clever, myself," Phil said smugly. "I had relied on Bert Pickens to ignore the murder, saying it must have been an accident, but old Bert got stubborn on me. So I found a drifter who was wandering through the area, and he suddenly became Bert's number one suspect. I thought it tied together the loose ends very nicely.''

Dev looked over at Carly, and saw that she was beginning to sway on her feet with the effort to remain completely still in the hot sun. When she caught his eye the next time she swayed, he gave her an infinitesimal nod of approval. He saw the understanding in her eyes.

A moment later she swayed again, nearly falling to the ground. Devlin leaped to catch her. While he bent over her, he whispered, ''I'm going to try and distract him. You see if you can slip behind one of those mesquite bushes. If you're out of his sight, you'll be able to get away.''

She squeezed his hand to let him know she'd heard. Dev turned to Phil. ''I'm going to set her down on one of the rocks over by the stream. She's weak from running through the mountains yesterday. She needs to drink more water.''

''Put her down and get away from her,'' Phil bellowed.

Dev set her gently on a rock, then brushed a kiss over her forehead. ''Get behind one of those bushes, then run like hell out of here.''

She squeezed his hand, then laid back on the rock as if she was faint. He gave her tiny smile, then stood and faced Phil again.

''You get over here, McAllister. Get away from her.''

Devlin walked back across the stream, deliberately placing his body between Carly and Phil. He glanced back once to see that Carly had slid her body off the rock and was now sitting behind it.

''What's going to happen once I'm out of the way?'' he asked Phil.

''I'll get the water I need, then the Tall T will be the ranch it should have been all along,'' the other man replied with fierce satisfaction.

''Shea might have something to say about that.'' Dev spoke without any inflection in his voice.

Phil spat out of the corner of his mouth. ''She's a woman. What does she know about ranching? I'll deal with her, then I'll own the source of the water.''

Devlin watched the other man's face redden. As long as Phil was ranting, Carly might be able to slip away without Phil noticing. He'd add a few logs to the fire.

"I don't know why you'd think so. It looks to me like Shea's done a pretty good job with the Red Rock."

Phil's face trembled with fury. "That ranch should have belonged to me when your father died. I made a fair offer. You weren't interested in running the place. But that sister of yours insisted on taking over the ranch herself. Now we'll see how she does when you're not around to bail her out."

Devlin sensed Carly's movement behind him. "Planning on killing Shea, too?" he asked Phil.

Phil spat again. "I won't have to do that. She'll turn tail and run after a few months of handling the place on her own."

Phil didn't know very much about Shea if he thought that was going to happen, Dev thought with grim satisfaction. "Do you think Dusty, Joe and Levi are going to stand by and let you get rid of Shea?"

"Those old cowboys of yours aren't worth the boot leather it'll take to kick them off the ranch. They won't be able to stop me, either."

Devlin hoped Carly was safely concealed behind the foliage. Phil was ranting like a madman, but he'd notice pretty quickly that one of his victims was missing.

"I've had enough of your questions, McAllister." Phil gestured with the shotgun. "It's time I dealt with you and the reporter."

"Are you going to shoot us here?" he asked, desperate to buy Carly a few more moments. "Or do you want our bodies found right away?"

"I'm taking you to the same place the Whitmore boy was found. Once folks know that Carly was his brother, they'll understand why you took her there to shoot her. A murderer always returns to the scene of his crime. And you know what they say. Like father, like son."

He cackled for a moment, then gestured with the shotgun. "Start moving. You too, Carly."

Devlin watched as Phil looked over at the rock where he'd left Carly sitting. She had vanished, and fury erupted in Phil's eyes.

Carly heard Phil's bellow of rage and paused for a moment. She'd been trying to circle around in back of Phil, hoping to take him by surprise. She knew that all Dev needed was a momentary distraction and he'd be able to subdue the older man.

The rock beneath her hands was hot, and the air was filled with the scent of sagebrush and mesquite. Dust coated her legs and arms and filled her mouth, and she brushed it out of her eyes as she began to edge along the ground again, moving more quickly. Clearly Phil had discovered that she had disappeared. She didn't think he would kill Dev before he found her, but urgency pounded through her blood.

She heard footsteps close by, and she froze. Flattening herself on the ground, she stared through the dense branches of the mesquite to see Phil waving the shotgun at Dev. He'd stepped closer, but still too far away for Devlin to push the gun to one side.

Her hand closed around a rock on the ground, and she desperately wanted to throw it at Phil, to draw his attention away from Dev. But she was too far away. She wasn't sure she could hit him, and if Dev acted too soon, he might get hurt.

So she waited, forcing herself to be patient. Phil sounded like he'd gone completely over the edge. His words didn't make sense anymore as he kept the shotgun aimed at Dev.

Suddenly Phil stopped the stream of invective. "It doesn't matter," he said to Devlin. "Let's go. I'll take care of you, then come back for her. She's not going to be able to find her way out of here."

There was no way she was going to let him take Dev away. Grabbing a handful of pebbles from the ground, she threw them behind Phil. He spun around. Carly saw Dev gather himself to jump Phil, but then Phil spun back around to face him. "I'm not that stupid," he taunted. "You think I'm going to turn my back on you?"

Staring at Dev, he called, "You can come out any time, Ms. Fitzpatrick. Or you can stay hidden and watch me blow a hole into your boyfriend. A shotgun is a messy way to die, you know. There won't be enough of McAllister left to scrape into a box."

Carly picked up another handful of pebbles and threw them in a different direction. Phil spun around to look, then quickly turned back to Dev. "I hear you moving back there, Carly," he called. "I'm losing my patience. How much longer do you want McAllister to live? Don't you want to give him one last kiss?"

Carly threw another handful of pebbles in a different direction, then another. Devlin smiled at Phil, seemingly perfectly calm. "She's not alone back there, Hilbert. I radioed my deputies first thing this morning and told them where to find me. Do you still think you're going to get away with this?"

"You're lying," Phil said, but Carly watched as his eyes scanned the area. "I would have heard if anyone else was out there."

"You wouldn't have heard Ben Jackson. No one hears or sees Ben if he doesn't want to be heard or seen. Tracking is in his blood."

Phil swung the gun wildly in one direction, then another. Carly threw another handful of rocks away from her, and Phil whirled and fired his gun into a clump of sagebrush.

Before he could turn around, Dev had leaped on top of him and knocked him down. Phil struggled beneath him, and Carly watched with horror as he tried to turn the double-barreled shotgun and fire the other load into Dev.

Scrambling out of her hiding place, she ran toward the two men on the ground. She reached down and picked up a rock, but found herself standing over the two men, unable to use it. Dev and Phil were rolling around in the dust, and she couldn't get a clear shot at Phil.

"Run, Carly," Dev panted. "Get out of here."

Ignoring his command, she clenched the jagged rock in both hands. But Dev's head was too close to Phil's, and she couldn't take a chance on hitting Dev.

Phil managed to get one hand away from Dev, and he swung his arm around. In moments the gun would be pointed directly at

Dev's chest. Without thinking, Carly crashed the rock down on Phil's arm.

He bellowed with rage and pain, but the gun dropped to the ground. Carly kicked it away, then picked it up.

Phil used both his hands to claw at Dev's face and eyes in a desperate attempt to free himself. But Dev was younger and stronger, and he grabbed Phil's wrists in his hands. He managed to flip the older man over, and he brought his hands behind his back.

"Carly, come here and help me."

Holding the shotgun carefully away from herself, she stepped over to Dev's side.

"Put the gun down, way behind us, and take the handcuffs out of my belt."

She set the shotgun down on the rock where she'd been sitting, then pulled the metal handcuffs out of the pocket on Dev's belt. "All right, I have them."

"Open them up, and snap one of them around Phil's wrist."

She fumbled with the unfamiliar device, but finally managed to open the bar on one of the handcuffs. Dev held Phil's wrist steady, and she placed the cuff around it and pressed the latch together.

"Tighter than that," Dev instructed. "Squeeze it together."

She squeezed until the cuff couldn't tighten any more, and Dev nodded.

"Good. Now do the other wrist."

It took only moments for her to secure the handcuff on Phil's other hand, and when it was tightened, Dev gathered himself and stood up.

He drew his gun from his holster and pointed it at Phil, who was still lying on the ground. "Don't move a muscle, Hilbert." He recited the Miranda warning, then he turned to her. "Are you all right? Are you hurt?"

"I'm fine. What about you? You're the one who was rolling around on the ground with him."

"I'm okay." He reached out to push her hair behind her ear,

almost as if he couldn't stop himself from touching her, then he let his hand drop away. "You're sure you're not hurt?"

"How would I have gotten hurt?" she demanded, needing his touch and angry at herself for her weakness. "I was hiding behind a bush the whole time."

Finally he smiled. "If your mouth is working, I guess the rest of you is, too. Are you ready to start walking?"

"Yes." Her voice was too fervent, she knew, but suddenly she ached all over. The scratches on her arms and hands burned, her throat was dry and her legs felt weak and wobbly. She wanted Devlin to wrap his arms around her and keep her safe. And she wanted to go home.

She must have spoken the last wish aloud, because Dev gave her an unreadable look. "You can go home as soon as we have all this settled. Let's get started."

As they began to walk, she opened her mouth to reply, then closed it again. It didn't matter anymore. But when she said she wanted to go home, she hadn't meant to New York. She'd meant the Red Rock Ranch.

Chapter 17

As soon as they reached the road, Dev radioed to Ben. "I've got Hilbert," he said. "We're on the road back to the ranch. Come and pick us up."

He turned to her. "Ben will be here soon. Do you want to sit and wait for him?"

"I'm fine, Dev." She glanced over at him, then back down the road again. "I'd rather keep walking." If she stopped, she wasn't sure she'd be able to start moving again. "But what about Phil? Maybe he needs to rest."

"He managed to hunt us down in the mountains," Dev said grimly. "He can keep walking."

"Think you're pretty clever, don't you, McAllister?" Phil sneered. "We'll see what my lawyer has to say about that."

Dev glanced over at him. "Your lawyer is going to be talking plea bargain faster than you can blink, Hilbert. If I were you, I'd keep your mouth shut. You've done more than enough talking to put yourself away for the rest of your life."

Phil shot Dev a look filled with hatred, but he didn't say anything more. Carly almost wished he would. It would take her mind off Devlin and what he was thinking.

Dust swirled around them as they walked, and the sun beat down relentlessly. Her blouse was sticking to her back, and sweat trickled down the side of her face. When she reached up to push her damp hair off her forehead, she saw Devlin watching, a frown on his face.

"I'm going to radio Ben again and have him call Doc Ellis," he said. "I want him to meet us at the ranch so he can take a look at your arms and your hands."

"Don't be ridiculous, Dev. There's nothing wrong with me that some soap and water won't cure. These are just scratches." She smiled wearily at him. "If you make Doc come and look at me, he's going to think I'm nothing more than an accident waiting to happen."

He scowled at her, but didn't answer. They walked on in silence, the air between them becoming more and more charged. But there was nothing she would say with Phil as an audience. And even if they were alone, she acknowledged, she wasn't sure there was anything that Dev wanted to hear from her.

Except perhaps that she was leaving Cameron.

Her heart contracted at the thought. She'd only been here for a little while, but the town felt like home to her. She would miss Shea, who already felt like a friend. She'd miss Gladys Jones, and Melba, and Phyllis, the waitress at Heaven on Seventh. She'd even miss Janie, the aloof owner of the restaurant, and the interesting non-relationship she had with Ben Jackson.

She wasn't sure how she'd become so attached to a small town in the middle of nowhere, but she had. And now she had to think about leaving. She'd accomplished what she'd come for, after all. She knew the truth about her brother's death, and the man responsible had been arrested. She should be looking forward to getting back to her life in New York. Nothing could have prepared her for the wrench of leaving Cameron. She couldn't have imagined how difficult it would be to leave.

She glanced over at Dev out of the corner of her eye. But she couldn't have imagined that she'd find Devlin McAllister in Cameron, either. He was the real reason she didn't want to leave. He was the reason she'd be leaving her heart behind when she drove out of Cameron for the last time. Dev was the reason that Cameron felt like home.

"You look serious, all of a sudden." Dev's voice roused her from her thoughts.

She tried to smile. "I'm thinking about some serious food and water," she said lightly. "A stack of pancakes from Heaven on Seventh would be perfect."

"Trust me. Maria will be setting huge platters of food on the table as soon as we walk in the door, and insisting that we eat it. That's her answer to any kind of crisis."

"Sounds good to me." She kept her voice easy and full of banter.

A few minutes later they heard the sound of a powerful truck engine, then Ben's police Blazer came into view. Ben looked worried as he jumped out of the truck and looked at them.

"Are you both all right? Anyone injured?"

"We're fine, Ben. Let's get back to the ranch."

Ben and Dev settled Phil in the back seat, then all three of them crowded onto the front bench. Sitting in the middle, between Ben and Dev, Carly held herself rigidly upright, trying not to brush against Dev. But every time they hit a bump or rounded a curve, she slid into him. It was only for a few more minutes, she told herself. She could survive anything for a few minutes.

But her heart wasn't sure that was true.

Dev didn't seem to notice the fact that she was practically sitting on his lap as they bounced down the road toward the Red Rock. He was too busy telling Ben what had happened with Phil Hilbert up by the stream. At one point, Ben turned to her, his serious dark eyes approving. "That was quick thinking up there, Ms. Fitzpatrick, to fake that you were going to faint."

"I wasn't faking." She gave him a weary smile. "Dev was just good enough to take my weakness and be able to run with it."

Ben's assessing brown eyes moved from her to Dev, then back again. "It sounds like you make a good pair," he murmured.

Before she could respond, the Red Rock ranch house came into view. Dev sat up straight and looked over at Ben. "You call the rest of the deputies and let them know we have Phil, then take our guest of honor into the office. I'll meet you there later."

Ben nodded. "Will do."

When the truck stopped in front of the house, Dev slid out, then turned and held out his hands to her. She only hesitated for a moment before taking his hands. But he slid his hands around her waist and gently lifted her out of the truck.

She wanted to tell him that she was perfectly capable of getting out of the truck by herself, but it felt too good to have him holding her, even if it was only for a moment. Too soon, he dropped his hands and turned away. Leaning into the truck again, he gave Ben a few more last minute instructions, then slammed the door and stood back as the truck pulled away.

Phil was gone and there was no one else around. Carly wanted to look over at Dev, wanted to know what he was thinking, but he said brusquely, "Let's get you something to eat and drink."

She wanted to scream at him that food and water was the last thing on her mind right now, but she didn't open her mouth. Maybe it was better to give them both some time, let them recover before they talked. If he looked at her right now, or touched her again, she was afraid she'd break down and embarrass herself. And him.

He didn't want to know that she loved him. He'd made that very clear this morning in the cave, and even more clear later on, when she'd challenged him about it. His lack of an answer had been all the answer she'd needed.

"Dev! Carly!"

Shea's voice came from the barn, and she turned around to look. Shea was loping toward them, her blond ponytail bouncing behind her. "Are you two all right? I was worried sick about you."

She threw herself into Dev's arms and held on tight. After a moment, she leaned away, holding his shoulders, and looked him over. "Are you hurt?"

Dev leaned down and planted a kiss on her cheek. "We're both fine, but we could use some water. And some food."

Shea turned to her and gave her the once over. She stilled when she saw Carly's arms, then grabbed her hands. "You're not okay. Look at her poor arms."

"It's all right, Shea. They're just scratches." Carly wanted to hide her arms behind her back. "They just need to be cleaned."

"Then come into the house and let's take care of that."

Shea swept them away and cleaned Carly's arms, applying antibiotic lotion and bandages to the deepest cuts. Then she stayed with them while they ate lunch, listening to the story and expressing outrage at Phil Hilbert's actions.

Finally Shea stood up, saying that she had work to do. When the door banged behind her, silence settled over the dining-room table. It was the middle of the afternoon, and Carly ached with weariness. Dev sat rigidly at the dining-room table, watching her.

"I imagine you'll want to leave soon," he said, breaking the uncomfortable silence.

"Yes," she said, but her heart ached. "I accomplished what I set out to do."

"Are you going to include this in your story about Cameron?" he asked stiffly.

"There isn't going to be a story about Cameron, Dev." She shifted and looked out the window at the magnificent mountains behind the house. "It was just a convenient reason to come to Cameron to begin with, but now I see that you were right all along. I don't want to share this place with the world."

"Thank you for that," he said after a while. He shifted on the chair. "You're welcome to stay here on the ranch, of course. Until you leave."

Her heart breaking, she couldn't bear to look at him. "Thanks, but I'll go back to Melba's. I want to say goodbye to her, anyway."

"What's the story with Melba? Why were you so insistent about staying there?"

"Melba was my third grade teacher." She continued to look out the window, but her eyes lost their focus. "It was...difficult

after Edmund was killed. I had a hard time. My mother wasn't..."
She compressed her lips. "Anyway, it was a bad time for me.
And Melba was very kind. She went out of her way to take care
of me. She made sure I had lunch every day, she made sure I got
help with my homework. She always asked how I was doing and
if there was anything I needed. All the other kids were scared of
her, because she was strict. But she was there for me when I
needed her. And I've never forgotten. So when I saw that she had
a boarding house, I had to stay with her."

She thought his eyes softened, but all he said was, "Does she
know who you are?"

"No. She told me once that I looked familiar, but I made a
joke and she never said anything else. But I'm going to tell her
before I go." It was the perfect excuse to leave the Red Rock,
and she grabbed at it. She was sure that Dev would be relieved.
"I need to go back today. I don't want her to hear who I really
am from someone else. I want to tell her myself."

She couldn't read a thing in his face. He nodded once. "Fine.
I'll drive you back whenever you're ready. I'll have someone
bring your car into town tomorrow."

"I'll get my things together."

She walked upstairs without looking back, afraid he'd see the
tears in her eyes. A lump swelled in her throat as she passed his
closed bedroom door. Forcing herself to ignore it, she walked into
her own room, then shut the door. She pressed her hands to her
eyes, forcing back the tears, then took a deep breath and started
packing her belongings.

Dev had had his chance, and he hadn't asked her to stay. So
she would go, and because she loved him, she wouldn't try and
make him feel guilty. You couldn't force yourself to love a person. It wasn't something you could turn on at will.

The ride into town was filled with an uncomfortable quiet. By
the time they pulled up in front of Melba's house, all Carly
wanted to do was jump out of the truck and run inside. But Dev
helped her carry her luggage into the house, then carried them up
the stairs while she went looking for Melba.

She said goodbye to him under the watchful eye of her former teacher. "I'll see you tomorrow," he muttered, then he escaped out the door. Carly listened to the sound of his truck until it faded completely away.

She and Melba stood in the hall for a moment. Then Melba said gruffly, "I heard you had a hard time with that Phil Hilbert."

Carly smiled at her. "The grapevine was at work quickly."

"That's the way it is in small towns. We all know each other's business. A bunch of gossips, that what we all are."

"I like that about Cameron. And I wouldn't call it gossip. Everyone cares about everyone else." It was one of the things she was going to miss most about this town.

"Come in and have some dinner," Melba said abruptly, but Carly put a hand on her arm.

"There's something I want to tell you first, Melba. Something I don't want you to hear from anyone but me."

"What's that?"

Carly took a deep breath. "You know I've been looking into Edmund Whitmore's death. I'm Edmund's sister. You were my third grade teacher."

Melba looked at her sharply. "I told you I thought there was something familiar about you." She cocked her head. "So you're little Carrie Whitmore, all grown up."

Carly nodded. "You were very kind to me after my brother died."

"You needed to have someone care about you," she said gruffly. "Your mother was too torn up about your brother."

"I've always wanted to say thank you," Carly said. She put her arms around the older woman and hugged her. For just a moment, Melba hugged her back. Then she stepped away.

"Well, come on. My dinner will be ruined if we stand here jawing about old times."

Carly watched Melba stalk into the kitchen, her back rigid. But just before the door swung shut behind her, Carly saw the older woman wipe at her eyes. Blinking some sudden moisture out of her own eyes, Carly went and sat at the dining-room table.

Devlin pressed the accelerator a little harder the next morning as he headed toward Cameron, driving past the mountains without seeing them. Melba's voice still rang in his ears. She'd called him a fool, telling him to get his rear end into town immediately if he didn't want Carly to walk out and never come back.

His heart panicked at the thought and he drove a little faster, afraid she'd already be gone. He and Shea had driven her truck into Cameron after dinner the evening before, leaving it standing in front of Melba's house. He'd been reluctant to leave it for her, but Shea had been insistent. She'd claimed that Carly might need the Jeep, and it would take a while for them to find the time to drive it into Cameron the next morning.

He'd been looking for any excuse to keep Carly in Cameron for a while longer, he acknowledged. If she didn't have her car, she couldn't leave. And leave him behind.

His hands were trembling by the time he turned onto Melba's street. Seeing her black Jeep sitting at the curb allowed him to take a deep breath. At least she was still here.

He pulled up behind the Jeep, but he didn't rush to get out of his truck. He waited until the trembling in his hands had lessened, until he was sure he could control himself. He wasn't sure what he was going to say to Carly, but he thought maybe he should suggest she write that article about Cameron, after all. Anything to keep her in town for a while longer.

Coward, he muttered to himself as he got out of the truck and slammed the door. He'd barely reached the front door of Melba's when she opened the door and stepped out onto the porch.

"It took you long enough, Sheriff," she said, her voice tart. "I'm going down to Heaven on Seventh for breakfast. Carly's inside."

Without saying anything else, she marched down the sidewalk and headed for the restaurant. She never looked back at him.

Taking a deep breath, he knocked on the door. After a few moments, Carly opened it. A look of surprise flashed in her eyes, then they were carefully blank again. So Melba hadn't told her he was coming.

"Good morning, Dev," she said, her voice too polite. "What can I do for you?"

"Can I come it?"

"Of course." She stepped aside and opened the door wide.

Once he was inside, they stood in the small hall, staring at one another. Tension, thick and heavy as a rope, coiled between them. Neither of them spoke, but he watched as Carly swallowed once, then again.

"What do you want?" she finally said.

"Why don't we go sit down?" he answered, gesturing toward Melba's living room.

"Do you want some coffee?" she asked, her voice filled with the impersonal tones of a stranger.

"No. Thank you. I know better than to try and drink a cup of Melba's coffee."

For a moment, a smile softened her eyes, then she shuttered them again. "Do you want to tell me what you're doing here?" she asked.

"I wanted to talk to you before you left," he answered, and her eyes became even more remote.

"Don't worry, I'll be available to testify against Phil. Just let me know when, and where I need to be."

He scowled. "That wasn't what I was going to say."

Tilting her head, she asked, "Then what were you going to say?"

This was it. Taking a breath, he said, "Maybe you should do that article about Cameron after all. Your boss at the magazine might not like it if you came back without something to show for your trip. I'm sure Melba could put you up for a while longer, and if she doesn't have room, you could stay at the Red Rock."

"Why would I want to do that?" Her voice was very low.

He scowled again. She wasn't going to make this easy on him. "I don't want you to leave yet, all right?"

For the first time since he'd walked into the house, there was a flicker of life in her eyes. "Why not, Dev?"

He stood up and paced around the room. "We haven't had a chance to get to know one another. I'd like to spend more time with you."

He sneaked a glance at her. Her eyes were filled with pain and a weary resignation that twisted his heart. "I think we've both had a chance to know everything we need to know about one another. It doesn't sound as if anything has changed, and there's no reason to think it'll change no matter how much time we spend together."

She stood up, and he felt panic shiver down his back. Now was when she was going to walk out the door and drive away from Cameron. Moving to stand in front of her, he said, "Don't go, Carly."

She stopped, but she didn't come any closer to him. She stared at him steadily. "Why not, Dev?"

"Because."

She didn't answer, didn't move. She just waited. And he knew this was his last chance. If he didn't find the right words, she would be gone. And she'd take his heart with him.

"Because I love you, Carly."

His hands were trembling. He shoved them into the back pockets of his jeans, curling his fingers into his palms. He didn't dare move, didn't dare touch her.

He watched her face, watched her eyes as they came to life. "What?" she whispered.

"You heard me."

"I'm not sure I did. Say it again, Dev."

"I love you, Carly. Please don't leave me."

She flew into his arms, wrapping herself around him so tightly that he could barely breathe. But he didn't care. He didn't need to breathe. All he needed was Carly, in his arms like this, forever.

"I love you, too, Dev," she whispered. "So much. And I was so afraid you didn't love me back."

He found her mouth with his, telling her with his kiss how much he loved her, how much he needed her. Pledging himself to her, now and forever. And he tasted the same promise on her lips.

He didn't want to break the kiss, but he finally leaned back and framed her face with his hands. "I wouldn't have let you leave Cameron," he said fiercely. "I would have arrested you if I had to, kept you in jail until you agreed to stay."

She smiled at him, the same cocky, self-assured smile he'd fallen in love with. "Who said I was going anywhere? I decided during the night that blasting powder and dynamite couldn't get me out of Cameron."

"You mean all the suffering I did since you left the Red Rock yesterday was for nothing?" he said, mock-frowning at her.

She grinned at him. "You deserved to suffer. I was convinced you didn't love me and would never be able to love me."

He brushed her dark red hair off her face, then smoothed his fingers down her cheeks, lingering at the corners of her mouth. "How could I not love you, Carly?" he whispered. "Your courage and honor would put most people to shame. You came back here after twenty years to find justice for your brother. I was angry at you at first, angry that you hadn't told me the truth, but I realized before long that you'd done the only thing you could do. From your point of view, my father was the most likely suspect. And you did tell me the truth, in the end."

The smile had disappeared from her face. "I should have told you much sooner," she said, her voice low and full of emotion. "It didn't take me long to see that your family wasn't capable of covering up for a murderer. I'll always regret that it took me so long to tell you who I was. Do you think you can ever forgive me for that?"

"It's already forgotten, love." He bent down and kissed her again, a lingering caress that brought desire leaping to life. "I should be the one asking you to forgive me. What we have together, what we shared yesterday in the cave was...unbelievable. And I ran away from it."

She touched his face. "You weren't ready to accept it. I understand that."

"I was scared to death," he said bluntly. "I had always sworn I wouldn't ever fall in love. And when I realized that was exactly what had happened, I wanted to run. Far and fast."

She smiled up at him, a slow smile that was full of love. "As long as you ran in my direction."

Spearing his fingers through her hair, he pulled her close again. "I knew as soon as I brought you back here yesterday that I'd made a mistake. But I was too damn stubborn to turn around and admit it then.'' He grasped her shoulders and held her away from him. ''Carly, I don't want to be afraid that I'll lose you, ever again. Will you marry me?''

''Yes,'' she whispered. ''I want to marry you, Dev. I love you.''

He closed his eyes and pulled her close again. His heart was pounding against his chest. ''I'll move to New York with you, if you like. They probably could use another police officer there.''

She tore herself away and stared up at him. He thought he saw tears glittering in her eyes.

''What about Cameron? What about the Red Rock? You told me that this place meant everything to you, that you never wanted to leave it.''

''That was before I met you. It's just a place, Carly. I love Cameron, but I love you more. You don't find happiness in a place. Happiness is the people you love. And I love you.''

''You would be willing to leave Cameron for me?'' she whispered.

''I'd do anything for you.''

''Oh, Dev.''

She threw herself into his arms, and he felt the wetness of her tears on his shirt. He bent his head to kiss her again, but she looped her arms around his neck and gave him a watery smile.

''Are you really set on leaving Cameron?'' she said.

''What do you mean?'' he asked, but his heart began to pound.

''I hope I can talk you out of it, because I'm going to miss you if you're determined to be a New York cop. I talked to Ralph and June Hanson yesterday evening. I'm going to buy the *Cameron Weekly Sentinel* from them, and start turning it into the kind of paper that Cameron deserves to have.''

''You never intended to go anywhere,'' he said, his voice full of wonder.

Her smile was pure love. ''Of course not. I was going to chase you shamelessly until you finally gave in and admitted that you loved me.'' Her smile faded. ''I love you, Dev. You changed my life. You showed me what I could be with you, and what we could be together. I found everything I've been looking for here in Cameron. I wasn't about to walk away from that.''

"But what about your life in New York? What about your job, your friends?"

"*Focus* will survive perfectly well without me," she said. "But the *Cameron Weekly Sentinel* won't. I love Cameron, Dev. I love the town, and I love the people. And I've already made more friends in Cameron than I have in New York. I have a lot of acquaintances, a lot of business associates, but here in Cameron, I have friends. Don't think that I'm making any sacrifices. This is exactly where I want to spend the rest of my life. And this is where I want to raise our children.''

He reached for her again, and she melted into him. Desire and passion spiraled together inside him, mixed with a love that left no part of him untouched. Carly murmured his name and sighed against his mouth.

Lifting his head, he looked down into her face. Her eyes were closed, and her face was flushed with passion. Slowly she opened her eyes. Her smile held a lifetime of promises.

"I love you," he said, bending to kiss her again.

"I love you, too," she murmured. "What are we doing here? Take me back to the Red Rock, Dev. I want to go home.''

Home. He tightened his arms around her. "I can't think of anything I want more. Today, tomorrow, and for the rest of our lives.''

* * * * *

THE CAMERON, UTAH SERIES

by
Margaret Watson
continues!

Turn the page for an exciting
sneak preview of Shea McAllister's
love story,

THE FUGITIVE BRIDE,

coming to you April 1999,

only from
Silhouette Intimate Moments.

The steer clearly had a death wish.

Shea McAllister let the rope attached to his halter slide through her hands as she narrowed her eyes and watched the Hereford put on a show. She'd tried four times to get him into the chute, and each time he'd managed to evade it. This time, he shook his head and snorted at her, danced sideways away from the chute, bucked a few times, then turned and ambled across the corral.

Reaching the animal's head, she grabbed his halter. "You're treading on thin ice here, buddy." Leaning into the animal's massive side, she pushed until the steer turned around. Then she pulled on the rope again, moving him slowly toward the metal contraption.

"Looks like you could use some help."

The low, slightly raspy masculine voice wrapped around her, strumming across nerves she hadn't even known she had. Despite the heat of the Utah spring sun, a shiver chased down her back.

Spinning around, she dropped the rope attached to the steer's halter. "Who are you?" she asked the stranger leaning against the corral fence.

Instead of answering, he vaulted across the fence and grabbed the rope from the ground. Jamming his shoulder into the steer's side, he swept off his hat and used it to smack the animal's tail. At the same time he let out a yell.

The startled animal jumped forward, and the stranger merely aimed him at the chute. A minute later, the steer stood secured in the metal apparatus.

"That was slick," Shea said, watching the man dust his hat off against his leg, then replace it on his head.

He shrugged, and his hazel eyes crinkled in a smile. "It was all in the timing. I surprised him."

"You surprised me, too." Shea let her gaze drift over him once more, then extended her hand. "Thanks for your help. I'm Shea McAllister."

If she hadn't been watching so closely, she would have missed the start of surprise in his eyes. It was gone in a moment, his face smoothly blank as he touched the brim of his hat with one hand and reached for hers with the other. "I'm Jesse Coulton."

His hand was hard and callused as it closed around hers. He gripped her fingers firmly, and for just a moment a sense of rightness swept over her, a feeling of belonging. But that was ridiculous. Slipping her hand out of his, she flexed her fingers and said, "What can I do for you, Mr. Coulton?"

Again, if she hadn't been watching so closely, she would have missed the flicker in his eyes. An instant later, he moved his gaze to look at the house, barn, the outbuildings, then lingered on the mountains behind them. "I heard you could use some help. The word in Cameron is that you're shorthanded. I need a job," he said with a smile.

Because her stomach fluttered when he grinned, Shea took a step backward. "We need another hand, but I have no intention of hiring the first person who drives through the gates," she said coolly. "I appreciate your help with the steer, but I'll need to see some references. And I'll check them. What experience have you had?"

His eyes flickered over the barn again, and when he looked back at her, his grin had faded and there was a hard edge to his gaze. ''I grew up in a small town back east, working on farms. I've worked all over, but mostly in Wyoming and Montana for the last several years, running cattle on the range and taking care of whatever needed to be done. I do a good job.''

He sounded like one of the drifters who was drawn to ranch work, staying at one place only until he got an urge to move one. It was a common enough story in the west, and no one thought twice about men showing up at a ranch, looking for a job.

But there was something different about Jesse Coulton. Shea studied him, wondering what it was. There was a determination in his eyes that she didn't see in the other drifters who wandered by, interested in work. His eyes glinted with intelligence, and a hardness that wasn't due to years of drifting. There was a dangerous edge to the look in Jesse Coulton's eyes.

She couldn't hire him, she decided abruptly. She would never be comfortable, never feel safe with those knowing eyes of his watching her. There was too much at stake for her, for the ranch.

She had too much to hide.

Don't miss Shea and Jesse's love story,
coming April, 1999, only from
Silhouette Intimate Moments.

INTIMATE MOMENTS®
™ *Silhouette®*

invites you to join the Brand brothers,
a close-knit Texas family in which each
sibling is eventually branded by love—
and marriage!

MAGGIE SHAYNE
continues her intriguing series

with

THE BADDEST BRIDE IN TEXAS, #907
due out in February 1999.

If you missed the first four tales of the irresistible
Brand brothers:
THE LITTLEST COWBOY, #716 (6/96)
THE BADDEST VIRGIN IN TEXAS, #788 (6/97)
BADLANDS BAD BOY, #809 (9/97)
THE HUSBAND SHE COULDN'T REMEMBER, #854 (5/98)
You can order them now.

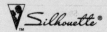
™ *Silhouette®*

Available at your favorite retail outlet.

Look us up on-line at: http://www.romance.net   SIMTXBRD2

If you enjoyed what you just read,
then we've got an offer you can't resist!

Take 2 bestselling love stories FREE!

Plus get a FREE surprise gift!

Clip this page and mail it to Silhouette Reader Service™

IN U.S.A.	**IN CANADA**
3010 Walden Ave.	P.O. Box 609
P.O. Box 1867	Fort Erie, Ontario
Buffalo, N.Y. 14240-1867	L2A 5X3

YES! Please send me 2 free Silhouette Intimate Moments® novels and my free surprise gift. Then send me 6 brand-new novels every month, which I will receive months before they're available in stores. In the U.S.A., bill me at the bargain price of $3.57 plus 25¢ delivery per book and applicable sales tax, if any*. In Canada, bill me at the bargain price of $3.96 plus 25¢ delivery per book and applicable taxes**. That's the complete price and a savings of over 10% off the cover prices—what a great deal! I understand that accepting the 2 free books and gift places me under no obligation ever to buy any books. I can always return a shipment and cancel at any time. Even if I never buy another book from Silhouette, the 2 free books and gift are mine to keep forever. So why not take us up on our invitation. You'll be glad you did!

245 SEN CNFF
345 SEN CNFG

Name	(PLEASE PRINT)	
Address	Apt.#	
City	State/Prov.	Zip/Postal Code

* Terms and prices subject to change without notice. Sales tax applicable in N.Y.
** Canadian residents will be charged applicable provincial taxes and GST.
  All orders subject to approval. Offer limited to one per household.
  ® are registered trademarks of Harlequin Enterprises Limited.

INMOM99   ©1998 Harlequin Enterprises Limited

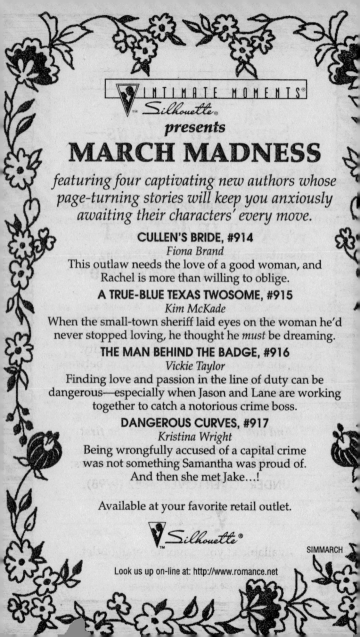

INTIMATE MOMENTS

Silhouette

presents

MARCH MADNESS

featuring four captivating new authors whose page-turning stories will keep you anxiously awaiting their characters' every move.

CULLEN'S BRIDE, #914

Fiona Brand

This outlaw needs the love of a good woman, and Rachel is more than willing to oblige.

A TRUE-BLUE TEXAS TWOSOME, #915

Kim McKade

When the small-town sheriff laid eyes on the woman he'd never stopped loving, he thought he *must* be dreaming.

THE MAN BEHIND THE BADGE, #916

Vickie Taylor

Finding love and passion in the line of duty can be dangerous—especially when Jason and Lane are working together to catch a notorious crime boss.

DANGEROUS CURVES, #917

Kristina Wright

Being wrongfully accused of a capital crime was not something Samantha was proud of. And then she met Jake…!

Available at your favorite retail outlet.

Silhouette

SIMMARCH

Look us up on-line at: http://www.romance.net

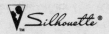

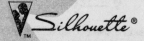

Silhouette

SPECIAL EDITION™

In March 1999 watch for a brand-new
book in the beloved MacGregor series:

THE PERFECT NEIGHBOR
(SSE#1232)

by

1 *New York Times* bestselling author

NORA ROBERTS

Brooding loner Preston McQuinn wants nothing more
to do with love, until his vivacious neighbor, Cybil
Campbell, barges into his secluded life—and his heart.

**Also, watch for the MacGregor stories
where it all began in the exciting 2-in-1 edition!**

Coming in April 1999:

THE MACGREGORS: Daniel—Ian

Available at your favorite retail outlet,
only from

Silhouette®

COMING NEXT MONTH

#907 THE BADDEST BRIDE IN TEXAS—Maggie Shayne
The Texas Brand

When Kirsten Armstrong was falsely accused of murder, she turned to her jilted but still unbelievably sexy lover, Adam Brand—the only one who believed in her innocence. Would Adam help her outrun the law before a long-buried secret destroyed their happiness all over again?

#908 THE MERCENARY AND THE NEW MOM—Merline Lovelace
Follow That Baby

No sooner had woman-on-the-run Sabrina Jensen delivered her beautiful daughter than she was found by sexy oil tycoon Jack Wentworth—the presumed-dead father of her baby! But their family reunion was put on hold when Jack's double life caught up with them....

#909 HOME IS WHERE THE COWBOY IS—Doreen Roberts
Rodeo Men

Rodeo man Denver Briggs knew that his desire for April had never gone away. Then he learned her ten-year-old secret, and the rugged cowboy came face-to-face with the woman and child he longed for—and hoped to hold on to forever....

#910 HEARTBREAK RANCH—Kylie Brant
The Sullivan Brothers

Returning home after seven long years, Julianne Buchanan was shocked to discover that her father's ranch had been sold—to Jed Sullivan! Growing up together, they had long denied their attraction to one another. Would the hurt and betrayal she felt get in the way of their long-overdue happiness?

#911 THE COWBOY SHE NEVER FORGOT—Cheryl Biggs
Way Out West

When former lovers Kate Morgan and Shane Larrabee were reunited, the sparks flew as though time had stood still. He thought she had finally given up on her dangerous career as a cop, but he was wrong. And when Shane became the focus of her undercover mission, could she save his life before she lost him again—for good?

#912 SUDDENLY A FAMILY—Leann Harris
Families Are Forever

When he discovered he was the father of twin four-year-old girls, Zachary Knight found that his bachelor life suddenly went haywire. Then beautiful, sympathetic Antonia Anderson arrived and, with a compassion for children *and* sexy executives, offered to help him raise his newfound family. But when it came to love, did they have the courage to move ahead and greet the future together?